# BAD To The Bone

Small-town private eye and part-time assassin Bonnie Parker is back, in another high-voltage adventure set on the Jersey Shore.

Bonnie thought she'd put her troubles behind her when she killed mob boss Frank Lazzaro and got away clean. But nothing's that easy. Russian mafia kingpin Anton Streinikov has taken a personal interest in the killing—and in Bonnie herself. He wants her delivered to his greenhouse, where very bad things happen.

It doesn't help that Bonnie's latest client has set the cops on her tail, giving the local chief of police his best chance to put her behind bars. All in all, she's had better weekends.

As night falls, she finds herself hunted by bad guys and cops, outmaneuvered, outgunned, and in the fight of her life. Luckily, only the good die young—and Bonnie is bad to the bone ...

*Bad to the Bone* is the latest thriller from *New York Times* and *USA Today* bestseller Michael Prescott, author of *Cold Around the Heart*, *Blood in the Water*, and *Final Sins*. With over three million copies sold in both print and digital editions, Prescott is one of today's leading writers of crime fiction and psychological suspense.

# BAD

## TO THE

# BONE

## Books by Michael Prescott

*Manstopper*
*Kane*
*Shadow Dance*
*Shiver*
*Shudder*
*Shatter*
*Deadly Pursuit*
*Mortal Pursuit*
*Comes the Dark*
*Stealing Faces*
*The Shadow Hunter*
*Last Breath*
*Next Victim*
*In Dark Places*
*Dangerous Games*
*Mortal Faults*
*Final Sins*
*Riptide*
*Grave of Angels*
*Cold Around the Heart*
*Steel Trap & Other Stories*
*Chasing Omega*
*Blood in the Water*
*Bad to the Bone*

# BAD
## TO THE
# BONE

## MICHAEL PRESCOTT

Some day they'll go down together;
And they'll bury them side by side;
    To few it'll be grief
    To the law a relief
But it's death for Bonnie and Clyde.

—Bonnie Parker, "The Trail's End," 1933

# PROLOGUE

THE LATEST TWO were waiting for him in the greenhouse, among the orchids and the bromeliads. They lay on the floor, hands bound behind them, faces pressed to the brick pavers, necks seamed with sweat. Gregor and Ilya stood by, wearing long overcoats and dark suits, their 9mm Makarovs pointed casually downward. Somewhere, water dripped.

"What are their names?" Streinikov asked, striding through the leafy foliage and the heavy tropical air.

"Wong and Yao," Ilya said.

"They have the insignias?"

Gregor stooped. With the Makarov's barrel he nosed up the nearest boy's T-shirt, exposing a Chinese dragon rampant on his lower back.

Streinikov nodded. He sank into a crouch, arms resting lightly on his knees, and addressed the pair in his clear unaccented English. "So. You two are LFB?"

The one whose shirt had been lifted said nothing. His companion was a bit more talkative. "Not no more," he muttered.

"What is that? Speak up." Streinikov had heard him well enough, but he disliked mumblers.

The boy dared to raise his head. "We ain't part of 'em no more," he said slowly and distinctly.

He glared up at Streinikov with a fixed gaze. Trying to mad-dog him—to stare him down.

Streinikov studied the boy. A single Chinese character was tattooed on his neck. He had pale acne-scarred skin and long earlobes, a feature known to the Chinese as Buddhist ears. They were said to predict a long life. In this case the prediction would prove inaccurate.

"Which one are you?" Streinikov asked almost kindly. "Wong or Yao?"

"Yao."

"Well, Mr. Yao, you are quite correct. In point of fact, no one is part of the Long Fong Boyz any longer. Your former organization has ceased to exist, its membership scattered like so many autumn leaves."

"Scattered, fuck." The boy's eyes burned bright with hate. "Most of us is dead—thanks to you, you bitch-ass psycho."

"You flatter me. But I can't take all the credit. The Italians have done their part in thinning your ranks."

"You done more."

"I should like to think so. But my work is not yet finished." Streinikov fingered a gold cuff link. He wore only French cuffs with his suits, and he wore only suits—always. "Do you know why I'm going to kill you, Mr. Yao?"

To his credit, the boy didn't flinch at the question. He shook his head once.

"It is because you've cost me money. A good deal of money, as it happens. I don't like to lose money. I've already lost too many other things."

"Like your balls?"

The boy meant it to be a wounding thrust, but Streinikov was unfazed. "*Da*. Those. And other, more valuable items. You should not have killed Lazzaro. It was a reckless act, and it set in motion a chain of events that benefitted no one."

"We didn't have nothing to do with it."

"But your playmates did, and so you must pay." His gaze returned to the character printed on the boy's neck. It intrigued him. "What is the meaning of this?" he asked, pointing.

"My gang name."

"Which is?"

"Stupid."

"What?"

"That's my nick. They call me Stupid."

Streinikov nodded, digesting this. "It suits you." He snapped his fingers, and Ilya flipped his Makarov a few inches to the left and shot Yao in the head.

The red splash of brains doused his companion, spattering the dragon on his back.

"No, wait a minute, man, wait a minute." That was Wong. Suddenly he was interested in conversation. "He was right. It wasn't us."

"Guilt by association," Streinikov said complacently. "You wear your coat of arms on your back."

"You don't *get* it, man. It wasn't the LFB. We didn't ace Frank Lazzaro."

"*Ne svisti.*" Don't lie. "You're a sad little coward. Your friend, at least, died with a modicum of dignity."

Streinikov almost gave Gregor the nod, but Wong's next words stopped him.

"It was the *huang tou fa*. The woman. She's the one."

Streinikov's eyes narrowed. He leaned closer, drawing down on his haunches. "Just what are you talking about, dragon boy?"

"We wasn't after Lazzaro. We was goin' after the woman. I heard Chiu tell it to his guys, the ones he took with him— Kicker and Monkey, Mouse and Fire Ant and Bucket Head. He said they stuck a GPS thing on her ride. They was gonna track her that way and blip her when they got the chance."

"But they killed Lazzaro."

"Or *she* did. She's a stone killer, said Chiu. He told his guys about her. Said she pulled hits for money."

"A woman?"

"Yeah. A *huang tou fa*, Chiu called her." He saw Streinikov's nonplussed expression. "It means yellow hair," he added as if it were common knowledge. "You know, blonde."

"She's not Chinese, then?"

"Nah, she's a *lo faan*. A white girl."

"What's her name?"

"Dunno. Chiu didn't say."

"What more do you know about her?"

"She operates somewhere south of here. I remember the *dai lo* saying she'd be off her turf this far north."

Streinikov considered the story. "The police say the Long Fong Boyz killed Frank Lazzaro."

"Since when do cops know shit?"

This was a fair point.

"Cops don't know about the woman at all." Wong was talking faster. "Anyway, even if our guys did nail Lazzaro, it's only 'cause *she* brought 'em there. She set it all up. Bitch played us—played everybody. And she's the only one who walked away."

"If this is true, why haven't I heard about it before?"

"The ones who knew are dead, 'cept for me. They was the ones who went into the warehouse with Chiu. I just— well, I kinda got a line on what they was planning."

"You eavesdropped."

"I heard, is all. The walls in our crib was fuckin' cardboard."

"And you stayed quiet afterward?"

"I was on the run, like everybody. I'm speaking true," he added with a thin piping note of desperation.

"Perhaps. What's your gang name?"

"*Ha Gwei*. Black Ghost."

"And why did they call you that?"

"'Cause I'm stealthy. I blend into shadows."

"A useful skill. So tell me, Black Ghost—what else did your *dai lo* say?"

"Not much. He was pretty psyched, I remember. Kept calling her the bitch. The *huang tou fa* bitch. He was jonesing real bad for her scalp. She'd, like, got under his skin, you know?"

Streinikov thought it was a weakness to be thrown emotionally off-balance by an adversary, any adversary, and least of all a woman.

"And in the past two years," Streinikov said, "you never tried to hunt her down?"

"Why would I?"

"To avenge your comrades."

"No."

"Why not?"

"Man, she took out the whole fuckin' crew."

"You were scared of her. Is that it?"

"Yeah, motherfucker. I was scared."

Streinikov was convinced. A boy like Wong might lie about many things, but he would never feign fear of a woman.

"Well, then," Streinikov said, "it appears that all this time I have been hunting the wrong quarry. You have my apology."

Wong blinked. "So ... you cuttin' me loose?"

"You may go. But"—Streinikov held up his hand—"there is one small matter. Your late friend made an unkind remark about my medical condition."

"He wasn't my friend," Wong said thickly.

"Even so, his rudeness requires redress. Besides, I am lonely in my infirmity. I'm sure you understand."

Wong shook his head, bewildered.

Streinikov simplified it for him. "This is a greenhouse. We will do some pruning."

WONG WAS SCREAMING as Streinikov emerged into the January night. He crossed the wide lawn at the rear of his estate. His property was large, his house the last one on a dead-end street. Beyond it, there were only the wooded uplands of Palisades Interstate Park. He had few neighbors, and it was doubtful they could hear the cries. Even if they did, they knew better than to call the police.

Standing at the top of the hillside, Streinikov looked across the river at the lights of New York City and the distant span of the George Washington Bridge. He thought about what the boy called Black Ghost had told him.

A crazy story, yet somehow he was certain it was true.

So a woman was behind it. A lone woman.

In the greenhouse the screams went on, muffled by the panes of tempered glass. Streinikov did not enjoy hearing them. He was not a sadist. He did not personally employ the methods of torture. Such chores he left to others—Ilya, in particular. He understood that men like Ilya Kvint took a sexual thrill in inflicting pain. Streinikov was beyond such things.

He found himself touching the smooth and hairless place below his phallus. The incision had long since healed, barely leaving a scar. Why, then, could he still feel the bite of it? Why did the sensation come to him, sharp as a blade, at random moments? The human body was said to have no mechanism for remembering pain. And yet he did feel it, and often. Strange.

He had been the boy's age when he suffered his mutilation. That was in Donetsk, in a basement below a whorehouse. Three of the bastards pinned him down—it had taken three men to hold him—while Smolin applied the knife. Later they thrust him up the stairs and into the night, bandaged and weeping. He shouted at them, promised he would return and kill them all, and before he let them die, he would clip their balls—and their pricks, too. They laughed. He was only a kid. They knew he could do nothing.

They had been wrong.

In the years since, testosterone injections had allowed him to regain his virility. He was capable of orgasmic release. But oddly, he felt nothing. His doctors said there was no medical reason for it. It was as if the capacity for physical pleasure had been cut out of him by the same blade that had cut his body.

Still, there were advantages. A man devoid of sexual feeling or romantic attachments was little different from a machine; and like a machine he was tireless and implacable. He had no human weaknesses to exploit, no frailties to hamstring his remorseless pursuit of the things he wanted. No love and no joy, but wealth and power. A fair trade-off, he believed.

The cries from the greenhouse had died down by now. After a few minutes Gregor joined him. Ilya, he said, was cleaning up.

"How'd the boy like it?" Streinikov asked in Russian. When alone with his men he nearly always reverted to his native tongue.

Gregor lit a cigarette. "Not much."

"He'll adjust." Streinikov released a sigh. A low, bitter sound. "One can always adjust."

"You think he was telling the truth?"

"I do."

"Then ... what's our next move?"

Streinikov studied the black water, the unforgiving stars. "Without a name, we have little to go on. A blonde Caucasian female operating somewhere south of here, known for doing hits. That is all. I'll put the *domovyk* on the job."

"Okay," Gregor said, using the English word. He glanced at Streinikov. "Why are you smiling?"

"This new development—it pleases me. Do you know the story of the Zhar-ptica?" He used the term from his native Ukraine, the word his mother had used when she told him the story at bedtime.

Gregor did not answer. The question was purely rhetorical. Of course he knew the tale. Everybody knew it.

Streinikov told it, anyway. He enjoyed telling tales. "There was a czar whose orchard of golden apples was raided nightly. At last his youngest son spied the culprit, the Zhar-ptica, the Firebird, with its plumage of red and gold. He plucked a single luminous feather before the Firebird made its escape. When the czar saw this feather, he entrusted his son with a quest to capture the bird and bring it back alive."

"Yes," Gregor said, shifting his weight. Streinikov knew he cared nothing for myths and fables. An unimaginative man. A man who could not understand his master's moods.

"Tonight I am the czar of the story, and this woman of the yellow hair is the golden Firebird who has raided my orchard. I have caught one of her feathers. Now I will have her brought to me, as the Firebird was brought in captivity to the czar."

Gregor blew out a jet of smoke. "The stories say the Zhar-ptica is both a blessing and a curse. To capture it is to risk misfortune."

"Very good, Gregor. An intelligent objection. But I defy augury. I shall have my golden bird in my cage of glass." Streinikov breathed deep, inhaling the dark night air. "And I shall make her sing."

# 1

GIL KRAUSS WAS flat on his back on the creeper, shining his headlamp at the chassis of a Porsche Boxster as he tracked down a leak, when he heard the clack of hard-soled shoes on the concrete floor.

Shit. He'd been robbed twice already. By now he should have learned to carry a gun.

Outside, night had fallen, a cold, wet night in February. He'd closed up shop an hour ago. The only light in the shop was the headlamp on his forehead. He detached it, thinking vaguely that a spotlight on his noggin would make him a better target.

With the headlamp in his hand, he decided he'd better get this over with. He rolled the creeper out from under the Porsche and sat up, aiming the light across the garage. The beam picked out a slim figure near the doorway.

Gil relaxed a little. His visitor was a woman, and she didn't look like any burglar. Maybe he'd forgotten to lock up, and she'd wandered in to talk about car trouble.

"Can I help you?" he asked, making his voice big in the stillness.

She took a few steps forward, her hands in the pockets of her jeans, a handbag slung over her shoulder. She wore a snazzy little beret, an unzipped nylon jacket, and a shirt that read, *I'm Not Always A Bitch*, and underneath, in smaller letters: *Just Kidding*. She was blonde and young. A pretty face, but hard.

"I'm thinking maybe I can help *you*," she said. Unlike him, she didn't raise her voice.

He wasn't too happy with that answer. It pretty much blew his car-trouble theory away. "How'd you get in here?"

"Your office wasn't locked in any serious way."

He didn't like that answer, either.

Carefully he balanced the headlamp on the floor, then stood up. The upward glare threw long shadows on the ceiling. Rain pattered on the roof.

"What do you want?" he asked.

"I understand you're looking for a professional."

"What are you talking about?"

"A hired gun."

"Where'd you get that idea?"

She tipped the beret farther back on her head. "Heard it through the grapevine."

He wasn't so sure he liked that. He might not know this lady, but she seemed to know a hell of a lot about him.

Because she was right. He had been trolling for a hit man. Dropping casual hints in the company of certain acquaintances who, he thought, were in a position to help. Guys who weren't made men themselves, but who bragged often enough about the mobsters they knew. One of them had even supplied a phone number, which Gil had called, hoping to set up a meet.

The guy hadn't called back. Maybe he'd sent this girl instead.

"You with Marco?" he asked.

"Nope."

Another theory shot to shit. "So who sent you?"

"I sent myself."

"Sure. Or maybe the Maritime PD did. Can I see your badge, Officer?"

She looked bored. "Cut the crap, Gil. I'm not a cop. You're shopping for a triggerman. Here I am."

It all came together for him then, the way it did when

he worked out a tricky diagnosis on a malfunctioning engine. "Hey. You're the woman."

"Real perceptive."

"I mean the PI. The one who moonlights as a hitter. Bonnie Parker."

"Like the outlaw," she agreed. "Bonnie and Clyde."

"I heard about you. Just rumors, you know?"

"The grapevine works both ways."

"You got an office in Brighton Cove, name of Last Chance or something like that."

"Last Resort. That's me."

"Yeah," he said slowly. "Okay. I made some inquiries about you."

He kicked the creeper out of his way and moved to a sink in the corner. He turned on the water and washed his hands, keeping an eye on her in the mirror. He toweled off with an old chamois.

Without turning, he said, "I might be in the market for what you're selling—if the price is right."

She hadn't moved. "Three grand up front, and thirty when the job is done."

"Pretty steep."

"No, it's not. If you've done your homework, you know it's at the low end of the price curve."

"In that case, why don't you charge more?"

"I'm a humanitarian."

Near the sink was a wall switch that would turn on the overhead lights. He thought about using it, decided not to. This felt like a transaction that ought to be conducted in the dark.

"Maybe you could go a little lower," he said, turning finally to face her across yards of oil-stained concrete. "Cut a working man a break."

"I don't haggle. Thirty-three thousand total, all cash. Take it or leave it."

"You're not working too hard to close the sale."

"I got other prospects."

"I'll just bet you do." All kinds of prospects. A hot babe with a gun. She ought to be airbrushed on the side of a van. "You know, maybe if we work out an arrangement, we could go someplace and celebrate."

"That wouldn't be such a good idea, Gil. Gotta keep our heads down."

"Yeah, I guess. Too bad, though. I'd like to see what's inside those jeans."

"Flesh and bone, mostly, just like anyone else. Gotta say you're treating this whole thing kinda light. You serious about this job?"

"You bet I'm serious. When I make up my mind to do something, I don't dick around."

"So you're not gonna get cold feet, like some people?"

"No way, honey. I'm in. I am *all* in."

She appraised him for a moment, then nodded. "Good to know."

He noticed how she stayed close to the doorway, away from the windows set in the garage door. Not much traffic on the road outside, only the occasional sweep of headlights and whoosh of rainwater spray, but she wasn't taking any chances on being seen.

"So who's the target?" she asked.

"Grapevine didn't tell you?"

"Grapevine says you didn't say."

He hadn't. He was cautious like that. Even now he didn't like to come right out with it.

She noted his hesitation and added, "I've pretty much gotta know, unless you want me to just start shooting people at random."

"It's my wife. That a problem for you?"

"Why would it be?"

"What I heard about you ..." He wasn't sure how to put it. "They said you might not take this kind of job. They said you got, um, moral standards, or something."

"I'm still here, aren't I?"

"So they were wrong about you?"

"Let's just say I can be flexible. And times are tough all over."

Gil nodded. "Fair enough. Can you get it done?"

"I always get it done. What's the timetable?"

This part of the conversation was easy. He'd rehearsed it a hundred times. Now it was really happening, and even the atmosphere was right—the dark garage, the spatter of rain on the windows, the girl with an outlaw's name watching him with her hard blue eyes.

"I'll be out of town next weekend. It's a perfect alibi. On Saturday night she'll be home alone. We have a townhouse on Seascape Island. End unit, and the one next door is empty. Very isolated. You can do her and make it look like a break-in that went wrong."

He'd spit the words out in a rush. He was out of breath when he finished.

She studied him. "You've given this a lot of thought."

"Hell, yeah. It's all planned. The last piece of the puzzle is you."

"Can I ask a question? Why do it? Why take the risk?"

He noticed he was still holding the chamois. He rubbed his hands with it, although they were clean. "She's been talking about a divorce."

"Might be simpler to just cut her loose."

"I can't do that." He rubbed harder. "See, her dad started this garage. She inherited it from him."

"And if she leaves you, you'll lose the business."

"I built it up," he said fiercely. "Her old man never did shit. I'm the only decent mechanic he ever hired. I put in eighteen-hour days. I don't deserve to lose everything."

"Killing your wife just for a gas station. Pretty cold."

"It's a *service* station." He balled up the chamois and flung it into a corner. "Full service. And what the fuck do you care? You here to pass judgment or do a job?"

"Both, actually."

A moment passed while the rain tapped on the windows, a low rhythmic sound.

"So," he said finally, "can I hire you?"

"Too late, Gil." She reached into her handbag. "Your wife already did."

She fired three shots, but Gil heard only one.

# 2

BONNIE SPENT FIFTEEN minutes in the garage, tidying up. Even in this modern world, some things never changed. It was always a woman's job to clean up after a man.

Her main concerns were to erase any traces of her visit to the repair shop and to make Gil Krauss's death look like a robbery gone bad. Which, incidentally, was the same scenario he'd had in mind for his wife. She guessed that would qualify as irony.

She pulled on gloves and wiped down the door that led from the office to the garage. It was the only thing she'd touched with her bare hands. In the office she removed all the bills from the cash box. She stuffed the money into her handbag, alongside the special compartment containing her handgun. The gun was a black-market .22 she'd acquired from a small arms dealer named Mama Blessing who, as it happened, lived right here in Maritime. It was not silenced. A silencer would only have bulked up the handbag, possibly raising Gil's suspicions. Anyway, in a closed garage alongside a mostly empty highway, there was little danger of anyone overhearing a few small-caliber gunshots.

The last thing she did was approach the body. Gil Krauss lay dead on the floor with three holes in his chest. His eyes were open and shocked.

He was a big man with hairy arms and a broad, unintelligent face. She hadn't particularly wanted to kill him, but she hadn't minded it, either. She'd held off doing anything final until she was sure he was serious. If he'd just been venting steam, she could have let him off with a warning. Some guys were all talk. Some wouldn't go through with it when it became too real. But Gil had worked it all out, had a definite date, an alibi, and apparently cash on hand. He would have hooked up with a shooter soon enough.

She checked his pockets for a throwaway cell phone and found it. No surprise that he had it on him; he'd been waiting for a callback from the shooter he'd contacted. She didn't want the police checking the call log and figuring out that he was trying to meet up with a mob guy. That would only complicate things. It had to be an open-and-shut case, the kind of thing the cops could confidently declare closed so they could go back to writing traffic tickets and scarfing down crullers with a clear conscience.

She slipped the phone into her purse. From the back pocket of his trousers she recovered his wallet. She pulled out all the cash, stuffed it into her purse, and left the wallet on the floor.

Anything else? She rolled back his sleeve and found a wristwatch. It looked pricey. She undid the clasp and flipped it over. His initials were engraved on the back. Sweet. She dumped it into her handbag also.

Before leaving, she took a last look at Gil Krauss. She hadn't done a hit since the Alec Dante case. That was more than two years ago, during the big hurricane. The job had led to its very own shit storm and several more deaths, but nobody had hired her for those. Frank Lazzaro's wife had been in touch once, offering reimbursement for getting rid of her sadistic, psychopathic, crime-lord husband, but Bonnie had told her to forget about it. It wasn't generosity on her part; she didn't want anything that could tie her to Lazzaro's death. That particular bit of business was the sort of thing that could come back to bite a girl in the ass.

It hadn't, though. By now she was sure—almost sure—that anyone who knew about her involvement had died in the warehouse that night. Well, except for Mrs. Lazzaro, and she wouldn't talk.

So everything was copacetic in that department. In most departments, in fact. Even her personal life was surprisingly okay. She might have turned thirty last June, a dubious milestone that she'd acknowledged by drinking alone and passing out on her sofa, but she was still alive and still kicking ass.

She'd outlived her namesake by seven years, and she'd survived the hostile intentions of one international hit man, one crazy mob underboss, and one ultraviolent Asian street gang, not to mention a disgruntled individual with a crossbow and a pissed-off former client with a gun. By all rights she should have been dead many times over, starting when she was fourteen years old and listened from hiding as her parents got shot to death in the next room.

So yeah, she couldn't complain. For the first time in a long while—maybe for the first time ever—life was good. And she intended to make it last.

# 3

AS SHE DROVE out of Maritime, Bonnie lit a cigarette, her first since the hit. It tasted fine.

She dialed through the radio, looking for some balls-to-the-wall rock music, settling on an oldies station playing Jefferson Airplane. The song was older than her ride, and that was saying something, because her ride was a well-used vomit-green Jeep Wrangler that had been with her since she'd started the detective agency eight years ago, and it hadn't been remotely new even then.

Heading south, she hit Miramar and stopped at a public park, where she tossed the .22 into the inlet. It made a dim splash in the darkness.

By now, her tummy was rumbling. A hit always made her hungry. Horny, too. She really ought to talk to somebody about that.

She drove to a McDonald's with a twenty-four-hour drive-through. She ordered a combo and ate it in the Jeep. The radio was playing Creedence. "Bad Moon Rising." It seemed appropriate.

So far, the job had gone well enough, but the toughest part was still ahead. That was the part where her client had to handle things on her own. Bonnie hoped Mrs. Joy Krauss could hold it together. She wasn't completely sure.

It was sheer good luck that Joy had tumbled to her hubby's plot to put her in the ground. Late one night, she'd overheard him leaving a phone message with a potential hitter. He wasn't dumb enough to use their home phone—he'd used his disposable cell—but he called from the den in their condo when he thought his wife was asleep.

The next day Joy came to Bonnie's office. How she knew about Bonnie Parker and her highly illegal sideline, she didn't say. Some people knew, that's all. Like Gil had said: rumors.

A hit on the husband was the obvious way to proceed. Sure, Gil could have been sent to jail, but Bonnie didn't see the percentage in that. He would get out eventually. And a hit on his wife was something that could be arranged from inside a prison, maybe even more easily than on the outside.

The only way for Joy Krauss to be really safe was to put her husband permanently out of the way. And since that was the same fate he'd had in store for her, it seemed only fair. Sauce for the gander and all that.

If only Joy could remember to see it that way, and keep from going all squishy now that the pressure was on.

Finished with the meal, she carried the food wrappers to a trash bin at the rear. She popped the SIM card out of Gil's phone and smashed it under her foot, then tossed the phone and the shattered card into the bin, along with the gloves she'd worn.

That took care of everything that could tie her to the crime scene except the victim's cash and his wristwatch. She had plans for the watch. After a couple weeks, she would fence it through an intermediary. She didn't give a crap about the money. She just wanted the watch to end up in police custody, where it would add weight to the robbery scenario. Gil's engraved initials on the back would make it easy to spot.

As for the cash—hell, the job ought to have some perks. It wasn't like she could take a tax deduction for the black-market guns she bought.

On the highway again, she doubled back to Seascape Island. Under the circumstances, there was some degree of risk in going to see Joy Krauss in person, but she decided to chance it. She had a feeling Joy might need a little more handholding than her average client.

She'd never been to the Krausses' condo. Joy had met with her twice, first in her office for the initial consultation, and later, when the down payment was made, at a coffee bar in Sandy Hook—miles away, where no one who mattered had seen them together.

The condo was a narrow two-story unit overlooking the Crab River inlet. Bonnie parked on the far side of the development and walked there in a light drizzle. She was grateful for the rain; it meant no one was around.

Joy was reassuringly composed as she answered the door and let her into the kitchen on the first floor. She maintained her poise as she offered Bonnie a seat at the kitchen table, where a honey dispenser in the shape of a bear stared up at her from a lazy Susan.

But as she poured herself a cup of coffee, her hands began to shake. The reality of the situation was beginning to catch up with her. Bonnie had seen it before. There were a lot of ways people could react. The key was to be sure Joy didn't go the wrong way.

"Okay," Bonnie said briskly, "here's how you're gonna play it. You sit tight, do nothing until ten o'clock. That's 'cause your hubby works late a lot, and sometimes he goes out for a drink after." Having shadowed Gil for the past two nights, she knew this to be true. "So you aren't worried until a fair amount of time has passed. Got it?"

Joy sank into the chair on the other side of the table. "Yes," she murmured. She didn't sound very sure.

"Righty-o. Around ten you call the gas station. Do that, so there's a record of the call. When you don't get an answer, you try to buzz him up on his cell. Leave a voicemail message both times. Don't get all dramatic about it. You could be sorta pissed off. Like, where the fuck are you?"

Joy nodded. "I can do that."

"'Course you can. You're a Jersey gal. Attitude comes naturally to us. Now it's around midnight, time for you to get officially concerned. You call the cops. Not nine-eleven, the local number. It's not an emergency, you're just saying, like, if they happen to have a prowl car in the area, maybe they could check on the gas station."

Joy stirred the coffee with her finger, a pointless gesture since she hadn't added milk or sugar. "I could say the place has been robbed before, and I'm worried—"

"Ixnay on at-thay. Don't bring up the subject of crime. You don't go there. You let *them* tell you about that."

Another nod, shakier than the last one.

"Which they will," Bonnie went on. She thought about lighting a cig but decided against it. She didn't want the odor of smoke lingering in the condo when the police showed up. "There's not a whole lotta action in this burg, and it won't take long for a patrol unit to drop by the gas station and see the door's open. They'll find him inside."

Joy gazed into the black depths of her coffee. "Where ... did you do it? In the office or ...?"

"It doesn't matter and you don't want to know." The less she knew, the less chance there was of her blurting out something she shouldn't say. "It may take them a while to get back to you. They won't make the notification by phone. They'll come over. You need to be in your nightgown and robe."

"Like I was asleep?"

"No, you were too worried about your husband to sleep. You were watching TV. And I want you to *really* watch TV, so you can tell them what you saw. Turn on a movie or whatever and pay enough attention so you can talk about it if you have to."

She swallowed. "Will I have to?"

"Probably not, but we need to cover all our bases. *Capisce?*"

"Mmm-hmm."

"So the boys in blue are here. I don't want you getting all hysterical. You're not Sally Field and you're not going for a friggin' statuette. Stunned and speechless is the way to play it. A few tears won't hurt, but don't go crazy with the waterworks. Be like you can't take it all in, like you don't know how to react."

"I'll try."

"Don't worry that they'll suspect you if you're under-playing it. They expect you to be kinda numb and spaced out. That's natural. It's the ones who overdo it who get in trouble."

"Right. Right." Distracted, her head nodding mechanically.

"Everybody thinks they can act, but not everybody can. Look at Steven Seagal."

Okay, the reference was dated, but Joy didn't even crack a smile. She was really scared. It occurred to Bonnie that maybe coffee wasn't such a great idea.

"You got any sedatives in the house?" she asked gently. "Valium or something?"

"I think so. It may have expired."

"Take some anyway. Just enough to take the edge off. But don't go near the liquor cabinet."

"I don't drink."

"Good. Don't start. Nasty habit. Like smoking."

"Don't you smoke?"

"I drink too. I also kill people for money, and sometimes I wear the same underwear two days in a row. I'm not exactly a role model."

This, at least, got a grin out of her. But the grin faded as she asked, "Will they make me identify the body?"

"No, they don't do that. You'll never have to see him again, unless you opt for an open casket." Bonnie winced.

"Sorry—shouldn't have said that."

"It's all right. You're sure he's dead?"

This was a seriously dumb question, but Bonnie didn't judge her for it. Civilians generally lost their bearings when shit got real.

"Yeah," she said. "He's dead and gone. But hey, listen, kiddo. He was serious about bumping you off. I made sure of that. If it hadn't been him, it would've been you."

Joy set down the coffee cup with a hollow clunk. "Yes."

"He chose to play this game. We just played it better than him, that's all. You practiced the golden rule: do unto others before they get the chance to do unto you."

This line, at least, did coax a smile from her client. Bonnie was satisfied with that.

"You got the phone on you?" she asked.

"The one you gave me? Yes."

Joy dug in her pocket and handed over a TracFone that Bonnie had picked up at Rite Aid. Bonnie dumped it into her purse and gave Joy a new phone, same make and model, and equally cheap and disposable.

"This one's activated, but it's never been used. No call history. I'll reach you on it in a couple days so we can work out a meet. You know, so you can pay me the rest of my fee. It's thirty grand, remember." Not long ago she had raised her going rate; everything cost more these days.

"Blood money," Joy murmured.

Bonnie was getting a little pissed off. "Yeah, that's right. Money that stopped him from shedding your blood. You knew this was how it would play out. I didn't come to you, remember? You came to me."

"Yes. I did."

"And you did the right thing." She lowered her voice. "You're just freaking out a little. It's natural. No biggie. But things will be fine. Just fine."

She hoped this would prove true. She stood, shouldering her purse.

"Gotta get moving. There's stuff I need to do. Plus there's always a chance the cops have already noticed the unlocked door and found the body, in which case they might be on their way over. Needless to say, it wouldn't be too good if they found me here."

The tremor that passed through Joy Krauss was almost strong enough to qualify as a shudder. "No," she whispered.

It wasn't unusual for a client to go blood simple on her, but Gil Krauss's widow seemed more poleaxed than most.

Bonnie took one last stab at reassurance. "All you need to do is hold it together for the next few hours, and it'll be all over. Okay? Just a few hours."

Joy didn't answer. Her gaze was fixed on Bonnie's jacket.

She looked down and saw a long smear of red on one nylon flap. It would be nice to think it was ketchup. It wasn't.

She must have picked up some blood while rifling the body. Damn. She'd liked that jacket, too.

Bonnie didn't say anything. Neither did Joy. Really, there was nothing to say.

She turned and left the kitchen. As she was opening the front door, Joy spoke up from where she sat.

"I don't know how you can deal with it," she said in a low, frightened tone. "With ... with death."

Bonnie shrugged. "It's a living."

As an answer, it was utterly inadequate, but it was all she had.

# 4

THE JACKET WENT into another trash bin, this one hidden behind a Whole Foods store that was still under construction. Bonnie pushed it way down among the refuse. Maybe she could have cleaned the stain off, but she wasn't taking any chances. The things they could do in forensic labs these days were pretty amazing—and downright scary if you had something to hide.

Back in the Jeep, she headed in the general direction of Brighton Cove, where she owned half of a little duplex on Windlass Court, a real fashionable address, right near the railroad tracks. But she didn't stop there. She kept going.

In Algonquin, just south of Brighton Cove, she slotted the Jeep into a space behind a store that sold used timepieces, called Second Hand. Get it?

She walked a block and a half through a mist of rain to a brick apartment building, climbed the outside stairs, and rapped on the door of unit 2A.

After a half minute, the door opened on Patrol Officer Bradley Walsh of the Brighton Cove Police Department.

"Where'd you disappear to?" he asked. "I was hoping we could catch dinner."

She went inside fast, because it wasn't smart to loiter in his doorway.

"Got stuck on a job," she said as the door closed behind her.

"Doing what?"

"Tailing a guy who may or may not be cheating on his wife."

"Sounds like a fun night."

"Oh, yeah. Snore."

"Care to give names?"

"You know I never tail and tell."

Naturally she couldn't tell him what she'd really been up to. He was a small-town cop whose most dangerous assignment on any given day was herding a flock of jaywalking geese across the street. How would he react if he knew that less than two hours ago she'd been rifling a dead man's pockets? She didn't have to ask the question. She knew.

He lived in a two-room apartment that was much tidier than the slovenly shit hole she called home. The living room was decked out in fake ferns, art prints from Kmart, and two goldfish in a bowl, whose names were Turner and Hooch. Scattered wireless speakers played low music throughout the premises—a Pandora radio channel, easy listening stuff. Elevator music. Bonnie hated it but hadn't said so, mainly because she hadn't been asked.

"You're soaked," he observed. "Still parking a mile away?"

"It's more like a quarter mile. What can I say? I'm the cautious type."

Though there was little chance the Algonquin cops would pay attention to her Jeep, she didn't want an alert patrol unit making a connection between her and a member of the Brighton Cove PD. It would do Brad no good at all if anyone figured out he was dating her.

They'd been seeing each other for six months, but almost never in public. On the rare occasions when they did go out, it was always to some distant spot like Atlantic Highlands, where there was little chance of being recognized. They never went shopping together or went to the movies or got a cone at the local ice cream parlor, or did any of the things normal couples did. That was okay. It was Bonnie's first clandestine relationship, and sneaking around made it even hotter.

Brad was a good guy, too. Totally straightforward, not a user, not a manipulator, like a certain former boyfriend she could name. No, she'd finally hooked up with somebody who would be completely straight with her about everything. This time the deceit was all on her side.

"You shouldn't be going around without a coat in this weather," Brad said reproachfully.

She'd had a jacket until she'd left it in a dump bin. "Aw, you know me—I got ice water in my veins. Don't even feel the cold."

"Let's warm you up anyway."

He drew her close and gave her a long kiss. When he pulled away, he was frowning. "You taste like french fries."

"Mickey D's."

"That stuff will kill you."

"It'll have to get in line. Behind your boss, at least."

"Dan doesn't want to kill you."

"Nah, he just wants me in a six-by-nine cell for life."

"You know, I sometimes get the impression you don't like the chief."

"What's to like? The guy's got all the charm of a urinal cake."

"You're a girl. What do you know about urinal cakes?"

She shrugged. "I hear things."

He followed her into the bedroom. She kicked off her shoes and unzipped her jeans. They had been together long enough that undressing in front of him was no longer an act of seduction.

"Dan's just doing his job, as he sees it," Brad said, lingering by the bedroom door.

"If his job as being an asshole, mission accomplished."

"That's not really fair to him."

"How fair would he be to you if he found out me and you've been shacking up?"

"With you, he's got a blind spot. I admit that. Nobody's perfect."

Bonnie chuckled. "Officer Walsh, your loyalty to your superior is admirable."

She wriggled out of her shirt, the one that basically proclaimed she was a bitch. She liked it because, you know, truth in advertising.

In her bra and panties, she sneaked a glance at herself in the mirror over his bureau. Lately she had been making more of an effort to stay in shape. She'd never been a big one for hitting the gym, but dating a younger guy with washboard abs had a way of changing her perspective on the virtues of working out. She thought she looked pretty damn good for a woman of thirty. Brad was fitter than she was, which kinda bugged her. Still, she hadn't heard any complaints.

She couldn't say exactly what had changed her mind about Brad. For a long time she'd put up an impenetrable wall of resistance to his advances. She hadn't wanted to risk getting him in trouble with his boss, and more than that, she just couldn't see herself hooking up with a guy she thought of as still a kid, and a Boy Scout at that. In her more cynical moods she'd thought it would be like dating Opie.

But maybe Opie was what she needed. Who could say? What did women want, anyway? She sure as hell didn't know.

The bottom line was that one night, lonely and bored, she'd shown up at Brad's door. And yeah, she'd already known where he lived. So the idea of paying him a visit must have been crouching at the back of her mind, at least.

Lonely and bored. But to be really honest about it, the operative word was *bored*. She could handle loneliness. She'd been immersed in it for most of her life, and it felt natural to her, the way the goldfish bowl must feel natural to Turner and Hooch. Boredom, however, was a different matter. To escape boredom, she was willing to take reckless and stupid chances, like moonlighting as an assassin or dating a cop who would feel duty-bound to put her ass in prison if he ever found out.

"Dan was talking about you just today," Brad said, breaking the silence.

"Yeah? What'd I do this time? Poison a puppy? Push an old lady down the stairs?"

"You cut off a kid's balls."

She turned to look him in the face. "Say what?"

"Some kid. Gangbanger up in Newark. He was pulling a B 'n E, got chewed up by a K-9 when he tried to book. They took him to the ER for repairs, and that's when they found out his dick had lost its two best friends."

She was having trouble following the story, maybe because of all the acronyms. "The dog did that?"

"No, it happened a while ago. A month or so. The wound was almost healed."

"You're saying he was ... neutered?"

"Fixed. Spayed. Not professionally, either. This was amateur work."

"So who did it?"

"He wouldn't say. Which is weird. Why the heck would he protect a person who did that to him?"

"Because the person in question could do a lot worse."

Brad seemed dubious. "I guess."

"If this went down in Newark, how does Dan even know about it? It's not exactly his jurisdiction."

"One of the guys in Homicide and Major Crimes is a friend of his. He knew Dan would be interested."

"Why? He in the market for the same kind of surgery?"

"He's put out the word that he wants to be kept up to date on the Long Fong Boyz. Remember them?"

She flashed on a memory: a machine gun stuttering, bodies dropping, screams. "Um, yeah, think I do. What've they got to do with some nutless wonder in Newark?"

"He had a tat identifying him as one of the gang. Chinese dragon. It's their symbol."

"Okay." She sat down on the bed, folding her legs under her. "And just for shits 'n' giggles, how does Danny think this relates to me?"

"He knows the Boyz were gunning for you a couple of years ago. And that ever since, they've been turning up dead."

"The mob's doing that. Because the LFB offed that Mafia guy, Frank Lazzaro."

"Yeah, that's what the newspapers say. But Dan's pal in Newark thinks some of the hits aren't mob related. He thinks there's another player involved."

"Another player? Who?"

"Dan thinks it's you."

"You gotta be shitting me."

"Look, it's not totally crazy."

She tilted her head. "It's not?"

Brad crossed the room and sat beside her, but she noticed he stared straight ahead, not meeting her gaze. "You could have a motive. That's all."

"Terrific. So Dan thinks I'm going around whacking gangbangers in my spare time."

He shrugged. "It's a theory."

"And this theory includes me turning the latest victim into a soprano?"

"It doesn't work like that. If you lose your testicles after puberty, you still have a normal speaking voice. I saw it on the Discovery Channel."

"Good to know. Can we stay on point?"

"Yeah, Dan thinks you could've mutilated this kid. His exact words were: I wouldn't put it past her."

"Huh. How about you, buckaroo?"

"How about me what?"

"Would you put it past me?"

"Oh, hell, Bonnie." She knew he was flustered, because for him this was a strong oath. "I know you could never do anything like that. It's Dan's idea, not mine." But he still wouldn't meet her gaze.

"You said it wasn't totally crazy." She couldn't let go of those words.

"If you look at it the way he does ... Like I said, he's got a blind spot about you. But I know he's wrong. And not just about any specific case. He's wrong about the kind of person you are."

"What kind is that?"

"You're one of the good guys, Bonnie. Even if you don't want to be."

She heard the compliment—and the caveat. "Why wouldn't I want to be?"

"Because you want to see yourself as an outlaw and a rebel. But deep down you believe in the same rules as everybody else. You just do your best to hide it."

"Maybe I'm hiding more than you think," she said a little recklessly.

"From other people, maybe. I know you for who you are." He smiled. "But don't worry. I love you anyway."

It was the first time she'd heard those words from him. She was caught off guard, not sure what to say, so she did the first thing she could think of. She moved her hand to her bra strap and undid the hook.

"Don't kid yourself, Walsh. I'm a bad, bad girl." The bra fell away, and her lips brushed his ear. "Bad to the bone ..."

# 5

BONNIE'S CELL PHONE rang at eight in the morning, waking her with a tinny rendition of "A Hard Day's Night." She glanced at the other side of the bed to see if Brad had heard it too, but there was no Brad. It was Saturday, and he'd left already. Lately, on the weekends, he'd been working the day shift, which began at seven.

She plucked the phone out of her handbag. It was a Samsung Galaxy, and it was named Sammy, which was short for Sammy II: Son of Sammy. Sammy II, like his predecessor, wore a shocking pink plastic case that did nothing to diminish his rugged masculinity.

She glanced at the screen. Caller ID didn't recognize the number, but she did. It was the throwaway phone she'd given to Joy Krauss.

Suddenly she had a feeling in her gut that, if translated into speech, would have been: *Uh-oh.*

"Bonnie? Bonnie?"

"It's me, Joy. I'm here. What is it? What happened?"

A beat of silence. "I screwed up."

Definitely not what she wanted to hear a client say. "Okay, Joy, take it slow."

"It happened the way you said. The police came by at eleven thirty last night and told me about Gil. I didn't overreact. I played it cool, like you told me to."

"Good, good." She'd never particularly cared for the expression "waiting for the other shoe to drop," but she got it now.

"But I made a mistake. When they told me Gil was

dead, I said his shop had been robbed before. But that was before they'd told me any details. It was even before they said he had been murdered."

Bonnie shut her eyes.

"So they got suspicious, I guess. I didn't realize at first. I mean, they were so nice to me."

I'll bet, Bonnie thought.

"I said there'd been robberies before, so I just assumed. But I don't think they bought it."

Bonnie was sure they hadn't bought it. There were too many other ways to die. Even in a redlined district like Maritime, death by gunshot was a rare occurrence.

"And they kept me talking a long time."

Without a lawyer ...

"They kept coming back to the robbery thing. That's when I knew I'd messed up. I shouldn't have said anything about that."

"It's not too bad, Joy. It's manageable." Gently, gently. "Why didn't you call me sooner?"

"They were with me all night. I got home at six. And then—then I was scared maybe they could listen in on the call."

"You're using the burner I gave you, so how could they listen in?"

"I don't know," she snapped, her voice worn ragged. "Maybe they could intercept the signal if I made the call from the townhouse. Maybe they have listening devices outside, like in the movies. So I went to the beach. That's where I am now. South Beach, where the snack shack used to be."

The shack was a casualty of Hurricane Sandy. It had been replaced, in season, by a food truck. Bonnie wondered why her mind was running to irrelevancies until she realized she just didn't want to deal with this. She forced herself to focus.

"Okay. How'd the cops leave things?"

"They want to talk to me some more."

"You got a lawyer?"

"Gil had one, for business."

"Get one of your own. A criminal defense lawyer. Chase Benedict's got a good rep, and he lives in Maritime. Call him."

"Won't it look suspicious if I, you know, lawyer up?"

"It doesn't matter how it looks. What matters is that you don't say anything else they could use against you."

"I'm scared, Bonnie. I didn't think it would be like this."

"Just keep it together. They're wondering how you knew it was a robbery before they told you anything. It could have been a heart attack, car accident, whatever. They're curious, that's all. They're not itching to arrest you. They just have questions."

"Questions I can't answer."

"Yes, you can. If they ask why you assumed it was foul play, say Gil was receiving threats that had him spooked."

"Threats from who?"

"You don't know. He wouldn't say. He kept it to himself."

"Why would somebody threaten Gil?"

"Let the police worry about that. Gil sold gasoline at his station. There's a lot of organized crime activity in the oil and gas business. Maybe somebody was trying to make him pay for protection, or trying to force him to sell out or use a different supplier. It doesn't matter, because you don't know. He never shared his concerns with you. All you know is that somebody was giving him shit, and he was nervous. And that's why you assumed foul play."

"But they already asked me about what I said, and I didn't tell them about any threats."

"Because you were scared. Gil made you swear never to talk about it with anybody. He was trying to shield you. Got it?"

"As if Gil gave a damn about me."

"The cops don't need to know that. As far as they're concerned, you had a happy marriage and Gil was looking out for your best interests."

"I understand."

"You can hold it together, can't you?"

"I—I think so."

"Say it with more confidence. Say: I can handle this."

"I can handle this," she said shakily.

"Again."

The second time her voice was stronger. "I can handle this."

"Bravo—or brava, I guess. That's what you say for women, right?"

"I wouldn't know."

Bonnie didn't know, either. Vaguely she thought it was something people yelled at the opera. Her total exposure to opera was limited to Bugs Bunny cartoons.

"You're doing great, Joy. One little slip-up isn't the end of the world. You'll be fine. I wish all my clients were as dependable as you."

This was a blatant lie, but she was past the point of telling the truth to Joy Krauss. What was needed was reassurance and an ego boost.

She ended the call, smoked her first cigarette of the day, and worried.

# 6

JOY'S CALL HAD made her jumpy, and maybe that was why she noticed the black Mercedes.

It was an E-class sedan, late model, with Jersey plates, and it was parked on the side street just south of the building that housed her office. It interested her, and it bothered her, because she'd never seen it before.

She'd taken a shower at Brad's and changed into some spare clothes she kept there. Her selection was limited. The shirt she'd ended up with was more of a warm weather item, one that showed a lot of boobage. In large letters it asked the timeless question: *Who do I gotta blow to get a drink around here?* She put on a fall jacket that ought to be warm enough, and of course a new hat. She was a big believer in hats. This one was a black wool cloche, which gave her kind of a 1920s look, she thought. Not that she actually knew anything about the 1920s. Well, she had watched an episode of *Boardwalk Empire* once.

After grabbing a hard-boiled egg and some coffee that was still in the carafe, she'd left Brad's place and driven straight to her office. She kept Saturday hours when she felt like it. Habitual caution kept her alert as she approached her building, and that was why she noticed the Mercedes.

She circled the block and drove past the vehicle again, sidling alongside the mystery car to look inside. Tinted windows were illegal in Jersey, which meant she could see into the passenger compartment without difficulty.

The sedan was unoccupied.

She parked in her building's lot, as usual. Before getting out, she studied the rearview and side view mirrors. She didn't see anyone lying in wait. Then again, if they were any good, she wouldn't see them.

From the glove box she removed a Walther .32 to replace the gun she'd ditched in the inlet last night. Unlike the murder gun, the Walther was nice and legal, the kind of thing the police couldn't charge her for if they found it on her person. It fit snugly in her handbag's special compartment.

She left the Jeep, keeping one hand on the clasp of her purse. No shots were fired at her, but she kept her guard up as she walked around to the building's front door. Yeah, she was paranoid, but on the other hand, she was also still alive, and the two facts were not unrelated.

Nobody was loitering by the door, which was still locked and showed no sign of tampering. But as she opened up, she saw a ripple of movement reflected in the window to her left. Somebody was across the street, moving from the doorway of a flower shop to the storefront of a deli next door. His back was to her, but he could have been watching her reflection just as she was watching his.

Stout, wide-shouldered guy. Tan overcoat. Briefcase.

Leaving the front door unlocked, she climbed the stairs to the second floor. She didn't open up her office until she'd checked the lock. The guy on the street might have nothing to do with anything. Somebody could already be inside the premises, hoping to catch her unaware.

Okay, so she was *super* paranoid. But she'd learned to trust herself about stuff like this. That Mercedes gave off a bad vibe, maybe because it reminded her of the vehicle Jacob Hart had been driving on the night when he'd tried to gun her down.

She got the door open and entered fast, her hand still on

the Walther, ready to fire through the purse if necessary.

The anteroom and the office of Last Resort were empty of life, other than herself and a buzzing housefly who'd been her unwanted companion for the past three days. She'd tried killing the damn thing, but it was smart and resourceful, not unlike herself. Eventually she'd developed a grudging respect for the tenacious little bastard.

She peered out the office window. This vantage point offered only a partial view of the street, and she couldn't see if the man in the raincoat was still window-shopping.

From below came a squeal of hinges—the door to the street, opening. Then a slow, heavy tread on the wooden stairs.

She seated herself behind the desk, leaving the purse within reach. Also within reach was a Smith .45 duct taped to the side panel of the desk's knee hole. A little insurance for emergencies. The gun was loaded and the safety was off.

The visitor reached the top step, identifiable by its telltale creak, and hesitated, orienting himself. Then, not at all to her surprise, he moved in the direction of her office.

The door to the hallway was closed, and unlike the doors of detective agencies in old movies, it wasn't made of frosted glass. She wouldn't see him until he opened it. She got ready to duck and cover. The desk, a garage sale find, was sturdy enough to stop most ammo, and she could fire back with the .45 before he had time to retreat.

If it came to that.

The door opened. The man in the tan overcoat stood there. It would have been more dramatic if he'd been in silhouette, but in fact he was lit by sunbeams slanting through the window at her back. He blinked in the glare.

The briefcase was still in one hand. The other hand was empty and hung relaxed at his side.

"You are Parker?"

His voice was gruff, with a strong Slavic accent.

"Who wants to know?" she asked, just to be a dick.

He moved through the anteroom into her office. She kept her eyes on his hands.

"I am Pavel Gura. I am faced with something of a delicate situation."

This was unexpected. Nothing about Pavel Gura struck Bonnie as delicate. He was medium-sized and very hairy. Squat build, long arms. Like an orangutan.

"Okay, Pavel." She leaned back, but not so far back that she couldn't grab the concealed .45 if she had to. "Take a seat."

He glanced around. His nose wrinkled, and she guessed he was picking up the mildewy odor of her sofa, another item rescued from a yard sale years ago. She really ought to think about replacing it.

After a moment of indecision he shrugged off the coat and settled into one of two ratty armchairs, the one positioned in front of a tacked-up poster of the original Bonnie Parker, posing on the grille of a roadster, a stogie in her mouth, a gun in her hand.

She took a closer look at Pavel Gura. He had a sallow face and graying hair, and he wore a gray suit. Nothing about him was the least bit colorful except the blood red scarf tied around his neck and, at his waist, a gold belt buckle with an elaborate embossed pattern.

"You were waiting for me to open up," she said.

"So you noticed? Most people would not." He cracked a knuckle. It popped like a firecracker. "I saw that you circled the block twice. You are cautious. I like this."

"I'm paranoid."

"It is not such a bad thing, paranoia. It can save your life."

"You know, I was thinking that exact same thing right before you showed up. You enjoy chitchat, Pavel?"

"Not much."

"Me neither." She lit up a Parliament White, not asking permission. Her office, her rules. "So how about we cut to the chase?"

"Very good." He cracked another knuckle. "For the past month I have been seeing a girl."

She glanced at his left hand. No ring.

He caught the flicker of her eyes. "I am not married. Nor is she, so far as I know. I met her a month ago, in Atlantic City. We began a conversation at a bar in the Tropicana. She is beautiful, intelligent, lively. About half my age."

Bonnie judged him to be in his late forties. "Okay."

"Her name"—crack—"is Clarissa Lynch. Blonde and trim. In bed she is exceptionally nubile and, how you say, uninhibited."

"Sounds magical."

Gura regarded her coolly. "You make a joke, but I am not laughing. We see each other whenever I get to that part of New Jersey. It is all good at first. But then I start to think maybe ... maybe it is too good. I begin to be"—crack—"suspicious of this girl."

"Suspicious?"

"I began to think she is too good to be true."

"Aww. Sounds kinda sweet."

"Do you take this seriously or not?"

"Sorry."

"I was divorced a few years ago. I have not played around much since. I could be seen as a, shall we say, soft target."

Soft. Another word she wouldn't associate with him. "Is there any reason somebody might want to set you up?"

"Nothing specific. But I work in a field where one cannot take chances."

"What field?"

"I prefer not to say."

"Gotta give me something."

He cracked two more knuckles in quick succession. "Personal security."

"Sorta like me."

"Very much like you," he said with a slow smile.

That smile annoyed her. "Okay, Rasputin. Quit being coy and tell me what you do for a living."

"I work for a business organization based in Ukraine, with branch offices in the USA. An organization that keeps a low profile and prefers not to be named. Need I say more?"

"No, I don't think so." The guy was Russian mob. Terrific.

"My employer is an unforgiving man," Gura said with another knuckle crack. "Should he discover that I have been on intimate terms with an agent of a rival faction, he would be ... displeased."

Bonnie took a slow drag on her cig. "Why? What could this chippy do to you? You're not married. There's no blackmail angle."

"I am thinking there are other angles. Perhaps she wishes to get close to me in the hope that I will spill my secrets. Perhaps she wishes to track my movements or access my computer or mobile phone. Perhaps she merely wishes to establish a relationship and use it to discredit me in my employer's eyes."

"Or perhaps"—she was picking up his diction without meaning to—"she's just a good-time girl who goes in for older men."

"You do not have to sound so flip."

"I'm always flip. It's part of my charm."

"What you say of her could have been true. But I could not go on faith. Do you see this ring?"

The change of topic took her by surprise. He showed her a small ring on the middle finger of his left hand.

"What about it?"

"It is called the Roundstone. A small circle with a dot on the inside. You see?"

"So?"

"It is symbolic. Trust no one—this is the meaning. All my life I have worn it, and it is always there to remind me." He turned his gaze on her. "Perhaps you should wear one, Bonnie Parker."

"I don't need any reminders."

He chuckled appreciatively. "A good answer. So because I trust no one, I look into this woman, this Clarissa Lynch."

He hefted the briefcase onto his lap, unsnapped the latches, and withdrew a manila folder. He tossed it onto her desk.

"Here is what I found."

Bonnie opened the folder and spent a long time studying its contents while Pavel Gura watched without comment. Occasionally he cracked another knuckle. That was all.

When she was done, she raised her head.

"Okay," she said simply.

"You see it, yes?"

"I see it." She flipped through printouts of online searches. "There's no Clarissa Lynch in any New Jersey database. There is a Clarissa Lynch on Facebook, but the page was created a month ago, and the photos are mostly selfies. Her Facebook friends—there aren't many—have pages that are equally new. The posts are all generic bullshit. In other words, Clarissa Lynch is a cypher."

"Very good," he said, nodding.

"She supposedly runs her own consulting business in Ventnor, but the WhoIs database lists her website's mailing address as a PO Box in Teaneck. That's at least a hundred miles north of Ventnor. Teaneck is where she really lives. Her car is what gives it away."

"You are quick, Parker."

"It's obvious. You ran her tag number and got her vehicle history. It shows smog checks conducted every two years at an auto shop in Teaneck. Did you call them?"

"Why do you ask?"

"It's what I'd do."

"Yes, I called. I concocted a story about Clarissa Lynch wishing to sell me her car."

"Lemme guess. They never heard of her."

"Correct. They knew no one of that name. But they did know the car."

"Did they tell you the owner's actual name?"

"This they would not divulge. They became suspicious, and I ended the call."

Bonnie tapped the folder with a fingernail. "How would she know you'd be at the Tropicana the night you met?"

"I always stay there."

"You go to AC a lot?"

"Very often."

"Business or pleasure?"

"Pleasure. I win at blackjack. Unlike most casino games, blackjack requires and rewards skill."

"How sure are you that she's dirty?"

"Let us say, eighty percent. There is always the possibility of an innocent explanation."

"Yeah, miracles do happen. Have you told your boss about this?"

"No. If it is known that I have been targeted in this way, I may become a liability. My employer does not tolerate liabilities."

He punctuated the statement with another knuckle crack, his loudest yet.

"All righty." Bonnie was nearly done with the cigarette, and already wishing for another. "So you've come to me. Somebody outside your, uh, business organization."

"That is right."

"And I'm guessing you want me to do a little more online digging into your sweetheart."

"That is unnecessary. I have dug deep enough."

She felt a little frisson of apprehension. "If you don't want me to run a background check on her, what do you want?"

"I have invited the maiden to spend this weekend with me—here, in this charming town. I booked her room at your Prince Edward Hotel. She will be here later today."

"Okay ..."

"While I dine with her this afternoon, I want you to enter her room and go through her things. Perhaps you can learn her true identity. At the very least, you can learn if she is a professional setting me up."

"Then I report back to you?"

"Yes."

"And depending on what I find, you take care of things?"

"That is right."

"Yeah, I don't think so."

Gura seemed unperturbed by her refusal. He resumed cracking his knuckles with methodical regularity "And why not?"

"Because if I confirm that your lady friend is a spy, or a plant, or whatever the hell she is, I have a feeling you'll take it out on her in a really bad way."

"This would trouble you?" He lifted an eyebrow.

"I'd rather not be responsible for a young lady getting whacked, even if she is doing a number on you. Which we don't know yet, by the way. Not beyond any reasonable doubt."

"This is not a courtroom, Parker."

"Yeah, but you and me aren't judge, jury, and executioner either."

"Aren't we?" His shrewd gaze was unsettling. "I know

about you, poppet. I know all about you."

"What's there to know?" she said as casually as possible. "I'm just a small time PI trying to pay the bills."

"A small time PI, yes. And also an assassin."

He really should have cracked a knuckle after that last remark. Would've been the perfect time for it. In terms of dramatic effect, it was a missed opportunity.

She sat back slowly in her chair. "Come again?"

"You are an assassin, Parker. There is no use pretending otherwise."

There were clients she would trust with that information. Pavel Gura wasn't one of them. She had absolutely no interest in going into business with Russian organized crime.

"Look," she said with a wave of her hand, "I don't know where you got your information, but you're way off base—"

"Do not try my patience. I have heard of your, shall I say, after-hours activities."

"Whatever you've heard isn't true."

"All of it? Even the fact that two years ago, you eliminated several members of an Asian street gang in a Jersey City warehouse, along with Mr. Frank Lazzaro?"

Her mouth was suddenly dry. She wished she had a glass of water. Or better yet, booze.

"That's horseshit." She didn't play poker, but as far as she knew, she had no tells. "I don't know what the fuck you're talking about."

"You are lying, poppet."

There was that word again "What the heck's a poppet?"

"A term of endearment. I am growing quite fond of you."

"Wish I could say the same. Look, you can believe whatever stupid shit you want about me. Bottom line, I'm not playing."

"But you are. You have no choice but to do as I say."

"Is that so?"

He nodded complacently. "Indeed, yes. I hold your little life in my hands. And do not lean forward, please. I would prefer it if the gun under your desk is not within your reach."

She sat very still. "You're on to the gun? How'd you pull off that trick? You can't see it from where you're sitting."

"I did not need to see it. Your body language betrayed its presence."

"Think I got any other guns around?"

"In your handbag."

"My body language gave that away too?"

"No. It is self-evident. You wear no shoulder holster, yet a woman in your line must be armed at all times. Ergo, the handbag."

"Ergo," she said quietly. "So how exactly do you hold my future in your hands?"

"I have not researched you on a whim. It was my job to find you."

"I'm not that hard to find. People do it every day."

"But in this case, I had little to work with. I began only with word of a female assassin. Blonde, from somewhere south of Jersey City. No name, no other details. I dug through many rumors and pursued many false leads before I found her."

"You still haven't found her. I'm another dead end." Her mouth twitched. "So to speak."

"I found her," he said again, "and now she will do as I ask."

"And why's that?"

"Because if she does not, I will give her to Streinikov."

Again, this would have been a perfect time for a knuckle crack, and again he missed his cue.

"Who?" she asked.

"My employer. Streinikov. You have heard of him?"

"Nope."

He looked disappointed. "He is an important man. He is most anxious for me to deliver you to him."

"Why?"

"For a conversation."

"About what?"

"I suspect it has something to do with that warehouse."

"I told you, I didn't have a damn thing to do with that."

"And I told you that you are lying." Gura showed her a wide smile made of too many teeth. Most were cracked and yellow. Dentistry had not been a big part of his life.

"So you're supposed to hand me over to the boss man, but you're willing to say you couldn't find me, as long as I help you out with Clarissa Lynch?"

"This is the bargain, yes." He steepled his hands. "I have you in a trap, poppet. No way out."

She looked down at the printouts of Clarissa's Facebook page—a few selfies of a smiling woman with gray eyes and ash blonde hair.

"So it's her or me," she said in a monotone. "I trade her life for mine."

"That is business." He shrugged. "For people like us, anyway."

"You know something, Pavel? I don't think I like you."

"Your opinion is of no significance. Do we understand each other?"

Bonnie didn't answer. She was afraid she understood Pavel Gura only too well.

# 7

BONNIE SAT AT her desk for a long time after Gura left. She found herself staring at the poster of her historical namesake. She had the unsettling impression that her namesake was staring back.

She was under no illusions about the original Bonnie Parker. The girl hadn't been any trailer trash saint, much less a Faye Dunaway look-alike with a retro fashion sense. She'd been a bony, dirt poor, hash-slinging waitress without a future, who remade herself into a gang moll and went on a multi-state crime spree that left a lot of innocent people dead. Bonnie could hardly blame the authorities for blasting the hell out of the roadster that she and Clyde Barrow had taken on their last ride. A photo of the bullet-riddled wreck occupied another wall of her office, as a reminder of where the first Bonnie Parker's path had led.

Still, she felt a curious connection with that other Bonnie, the one who had worked so hard at becoming a tough bitch that she had ended up really being a tough bitch. A blonde blue-eyed girl who had never been a winner, but who had been a survivor—at least up until the time when her luck ran out and her blue eyes were closed for good.

And though Clyde's Bonnie was a bad girl who came to a bad end and deserved it, today's Bonnie couldn't help feeling sorry for her. Sorry—and something more.

She didn't believe in reincarnation. At least she didn't think she did. But sometimes she would wake from a dream in which she was with Clyde and the Barrow Gang, pulling a bank job or outrunning pursuit or simply idling by the side of the road, and sometimes she dreamed of gunfire and breaking glass, an ambush laid by the law, blood in her lap and Clyde screaming.

Sometimes she thought she and the original Bonnie Parker were just roles played by the same actress, and the actress behind the scenes was the only real part of her.

Crazy stuff. But she'd always been a little weird.

Right now, of course, it wasn't the law that worried her—at least not primarily. It was her new friend Pavel. She was pretty sure he hadn't told her the whole truth, but she didn't know which parts of his story were bullshit. Whatever his story, he was sharper than he looked, and not a guy to be underestimated.

It probably didn't pay to sell the Russian mob short, in general. Not that she was any expert on the subject. There wasn't a whole lot of Russkie action in Millstone County. Any place with this many pizzerias and Italian delis was bound to be more of an old-school Cosa Nostra territory.

Still, she kept current on this stuff. It was part of her job—due diligence, and all. She knew the basics. In Russia, ever since the Berlin Wall came down, the mob had pretty much run the whole show. They were nasty boys, a murderers' row of psychopaths masquerading as *biznesmeni*, hulking brutes in black suits and opaque sunglasses, with close-cropped hair and scowling mouths, their bodies decorated in prison tats.

Ukraine, a separate nation now, was a hotbed of ROC influence. The Ukrainian mob was tight with the SBU, the security service that had replaced the KGB. The big bosses, or *vory*, ran the gambling houses, drug dens, and brothels, and a lot of other enterprises, too. She'd read that they were even into the archaeology trade, selling

Greco-Roman antiquities on the black market.

In the US, they were concentrated in Brooklyn and Miami. They smoked cigars and dressed well and carried Makarov pistols and lethal little banana knives with curved blades, usually sheathed in the small of the back. They spoke Russian among themselves, and they did not trust outsiders.

Now one of the *vory* was after her. And it had something to do with Frank Lazzaro and the warehouse. Why the hell a *vor* would give a damn about Lazzaro, Bonnie had no clue. But somehow this guy Streinikov had found out about her and put Gura on her trail. If she didn't cooperate, Gura would hand her over to his boss—or just kill her himself and deliver proof of her death.

Of course, he might do that anyway. Even if she did as she was told, he could still snuff her when it was convenient. And he probably would.

She puffed up her cheeks and blew out a big breath. As her pal Pavel had said, he had her in a trap, and she saw no obvious way out. She was like a wolf in a snare without even the option of chewing her own leg off.

The chair creaked irritably as she pushed it away from the desk. Suddenly she felt the need to get moving. Maybe it was the lingering memory of Gura in this room, or maybe it was the sense that the original Bonnie Parker was staring down at her from the wall in pity and disdain. *You're in it now, girl*, she seemed to say.

"Fuck you, bitch," Bonnie told the poster.

She slung her purse over her shoulder and left the building. A couple blocks down the street was the Main Street Diner, where she could get a proper breakfast. The food wasn't great, but on the plus side, it was really overpriced.

She hadn't gotten very far when she saw a white Dodge Grand Caravan with the words *Beach Cab* bannered across the side panels, discharging a passenger outside a shoe store. She strolled around to the driver's side and stuck her head in the window.

"Yo, Felix."

The cab driver smiled at her. He was a skinny guy with a broad, flat face, and he stood maybe five feet tall on tip-toe. She'd never been sure of his age. Somewhere between twenty and forty-five—that was the most she could narrow it down.

"*Bandida*," he said with a crooked smile. "You're up early."

"And you're up late. Aren't you normally in bed by now?"

"Gotta go the extra mile today. Got stiffed on a big fare last night."

She squinted, her face turning hard, and just like that, thoughts of breakfast were gone. "Who stiffed you?"

"Aw, don't worry about it."

Her voice was cold. "Just give me a name."

"It was that dude Alonzo. You know ..."

"Uh-huh. I know."

"It's no big thing," Felix Ramirez said nervously, watching her face.

She liked Felix. He was her type of guy. He worked mostly at night, and a lot of his clients were, not to put too fine a point on it, lowlifes. Drug dealers and their customers, pimps and their johns, people who needed quick transportation to one of the no-tell motels on the highway. You didn't hold on to a job like that unless you could keep your mouth shut about the people you'd chauffeured and the things you'd overheard and seen.

Felix, who'd crossed the border some time ago—illegally, no doubt—to make his fortune in *Los Estados Unidos*, could be deaf, dumb, and/or blind as circumstances warranted. The police had learned not to bother interrogating him. He never knew anything. His command of English was conveniently unreliable. His memory was just plain awful. It was amazing how little he noticed or recalled. As far as the authorities were concerned, poor Felix lived his life in a daze, unaware of any activities, criminal or otherwise, that were taking place around him.

"I thought you said it was a big fare," Bonnie pressed.

"Well, yeah. I mean, I take him over to the Roach House and wait around for like half an hour while he does business inside. Next we go to Alcatraz, and I wait there too."

The Roach House, more properly the Coach House, was a low-rent motel known for hot and cold running hos and convenient exchanges of cocaine for cash. Alcatraz was a bar.

"He comes out drunk, makes me take him home. This is why he hired me, see? Too many DUIs, so he don't drive after drinking no more. Which is okay, but when we get there, he just walks away. I tell him he owes me, and he yells at me to go fuck myself. He's an asshole," Felix added unnecessarily.

"Yeah, that's the word on him." She knew about Alonzo Duchenne, small time dealer and big time jerkoff. "Where's he live? In Maritime, right?"

"*Bandida*, you don't need to know."

"Gimme his address."

"Never mind. Just forget I say anything."

"I can get the info in other ways, Felix."

"I don't want no trouble."

"Like I would ever cause trouble. Come on, you know me."

"Yeah, I know you. That's the problem."

She was losing patience. "Quit dicking around and tell me where he sleeps."

Reluctantly Felix gave up an address in Maritime, close to the hospital, only a few blocks from where she'd done Gil Krauss last night.

"Good enough. I'll be in touch."

"You don't need to do this, *bandida*," Felix called after her as she walked away.

But she did. That was the thing. She really, really did.

# 8

GURA SAT IN his Mercedes in the parking lot of the Pussy-cat Cabaret, advertised as "a club for gentlemen," until 10 AM, when the club opened its doors. Business was minimal on a Saturday morning. He joined a handful of other patrons, none of whom appeared to be gentlemen in any accepted sense of the word, as they filed into a dimly lit room where sad, exhausted women performed on stage in skimpy lingerie.

It was not too early for a drink, or several. Gura drank vodka. He had an unlimited appetite for the beverage and never got drunk.

He was a man of animal-like habits and inclinations. He liked food, liquor, and women. Spiritual interests were as foreign to him as the carvings on an Egyptian sarcophagus.

He watched the scantily clad dancers and thought about this morning's meeting. He was pleased with how it had gone. Any doubts he'd had about Bonnie Parker had vanished. She might be a mere wisp of a thing, crude in her manner and speech—he'd noted the obscene text on her shirt, a childish bid for attention—but she was indeed a killer, and probably capable enough. Skill in that area was not dependent on breeding, manners, or taste.

She reminded him in certain ways of the woman called Clarissa Lynch. Both young, both blonde, both superficially glib but with a darker underside that spoke of past hardships. Neither was quite what she seemed to be. And neither had more than a few hours left to live.

A new song came on, but the dancers went on gyrating listlessly, their rhythm unchanged. Gura wondered if they even heard the music. He ordered another drink.

He had lied about where he'd met Clarissa. It was not at the Tropicana, but in a club like this one. Yes, it was in Atlantic City, but he had not gone there to play blackjack. He had no facility for card games. He had lied about that, too.

Soon Clarissa would die, and Parker would follow. And what did matter? No life was precious, not even his own. A life was worth what you were paid for it. Parker herself knew this. Gura had known it since he was twelve years old, when he agreed to kill a man for fifty of Mykola Petrovic's hand-rolled cigarettes.

The man was Dmytro Stavitsky, a drunkard who had raped Mykola's mother, a widow with no man to defend her honor. Afraid of Stavitsky, she had not reported the crime to the police or spoken about it to anyone. Mykola himself knew of it only because he'd found her bruised and weeping after Stavitsky stumbled out of their house. Mykola had sworn vengeance but lacked the confidence to do the job himself.

Pavel took the job. Though he was two years younger than Mykola and his experience as an executioner was limited to beheading the chickens that ran in his yard, he knew instinctively that he could do it. His only uncertainty involved method. After some thought, he settled on the hatchet that he had used on the chickens. The blade was rusty and dull; he took care to sharpen it.

He lived in a little windswept village in the Donbas, in eastern Ukraine. A miserable, hardscrabble life—a peasant's life, unchanged for centuries. Men tilled the land and herded goats and mowed down the high grasses with scythes. Squalor and privation were everywhere. Running water was unheard of. Every home had an outhouse and a *banya*—a makeshift bathroom where a bucket of well water, heated on the stove, could be ladled into a tub. Pavel Andreivich Gura bathed twice a month, and only because his mother insisted. His father, a shambling, sleepy-eyed hulk whose calloused fingers were permanently engrained with the dirt of the fields, did not care.

On the fatal night, long after bedtime, Pavel crept out of his house, hatchet in hand, and made his way across open land under the first sliver of a new moon, the slender sickle known as the *molodyk*, an auspicious sign. It was snowing—he remembered that detail, and remembered worrying that his trail of footprints would lead the authorities back to his house. But as the snow kept falling, he realized that any tracks he made would be erased by morning. God was with him. God—or the devil; to him it was all the same.

He avoided the one road that led through the village, though there was no local traffic other than state-owned tractors and a few horse-drawn carts. He gave a wide berth to the home of old Orysia, the *babka* who treated ailments with herbal concoctions and sometimes by more mysterious means. To diagnose illness, she would drip wax from church candles into a pail of cold water and interpret the resulting shapes. She was said, too, to have the *uroky*, the evil eye. Pavel was not sure he believed this, but he was a prudent boy.

Dmytro Stavitsky lived in a dilapidated shack. He had been a farmer, tilling a communal plot, until beer and vodka had consumed what little there was of his industry.

Breaking into the house was not difficult. There were no locks on the windows and no reason for any; the house offered nothing worth stealing. Stavitsky lay asleep on his bed, fully clothed. His boots, wet with snow, had left a puddle on the wooden floor. He was drunk—Pavel could tell as much from his stertorous breathing and the reek of alcohol on his clothes.

Seeing him this way, Pavel altered his plan. The hatchet was unnecessary. Better to smother the inebriated fool with his own pillow. That method would leave no mark.

The only complication was that the man's head lay on the pillow. Pavel had to work it loose, worrying the whole time that the movement might awaken his victim. But though he grumbled in his sleep and smacked his lips behind a mat of beard, Stavitsky remained asleep.

Until the pillow was pressed over his face. Then he was shocked awake, hands flailing, legs kicking. Pavel straddled the man, fighting to hold him down as the big body thrashed under him.

That was the worst part—the struggle, and the uncertainty of the outcome. Had Stavitsky broken free, he would have had the advantage. Even armed with the hatchet, Pavel might not have been able to subdue him.

But Pavel's victim was handicapped by lack of air, by liquor, by confusion and panic. In about a minute it was over. Pavel sat astride a cadaver, his hands gripping a pillow that was limp with sweat.

He felt nothing. No exhilaration, no triumph, not even relief. The job had needed to be done, and he had done it. Now he would get his cigarettes. That was all.

For some time he sat on the bed, watching the dead man. After a while he shoved the pillow under the corpse's head and arranged the sheets so there would be no sign of a struggle. The man had died in his sleep, that was all. No one would question it. Stavitsky had been a useless drunkard and a friendless *durak*, and the village doctor was a drunk also, incompetent and slow-witted. All would be well.

Pavel left the house and returned home. The whole adventure had taken less than an hour. He replaced the hatchet, climbed under the covers, and slept soundly, without dreams. His last thought before dropping off was that killing a man was not much harder than killing a chicken, and far more remunerative.

Though he had not known it at the time, on that night the whole course of his life was set.

GURA WAS ON his third vodka when Ilya Kvint took a seat beside him.

"You would want to meet in a place like this," Ilya said irritably.

"*Da*. I am crude, am I not? The peasant Gura. The rustic, the goatherd."

"I didn't say that."

Gura's shoulders moved. There was much Ilya did not say.

One of the women approached the table, her body moving in languid slow motion like something in an aquarium tank. Ilya waved her away.

Gura was disappointed. He had an ample lap and he enjoyed using it. But he supposed there was business to attend to.

"The cruiser?" he asked.

"Tied up at the basin in Miramar. There was no shortage of transient slips."

"No, there wouldn't be. Not in this season."

"You met Parker?"

"I just came from her shabby little office."

"And?"

"*Nyet* problem," Gura said, using a hybrid expression that had become part of his lexicon. "She will do as she is told."

"She put up no resistance?"

Gura gave another shrug. "Objections of conscience."

"Conscience? Disappointing. I would have hoped she'd discarded that vestigial organ."

"It did not override her instinct of self-preservation, at least."

"Does it ever?"

"Not for men like us," Gura said with a slow sip of vodka.

He looked at Ilya Kvint. Ilya was blond and sleek, with the bony elegance of a gazelle. Cyrillic letters tattooed on his fingers identified him as a made man. The black-ink dagger on his neck signified that he had killed someone in prison. An Iron Cross stamped onto his neck below his Adam's apple was the iconographic equivalent of the message: I don't give a shit about anyone. Gura had no reason to doubt it.

"Conscience or not," Ilya said, "you're sure she'll go through with it?"

"It is a certainty. I have put her in a box."

Ilya smiled. "Before long, I'll put her in a different kind of box."

"You enjoy your work a little too much, Ilyusha."

Ilya's face turned hard. He hadn't liked Gura's use of the diminutive. "And you lack imagination, *domovyk*."

Gura did not object to his nickname when Streinikov used it, but he disliked hearing it from this manicured boy. "Indeed," he said curtly, "I am a brute, an animal. But an intelligent animal. Always remember this."

"I've never doubted it. It does take a certain astuteness to enter Streinikov's inner circle."

"And still more to remain there. I have remained longer than you."

"Only because you were there at the beginning."

"*Da*. Because of that."

Gura was the only one of Streinikov's men left over from the earliest days, before Streinikov acquired the nightclubs and began his ascent. The only one who had known Streinikov even before Smolin had gotten hold of him and made him something less than a man—and at the same time, curiously, something more.

The thought made Gura touch his crotch self-consciously. He felt his *yajtza*, his balls, through the fabric of his trousers, reassuring him by their presence. He could not imagine life as a eunuch. The prospect was intolerable. Ilya, though—Ilya might adjust. A cold bastard, that one. A creature of frost and sleet.

"You seem worried," Ilya said, cutting into his thoughts.

"I am always worried."

"There's no need. The woman will play her part as scripted. Everything will go according to plan."

The boy was young. He did not know that nothing ever went according to plan.

"How did Parker react when you told her of Streinikov?" Ilya asked.

"She had never heard of him."

"Ignorant girl."

"Americans know nothing of importance. They do not know how life is."

Ilya stared into the darkness. He paid no attention to the dancers. His mind was on other things.

"Describe her," he said.

"You have seen her photograph."

Ilya shook his head impatiently. "I mean, describe *her*. Her manner, her psychology."

"Psychology." Gura made a spitting noise. "Everything with you is so complicated, when in fact all is very simple. She is a lost child who has made her way by her wits and ruthlessness. She depends on no one but herself. She keeps many secrets, has catalogued many sins, and she does not expect to live long."

"How can you know that? The last part, about her expectations?"

"She fears shadows, ghosts. Those fears are never groundless. She senses that her time is short."

Ilya smiled. A cruel smile, a wolf's fanged grin. "But she does not know just how short."

"She expects to see the sunrise, I am sure. But then, so do we all."

The wolfish grin vanished. "What does that mean?"

"Only that one can take nothing for granted."

"You wax philosophical, *domovyk*. It is not a mood that suits you."

"You asked the question," Gura said in a tone that suggested Ilya had asked too many of them.

He turned his gaze to the show. At some point the younger man left. Gura did not mark his departure. He was thinking of the village again.

It was gone now—just gone. The population had dwindled until there was no one left. Buses no longer stopped there.

He had been back once to see it, driving a borrowed Lanos while on a trip to Donetsk in springtime. Most of the houses still stood, including his own and Stavitsky's, but there was no human life, and no sounds save the creak of rusted playground equipment in the schoolyard and the dismal laughter of crows.

On a whim he entered Stavitsky's house and stood in what had been the bedroom. All the furnishings were gone, and the place had been taken over by mice and black beetles. He planted himself on the very spot where he had stood that night. After a while he felt tension in his arms and realized he was reliving the struggle to hold the pillow over his victim's face.

The memory did not trouble him. He was, however, vaguely annoyed with himself for having done the job for only fifty cigarettes. He should have asked for more.

But, what the hell, he had been only an innocent child.

# 9

THE JEEP GOT Bonnie to Maritime in twenty minutes. Alonzo Duchenne lived in a one-story bungalow at the ass-end of a giant Walgreen's. A car sat in the driveway, rusting decoratively. Baskets of brown plants, as dry and brittle as old newspaper, hung from hooks on the porch.

Since she had no intention of actually using her firearm, she was comfortable carrying her licensed piece. She knew about guys like Alonzo. They were all bluster, cowards at heart. She'd encountered plenty of them when she was growing up on the street, after her folks died and she was on her own. They could intimidate the weaker ones, but they'd never scared her.

Before announcing herself, she prowled around the house, looking in through the windows. The place was sparsely furnished, and the décor consisted mainly of pornographic pinups. Hip-hop played from unseen speakers, loud enough to make the glass panes tremble.

The rooms were empty except for the bedroom, where Alonzo, half undressed, lay sprawled on an unmade twin bed that was too small for him. The TV was on, blaring in competition with the music. It was tuned to an adult-movie channel. Naturally.

Probably she could just break in and take the money. He had to have cash somewhere, if he'd done a deal at the Roach House last night. Felix hadn't said anything about stopping at a bank, so Alonzo hadn't had a chance to make a deposit.

But she didn't want to play it that way. She wanted to

62

teach him a lesson.

At the front door she leaned on the buzzer and let it drone for a full minute, long enough to rouse the sleeping giant from his coma. Eventually she heard a tramp of feet on the wooden floor. The door was yanked open, and Alonzo stood blinking down at her from a height of six foot something. In a gesture of compliance with society's norms, his pants were on, but the rest of his clothes weren't.

"Yeah?"

"Hey, Alonzo. You don't know me. Mind if I come in?"

He probably did mind, but she'd already scooted under his outstretched arm and slipped into the living room. The air in here carried an ammonia smell she associated with stale cum. There was a coffee table scattered with superhero comic books, and a leather sofa flanked by expensive-looking end tables bearing lava lamps. Actual freaking lava lamps. She wondered if he had a bong and a black light too.

"Who the fuck are you, Barbie doll?" Alonzo asked, turning. He had a surprisingly high voice for a big man.

The hip-hop was still throbbing like a migraine. The heat was turned up high. Alonzo's broad, hairless chest was shiny with sweat.

"Friend of a friend. Somebody you did business with a few weeks back."

"Who?"

"I'm not mentioning any names. He purchased some product from you. Turned out to be mostly baby powder. Very unprofessional, Alonzo. Very bad for your rep."

"White girl, what the fuck brand of bullshit you tryin' to sling?"

He wasn't buying her story, but that didn't matter. She just had to keep Felix safely out of it.

"My friend says you owe him restitution for the bad shit you palmed off on him. He wanted five bills, but I talked him down to two. You're welcome. Now pay up."

Alonzo looked her up and down. He opened his mouth and emitted a deep belch.

"Is that a no?" she asked.

He smiled. "How about you and me talk it over in the bedroom?"

"That ain't gonna happen."

"Maybe I make it happen," he said, stepping forward with the beginning of a leer on his fat mouth.

Smoothly she drew the gun from her purse and pointed it in his direction. She enjoyed his look of stupid surprise.

"Get the money, honey," she said. "And don't shortchange me, or I'll be back. Next time I won't be so fuckin' friendly."

"I don't peddle no inferior, fucked-up shit. Your friend's lying."

"Or you are."

"My product is high quality, bitch."

"Seriously, Alonzo, I don't give a flying squirrel about your product. Think of me as your friendly neighborhood collection agency."

"Come clean, Britney. Who are you, for real?"

"A concerned citizen. Get the money."

He reached behind him, and she tensed.

"Hold it."

"Chill. It's just my billfold."

"Take it out slow."

He obeyed. She watched him peel off four greenbacks. He hesitated, the cash in his hand.

"Fork it over, big guy."

Grudgingly he held out the money. The fingers of her left hand closed over the wad. In that moment he grabbed her right arm, twisting the gun sideways. He pulled her close, her belly jammed up against his.

"Nice tits." His leer was back in a big way. "Now let's

see if you're worth two bills, golden girl."

He started to force her backward. If he got her on the floor, bad things would happen. So she wasn't going on the floor. Period.

She dipped her head and sprang upward on the balls of her feet, driving the crown of her head into his face.

She heard a wet crunch of bone. His nose, breaking.

Pain weakened him. She pulled free, grabbed him by the nuts, and gave them a hard squeeze and a firm twist. Applying torsion, she thought it was called.

He fell backward onto a sofa and lay there, a rain of bright red blood pouring from both nostrils.

"Fuck!" he howled. *"Fuck!"* He had one hand on his nose and the other one on his crotch. She wasn't sure where she'd done the most damage.

"Keep calm, Skeezix. No pain, no gain." Training the gun on him, she picked up the scattered cash. She was pleased to see that the blood hadn't soiled it. She slipped the folded bills into her purse.

"Fuck," he said again, having reached the limit of his eloquence. His nose was a fire hose streaming red. He had grabbed one of the comics and was using it to blot up the blood. It was a sorry fate for the Silver Surfer.

"You oughtta get somebody to look at that," she said from the doorway. "Good thing the hospital's so close."

She left, checking her six all the way to the Jeep to be sure he didn't come charging after her with a gun or something. Anything was possible.

But it didn't happen. He stayed inside, nursing his wound, and she got away clean.

Two hundred bucks. It was probably a dumb move to risk so much for so little. And it wasn't like Felix had insisted. But sometimes she just got pissed off. At such times, she was a teenager again, squatting below an underpass, cadging dollars from tourists, eating day-old donuts that the bakery put out for the homeless. There was no law on the street, and the only justice was the payback you got with your own hands. Either you scrapped for every morsel that was yours, or you gave up and died. There was no middle way. If you let them get away with filching so much as a nickel out of your pocket, you'd defined yourself as easy prey, and you might as well let them cut your throat.

It had been nearly fifteen years since she'd lived like that, but the life was etched deep into her bones. She could never escape it, never move past it. She could only keep fighting, making her own law, relying on no one but herself. One day it would get her killed.

But not today.

# 10

BY ELEVEN FIFTEEN Bonnie finally made it to the Main Street Diner, where it was now time for an early lunch. Her skull ached from butting heads with Alonzo, but it wasn't as bad as some hangovers she'd had. Felix, meeting her outside, had picked up his money. She hadn't taken a cut. "This one was on the house."

"I owe you a favor, *bandida*."

"I'll keep that in mind."

She would, too. It wasn't like she was Mother Teresa.

Now she was chowing down on a lobster roll and scrolling through news articles on her phone. She'd Googled the name Streinikov, finding a composer, a Russian writer from the Soviet era, a dancer, and a reputed mob boss located in north Jersey. The mob boss was Anton Streinikov, and from archived press reports she gathered that he was fifty years old and was active in all the usual things: drug trafficking, sex trafficking, auto theft, protection rackets, and various quasi-legitimate enterprises. He seemed oddly untouchable—a guy who either paid off the authorities on a regular basis, or knew where enough bodies were buried to keep the law at bay.

There wasn't much on him, not even a photo. She kept looking and got lucky when she found an e-book titled *The New Oligarchs*, detailing the rise of Russian organized crime. She didn't have an e-book reader, but with a little fiddling she was able to download an app to her phone and send the $8.99 purchase there. It was the first e-book she'd ever bought, and the first book of any kind she'd bought in at least a year. She probably ought to feel a little bit bad about that.

Worse, she wasn't even going to read very much of it. She used a search feature to find the passages that mentioned Streinikov, about ten pages in all.

He was raised in Donetsk, an industrial town in eastern Ukraine known for its large population of ex-cons. As a young man he was a petty criminal, nothing more. The turmoil surrounding the fall of the Soviet Union gave him his chance. He bought up three illegal nightclubs—places that offered gambling and prostitution, among other diversions. How he got the money for these purchases was unknown. It was rumored that he acted as a front for a Communist Party member. It was also rumored that this benefactor later disappeared, leaving Streinikov in full control. But lots of folks were disappearing in those days, and nobody could be bothered to look into it.

Streinikov upgraded the rundown nightspots and made himself a big man. Through the contacts he made among his patrons, he was able to open new businesses. Some were legal, some weren't, but for practical purposes there was no law in Donetsk in those days.

A decade later, Streinikov—who was now worth, like, a kajillion dollars—relocated to the US and bought an imposing residence in Edgewater on the bank of the Hudson, where he oversaw a thriving export-import business. He also dabbled in restaurants and bars, gas stations and auto service shops, and convenience stores. His other activities were more conjectural, but he was said to be a rival of the Italian and Albanian syndicates in New York City, and to be unpopular even among his fellow *vory*. Evidently he did not play well with others. His inner circle was small and loyal. There was no mention of Pavel Gura, but she hadn't expected one. Gura struck her as a guy who kept a low profile.

One story stood out among the scattered details of

Streinikov's life. It involved his days as a street criminal in Donetsk. He was probably no more than nineteen. Somehow he had ingratiated himself with the mistress of a local crime lord. The crime lord and his goons waylaid young Streinikov in an alley and dragged him into a cellar. And there, according to rumor, Streinikov received his comeuppance. He got neutered. Ouch.

Five years later, when Streinikov had attained power in the city, he sent his crew after the men who had cut him. They were never seen again.

Bonnie put down the phone and rubbed her forehead. She was thinking of all the Long Fong Boyz who'd been turning up dead—some killed by the Italians, but others supposedly offed by another faction. And one gangbanger in particular, the one Brad had told her about last night, the kid who'd been melon-balled. It seemed like the kind of thing Anton Streinikov would do.

It seemed this guy really was serious about what had gone down in the warehouse. And now he'd turned his sights on her. It was almost enough to make a girl lose her appetite.

The waitress, Lizbeth, drifted by with a pot of coffee. Bonnie and Lizbeth used to be pretty friendly with each other, but nowadays Lizbeth just served the food and poured the coffee without saying much. Bonnie had the idea that Lizbeth was scared of her. That wouldn't make her much different from a lot of folks in this town. No one knew what she did on the side, but there were rumors. Hardly anyone would be sorry if she closed up shop and relocated to another part of the country. Or just disappeared altogether, a missing person who was never found. Which, she reflected, was becoming a distinct possibility.

A low squawk of radio crosstalk drew her gaze to the counter. Seated on one of the stools was Dan Maguire, police chief of Brighton Cove and unofficial president of the No Bonnies Club. His feelings about her were roughly equivalent to most people's feelings about the Ebola virus.

Dan had probably spotted her as soon as he walked in, but he'd made no move to approach her table. He just sat at the counter looking over the dog-eared menu, even though he always ordered the same exact thing, a bacon double cheeseburger. Lizbeth had told her so, back when they were on speaking terms.

Bonnie went back to her lobster roll and her e-book. Though Streinikov had gotten his first break in nightclubs, the real money had come later, in the only part of the Russian economy that was worth a plugged ruble—natural resources. Oil and gas, mostly. By methods unknown, but undoubtedly involving the judicious application of force, he had acquired significant holdings in Ukrainian refineries and pipelines. In the US, he was said to run a variety of fuel bootlegging and gasoline fraud schemes, the simplest of which involved buying tax-free diesel fuel slated exclusively for off-road purposes and then selling it to no-name gas stations at the full wholesale price—taxes and all. Since no taxes had actually been paid, the supplier pocketed an illicit profit on every sale. If anyone found out about the ruse, the supplier's front company would fold up, and the schmuck who ran the gas station would be left holding the bag.

She raised her head, glimpsing the outline of an idea. She was still musing on it when Sammy interrupted, singing his Beatles tune. Funny how he never got tired of that one.

The phone's display screen showed the number of Joy Krauss's burner. Right away Bonnie knew this wasn't going to be good news.

"Hey, Joy," she said, keeping her voice low because Dan was only a few yards away.

"It's not working my God they know I did it they know they *know*!"

Rush of words, no pause for breath. The lady was flipping out.

Bonnie turned in her seat, away from the counter where Dan was observing her without trying to be too obvious about it. "Joy. Listen to me. Just keep it together."

"Keep it together? They *know*! It's all coming apart into a million pieces and you tell me to *keep it together?*"

"How exactly is it coming apart? Talk to me."

"It's no use pretending. I'll have to confess. It's the only way. I'll have to tell them everything."

Holy fuckamoley, she was planning to squeal.

"You haven't said anything yet, right?" Bonnie asked slowly.

"No, but I'll have to, I'll *have* to—"

"*Joy.*" Bonnie put some ice in her voice. "Calm the fuck down. You're getting fuckin' hysterical, and that's not good."

The woman hitched in a breath but said nothing.

Clearly she was losing her shit. Bonnie had to tread cautiously or risk having Joy hang up on her. And if Joy hung up in the state she was in, her next call would be to the cops for sure.

"Okay," Bonnie said more gently. "Now go slow and explain to me exactly what's got you so worked up. What is it that they know?"

"About you," Joy breathed. "They know about *you.*"

In Bonnie's gut, the lobster roll was suddenly threatening to make a comeback. "Tell me what happened."

"I was home. The doorbell rang. It was a cop. A different one. Not from Maritime. From Brighton Cove."

Oh, shit. "Yeah?"

"His name was Maguire. He's the chief of police there. Well, you must know him. Dave, I think. Dave Maguire."

"Dan," Bonnie said softly. She let her gaze swivel toward the counter, where Dan Maguire was still watching her, quite openly now. His small glittery eyes were bright with hunger. Rodent eyes. He was a rat, and he was looking at her like she was a prize chunk of cheese.

"He invites himself in," Joy was saying, "and right out of the blue he says, 'I know you hired Bonnie Parker.'"

Bonnie shut her eyes, wondering how the hell Dan could have tumbled to that. He wasn't exactly Sherlock Holmes. He wasn't even Dr. Watson.

"What did you tell him?" she asked hopelessly.

"I acted like I'd never heard of you. Like I didn't know what he was talking about. But he didn't believe it. He *knows*."

"He doesn't know. He suspects. Did he say why he'd even mentioned me?"

"He said he had a source in town who told him Gil was making inquiries about you. So the way he figures it, Gil found out I hired you and started asking questions about your reputation to find out what I was up to."

"Okay. I get it." Dan wasn't Sherlock Holmes, after all. He'd made the connection, but he'd gotten it backward. Gil had been asking about her *before* Joy had hired her. There weren't many locals with the right kind of reputation for the job Gil had in mind.

Even so, Dan had put Joy Krauss and Bonnie Parker together, a linkage that would not be good for either of them.

Sammy chimed with a text message from Gura, his signal for her to get moving. He and Clarissa must be heading down to the dining room for lunch.

She wished it was still legal to smoke in restaurants. She could have used a cig right now.

"Bonnie? You there?"

"I'm here. Where are you now?"

"At home."

"Okay. I want you to stay there for a while, drink some tea, think good thoughts. Then at one o'clock, meet me in the public library in Garrett."

One o'clock should be late enough to give her time to deal with the hotel thing.

"The library?"

"Yeah. Go into the stacks and make like you're browsing. I'll find you. Okay?"

"Yes. Okay."

"And, Joy?" She kept using the woman's name. It might help to center her. "Don't talk to anybody or make any decisions until you've met with me. Got it?"

"Yes ..." She sounded unsure.

"We'll work this out," Bonnie said firmly. "It's very doable. Believe me. I've got a plan in mind already."

"What plan?"

"I'll tell you at the library. Just hang tight. I'll see you in two shakes."

She ended the call. Two shakes? Had she actually said that? She really needed to work on her street cred.

She dropped some bills on the table to cover her tab, leaving the lobster roll half eaten. On her way out, she brushed past Dan at the counter.

"You look stressed, Parker," he said with that same shit-eating smirk. "Bad day?"

"Not until you showed up. You got a way of bringing me down."

"That is exactly what I'm going to do, Parker. I am going to bring ... you ... down."

She didn't have a good answer for that. She left him with his bacon double cheeseburger and his ugly grin.

As she slipped into the Jeep, she assessed the situation. As she'd told Joy, Dan didn't actually know anything. All he had was a rumor about Gil and a connection that could never be proved.

With proper management, the situation was probably salvageable. But it all depended on her client's emotional balance. If Joy was too far gone to cooperate, then she was a human hand grenade with the pin pulled, and it was only a matter of time till she blasted herself and Bonnie straight into the Edna Mahan Correctional Facility, the women's prison in Hunterdon County, where orange really was the new black.

Bonnie had no intention of doing time because a client wigged out on her. She would do her utmost to make Joy get with the program.

And if that proved to be impossible ...

She didn't like to think about that. It was a step she'd never taken, a step she never wanted to take.

But there was a way to keep Joy quiet. A foolproof way.

If it came to that.

# 11

GURA'S TEXT MESSAGE had consisted of just three digits: 317. It wasn't code. It was the number of Clarissa Lynch's room in the Prince Edward Hotel.

Bonnie arrived at the hotel about five minutes after leaving the diner. She spent the time worrying about what she might find and what she would do about it. She didn't want to confirm Clarissa Lynch as an operative if she could avoid it. Of course, even if she did find something, she could always lie. But she didn't think it would work. Gura was too sharp. He'd read her body language well enough to know about the gun under her desk. If she tried shining him on about Clarissa, he would know.

As she parked on a side street, she remembered Gura's voice saying, *I have you in a trap, poppet.*

What the hell was a poppet, anyway? She took a second to Google it on her phone. The definition was "small child." So that was how he saw her. Swell.

She was pissed off as she strode through the hotel lobby, her handbag swinging from her shoulder. She'd thrown on a winter coat salvaged from the mess of stuff occupying the rear compartment of the Jeep. The coat was warmer than the jacket she'd been wearing, and it served better at concealing the shirt she'd put on at Brad's. The shirt's message about trading blowjobs for booze was the kind of sentiment that might raise a few eyebrows in the Prince Edward.

She wasn't sure who the actual Prince Edward was. The guy they said was Jack the Ripper? Or maybe the one who abdicated so he could marry that chick with a dude's name—Wallace Shawn or whoever? Really, she had no clue. One of the disadvantages of dropping out of school at fourteen was that your Trivial Pursuit abilities were severely impaired.

The hotel was dimly lit but extravagantly decorated, like an upscale whorehouse. Red predominated. Red pile carpet, red velvet draperies, red uniforms on the bellhops. Lots of red. In season the place would be sold out, but in late February it was largely empty even on a weekend.

She knew the layout. The hotel restaurant, which went by the name of the Mute Swan, was to her left. Near the entrance, the menu was displayed on a table. It offered a bunch of stuff she barely recognized as food—truffles, tripe, sweetbreads, and a selection of mystery items categorized as amuse-bouches. No cheeseburgers or corndogs. Definitely not her kind of place.

She lifted her eyes from the menu to scan the half-empty dining room. Gura, with his blood red scarf, was easy to spot. He and a blonde companion were sharing a table and a drink. The blonde was the woman from Facebook, no question. Clarissa Lynch in the flesh.

By the doorway stood a big potted schefflera. Bonnie pretended to drop something, giving her an excuse to bend down and clip a camera the size of a cigarette pack to the pot. No one would notice it among the leaves. The camera, taken from a drawer in her office desk, ran on a CR2 battery. It had a 75-degree viewing angle, wide enough to take in the entire dining room through the doorway.

With a cell phone app she connected the camera to the hotel Wi-Fi. The video feed was now being uploaded to the web in real time.

She wasn't real big on surprises. If lunch ended early, she needed to know about it before Clarissa opened the door of room 317 and found a stranger pawing through her stuff.

On her way to the elevator she checked the video on her phone. Gura and Clarissa were roughly centered in the frame. She was about to put the phone back in her pocket when Clarissa stood up and walked away from the table.

Leaving already? What the hell?

Bonnie doubled back in time to see the girl disappear into the ladies' room. Not really leaving, just making a pit stop.

It seemed like too good an opportunity to pass up. Bonnie followed her into the restroom and busied herself at one of the sinks, pretending to fool with her hair. There wasn't really a whole lot she could do with her hair, which was straight and blonde and shoulder length, but she did her best to look busy until Clarissa emerged from a stall and washed her hands in the adjacent sink.

Stealing sideways glances, Bonnie checked her out. She was younger than expected, probably not more than twenty-five. Good looking in a hard-edged, slightly ano-rexic sort of way. Tall, ash blonde, with high cheekbones and a strong jawline. She had kind of a Taylor Swift thing going on. When Gura had said she seemed too good to be true, he hadn't been kidding. In person she looked way hotter than the blurry selfies on her Facebook page.

"Nice hotel," Bonnie said as she turned on the water and pumped liquid soap into her hands.

"Yes." Clarissa didn't look at her. "Very."

"Been here before?"

"First time."

"Staying long?"

"Overnight."

Okay, not exactly a great conversationalist. Or at least, not really into having a dialogue with a stranger in a bath-room. Bonnie respected that. She wasn't big on casual chatter herself. But it annoyed her that she couldn't get a read on the girl.

Clarissa was still soaping up when her wristwatch slipped a bit, momentarily revealing a white stripe of wrist marred by three purple punctures. Needle marks. Hastily she snugged the watch back into place.

So she was a user. She used a vein in her wrist to shoot up, and the watch, with its wide chain-link band, served as concealment. Interesting. It spoke of a vulnerability—weakness, even—that was rare for someone playing the kind of game Clarissa Lynch played.

Bonnie dried her hands on a cloth towel, then turned to Clarissa and said with a smile, "I'm Bonnie, by the way."

A moment's hesitation "Clarissa."

Her technique could be better. The hesitation made it a little too obvious that she was using an alias.

"Unusual name," Bonnie said. "I like it."

The woman turned to face her. "Did you want something?"

Her eyes were gray and cool and suspicious, and she wasn't smiling.

"I'm just a Chatty Cathy," Bonnie said. "Sorry if I came off like a pain in the ass."

She left without saying anything more. As she shut the door, she felt Clarissa's cold stare on her back.

Not the most revealing encounter, but at least she'd learned a few things about Clarissa Lynch. The girl was a hard case. She'd been around. She was an addict. And she didn't belong in a place like the Prince Edward, any more than did Bonnie herself.

Now it was time to find out what she'd brought with her in her luggage.

The elevator delivered her to the third floor. She looked up and down a corridor lined with closed doors and dim lightbulbs in fancy sconces. The lightbulbs were shaped like candle flames, but they weren't fooling any-one.

Room 317 was near the far end of the hall. Two doors down, a maid's cart stood outside an open doorway. The snore of a vacuum cleaner came from within. Other than the maid, there was nobody around.

It was go time.

Happily, she had prior experience in breaking and en-tering at the Prince Edward. Last year a worried wife had hired her to spy on her husband. Bonnie found that the hubby regularly checked into this hotel, unusual behavior considering he lived just two towns away. Even more damaging, he registered under an assumed name and paid cash. This was incriminating enough, but Bonnie wanted "ocular proof," an expression she'd picked up somewhere and used whenever possible. She wanted to catch the philandering son of a bitch in flagrante delicto with his bimbo *de jour.*

Doing so required planting a camera in the room—the same camera she was using today. She'd cased the hotel, learned the make and model of the keycard locks, and presented this information to a hacker pal of Mama Blessing. Two days later Bonnie had paid him a hundred bucks for a dry erase marker.

But not just any dry erase marker. This one contained a gizmo called an Arduino microcontroller board and some other junk. When you inserted the tip of the marker into the DC power port in the door lock, the micro-thingamajig instantly read the lock's 32-bit code and played it back, causing the lock to release.

Bonnie did not pretend to understand the details. The hacker guy could just as easily have told her that the dry erase marker housed a colony of army ants who'd been specially trained to march into the lock and disable it. As far as she was concerned, the thing was magic. That was okay. She could use a little more magic in her life.

And the ruse had worked. She'd planted the camera without breaking a sweat, and a few days later, wifey was suing for divorce.

She rechecked the video feed. Gura and his lady fair were giving their orders to a waiter. She hoped the service was slow.

At the door, she plucked the marker from her purse and jammed the tip into the socket. In less time than it took her to blink, she heard the satisfying click of the latch. She slipped inside and shut the door behind her.

Okay, she was in. Now she had to toss the room without making it obvious, and she had to do it fast. For all she knew, Clarissa was one of those bitches who would be satisfied with a stick of celery for lunch.

The girl traveled light—only one suitcase. It lay on a folding table. The toy-sized padlock was no match for Bonnie's collection of lockpicks. She got the case open in seconds, transferred it to the bed, and began removing the contents, laying them in separate piles corresponding to the items' original position. Everything would have to be repacked exactly the way it had been.

Blouses, sweaters, slippers, sexy lingerie. No hats, though. Bonnie could not entirely trust a girl who didn't like hats.

Toiletries, birth control, a paperback novel. Nothing suspicious. So far Clarissa was clean as a whistle. And what exactly was so clean about a whistle, anyway?

The thing was, Clarissa could have anticipated that Gura or one of his henchmen would search her luggage. If she was carrying anything she didn't want them to know about, it was probably hidden.

Bonnie ran her hands over the bottom and sides of the suitcase. Something could have been sewn into the lining.

She didn't feel any items in the lower part of the case. But when she checked the lid, her fingers found a long flat shape—something that extended along the entire perimeter of the case.

"Yahtzee," she said.

She glanced at Sammy again. Gura and Clarissa were already receiving their lunch order, or at least the first course. The food had come fast. Too bad.

With a pocket flashlight she examined the lining until she found a slit. Reaching in, she extracted the mystery object.

It was a belt. A wide black leather belt, with a large gold-plated buckle that bore an embossed design she'd seen just this morning, at her meeting with Gura.

Now, why would Clarissa, or whatever her real name was, be carrying a belt that was an exact duplicate of her boyfriend's? Only one reason: she intended to make a switch.

Sometime tonight, while Gura slept, Clarissa would replace his belt with this one, counting on him not to notice any difference.

Fair enough, but what was so special about this belt? Bonnie took a close look at the buckle. It was in two pieces, held together with tiny screws on the underside. Luckily she had a tool in her pick set that could serve as a tiny screwdriver. She used it to take the buckle apart.

Inside was a very flat, incredibly lightweight gizmo that she identified immediately as a GPS tracker, the kind that ran on a battery and recorded data for later retrieval. She was familiar with the tech, but she'd never come across one this small before. She was tempted to purloin it. It could come in handy.

She did not purloin it. Instead she switched Sammy to camera mode and took several pics of the tracker nesting in the buckle.

Anything else in the lining? Yeah, two smaller items. She teased them out. A capped syringe and a vial labeled with a chemical formula: $C_{21}H_{28}N_2O_5$. Probably a sedative, Rohypnol or something like that. Or—she remembered the needle marks on the girl's wrist—maybe it was some kind of dope for Clarissa herself.

She took pics of those items too. Now she had Clarissa dead to rights. Emphasis on dead.

Though she wasn't sure what the chemical was for, the basic plan was clear enough. The woman was a pro, and she was planning to switch out Gura's belt while he slept. Once he was outfitted with the tracker, she could download the data on his movements the next time they got together. What she wanted with that info, Bonnie had no idea, but somebody was paying her for it.

"Fuck," she whispered, with feeling.

She switched the phone from camera mode to the video feed and checked out the restaurant again.

Uh-oh.

Clarissa was on her feet. Gura sat rigid in his chair. Harsh words were being exchanged. The camera lacked audio, but the images spoke for themselves.

Lovers' quarrel. At the worst possible time.

Other patrons were looking. It must be quite a scene.

As Bonnie watched, Clarissa straightened her shoulders and harrumphed out of the restaurant.

Returning to her room, probably.

And the belt buckle was still disassembled, the contents of the suitcase distributed on the bed.

Bonnie stuffed the syringe and vial back inside the lining, then started to reattach the underside of the buckle, cursing the microscopic screws. Suddenly the tool she was using didn't seem to be grabbing the notches in the screwheads the way it had before. She kept throwing glances at the phone, hoping to see Clarissa reappear in the restaurant. No such luck.

Goddamned Gura could at least have texted her with a warning. He didn't know about the surveillance camera. Did the son of a bitch want her to get caught?

Finally she got Humpty Dumpty together again. Sliding the belt under the lining was another challenge. She threaded it through the slit and pushed it around until it was back in place.

Still no Clarissa. Maybe she'd gone for a walk. The beach was just across the street. Or ...

Rattle of the doorknob.

Bonnie turned as the door swung open. There was no way she could justify her presence in the room. And Clarissa was a pro, might be armed. She tensed for a fight.

Then the door finished opening, and Bonnie saw a maid standing there with a stack of bath towels in her hands.

"*Hola,*" the maid said with a smile.

Damn. She really should have hung a *Do Not Disturb* sign on the door.

"I bring towels," the maid added.

"What's that?"

"Plenty towels. You call for towels."

"Towels. Right. Thanks."

The maid went into the bathroom.

"I'm unpacking," Bonnie added unnecessarily.

No answer from the maid, who was already arranging the extra towels on a ledge over the sink.

Bonnie started replacing the items from the suitcase, working in reverse order from their removal. She was nearly done when she became aware that the maid, finished in the bathroom, was lingering by the door.

Oh, right. A tip.

She dug a bill out of her purse without bothering to check the denomination. "Thanks."

The maid beamed. The bill must have been a big one. "*Gracias.*"

"Yeah, uh, *hasta* lumbago."

The door closed, and Bonnie was alone in the room. Clarissa still hadn't showed up, a minor miracle. But she didn't trust her luck to last.

She shut the lid, secured the padlock, and returned the suitcase to the folding table.

When she eased open the door, she was sickly certain she would come face to face with Clarissa Lynch, waiting outside.

The corridor was empty. No Clarissa.

Bonnie found the stairwell and headed down. She didn't want to run into Clarissa getting on or off the elevator. After their tête-à-tête in the restroom, her presence on this floor might require an explanation she wasn't prepared to offer.

She retrieved the camera from the schefflera pot. Gura was eating his lunch in solitude. He appeared tranquil and composed. He still hadn't texted her. Maybe he'd known all along that Clarissa wouldn't go straight to her room. Or maybe he hadn't cared if Clarissa walked in and took her by surprise.

One way or the other, they were going to have a conversation about this.

Not here, though. Not in a public place. She didn't want anyone connecting her with Gura.

Her reputation in this town was crappy enough as it was.

# 12

SHE FOUND HER Jeep on the side street where she'd left it. From the driver's seat she sent Gura a text, telling him to finish his chow and meet her at the southwest corner of Atlantic and First.

With time to kill, she Googled the chemical formula of the stuff she'd found. It turned out to be doxylamine succinate, and yeah, it was a sedative. Pretty powerful, too. From what she read, that shit would put you to sleep faster than a Jane Austen movie.

She didn't see how it could be administered without Gura's knowledge, though. It had to be injected directly into a vein to take effect quickly. Maybe it was a last resort. Or maybe Gura was a user, and Clarissa figured she could trick him into injecting himself.

Bonnie doubted it. Gura didn't seem like the type.

She waited. She smoked a cigarette. She played Angry Birds on her phone. She wasn't too good at that game, which surprised her, because she was real good at being angry.

She was angry right now. And she intended to let Gura know it.

Twenty minutes after sending the text, she saw Gura in her side view mirror, approaching slowly, the red scarf flapping like a flag. She didn't bother to signal him. Having watched her building this morning, he would recognize the Jeep.

The passenger door opened, and he settled heavily into the seat next to her.

"Well?" he said curtly.

"We'll get to my homework assignment in a minute. First I want to know why you didn't give me a heads-up when Ms. Lynch left the restaurant."

He shrugged. "I assumed you were foresighted enough to monitor our activity in some fashion."

"That was a hell of an assumption."

"But an accurate one, poppet."

"I could've been caught red-handed. Maybe that's what you want."

"Why should I want this?"

"Fuck if I know. But you're starting to piss me off in a serious way. And incidentally, why the hell would that bitch need extra towels?"

"Towels?"

"Yeah, towels. She called down for 'em, I guess. A maid brought them when I was in the middle of repacking your girlfriend's unmentionables. What does she want with extra towels? She got, like, a towel fetish or some god-damn thing?"

Gura shrugged. "I do not know. Perhaps she antici-pates that we will do something exceptionally dirty to-night."

"Oh, yuck. That's a mental picture I didn't need to see."

"Calm yourself, poppet."

"Quit calling me that. I don't like it."

"It is a term of endearment."

She blew a jet of smoke at him. "Yeah, right."

He smiled. "I too have a nickname. It was given to me by Streinikov when I entered his employment. Like you, I did not care for it. Not at first." He took out a pack of ciga-rettes and tapped one into his hand. "I am called the *do-movyk*."

"If that means asshole, it fits."

"It does not mean asshole." Placidly he lit the ciga-rette. With the two of them smoking and the windows rolled up, the atmosphere was going to get pretty hazy, but right now Bonnie didn't care. "A *domovyk* is a creature of Slavic folklore. An odd, hairy, disgusting creature, more beast than man."

Privately she considered that name to be extremely appropriate. At least, she thought her opinion was private until he gave her a sidelong glance and said, "I see you approve."

Shit. There he went again, reading her mind.

"Whatever you may think," he went on imperturbably, "the name was not bestowed on me for my physical attributes. It was in recognition of my dutiful service. A *domovyk* is a protector of the household, a lackey who carries out all manner of useful chores. I was Streinikov's *domovyk*. His right-hand man, you may say."

"That's a beautiful story, Pavel. I'm guessing your useful chores included whacking people and making their bodies go bye-bye?"

"A good *domovyk* does what he is told. You could not be a *domovyk*, poppet. You are too headstrong, I think. Too contrary. And you are too much alone."

"Yeah, I got a real attitude problem. Just like your girlfriend, judging from what went down in the restaurant."

"It was a minor quarrel, nothing serious."

"It could have been serious for me."

"Could have been, but was not. Now tell me the results of your search."

"You're awfully friggin' cavalier about my safety."

He turned in his seat, facing her directly for the first time. His face was expressionless, but his eyes were alive with rage.

"That is because I do not give a *fuck* about you, Bonnie Parker. I do not give two *shits* about your worthless life. You mean"—he spat into his hand—"*this* to me. Is this clear?"

She didn't answer. Those eyes held her speechless.

"Now I have had enough of your fucking bullshit. Tell me what you found."

He turned away. She saw the rise and fall of his chest as he gulped a breath of air after his tirade. Other than that, he was immobile.

She knew better than to test him further. She could press her luck only so far. "Okay, Pavel. I'll tell you. Your gal is a pro."

"And you know this, how?"

"Because she brought a present for you. One you weren't supposed to know about, even after you got it."

"What present?"

"A new belt. An exact duplicate of that one." She pointed at his waistline. "Same buckle with the same design, whatever it is."

"It is the *tryzub*, the trident. The national emblem of Ukraine."

"And you wear it all the time, I'm guessing. Well, Clarissa noticed." She turned on her phone and showed him a photo of the disassembled buckle and the secret it held. "It's a GPS tracker."

"So I see."

"She's planning the old switcheroo."

"Yes. Like implanting a chip in a dog. But this dog has fangs."

And probably fleas, Bonnie commented silently. Then she wondered if Gura had picked up on that thought, too. Damn, the sly bastard really had her spooked.

He expelled another plume of smoke. "Did you find anything more?"

"A syringe and some heavy-duty sedative." She showed him those snaps too. "Doxy-something-or-other."

"Is that it?"

"Isn't that enough?"

"*Da.* Quite enough."

The interior of the Jeep was starting to resemble a

fogbound London alley. Bonnie cranked down her window a few inches, letting in some of the cold.

She didn't want to ask the next question, but she had to. "So what comes next?"

"I think you know."

"You can't just let her off with a warning? I mean, it's obviously business, not personal."

"In my profession, warnings are very seldom given."

"Yeah. I kinda figured you'd say that."

She asked herself if she could take him right here. They were on an empty side street, and the Jeep's windows were closed, or almost closed. The Walther in her handbag wasn't silenced, but the shot might not be heard, especially if she jammed the muzzle against his body to muffle the report.

It would require quickness. She'd have to grab the gun and fire before he could react. But maybe—

Then she saw him grinning at her, a hairy death's head with orangutan teeth, and she knew it was hopeless. He could guess her thoughts almost before she knew them herself. Maybe he really was some kind of mystical creature, part monkey, part devil.

She took a last drag on her cig and crushed out the stub in the ashtray. "Okay, Pavel. I held up my end. We're done here."

He made no move to rise. "You have performed competently. But we are not done. There is one more small task you must carry out for me."

"What task?"

"It is a little thing, really." Gura smiled at her. "You must execute Miss Clarissa Lynch. And you must do it tonight."

# 13

THE WORDS HUNG in the smoky air like some kind of evil incantation. Bonnie stared at the man beside her. Slowly she held up both hands.

"Whoa," she said quietly. "Just ... *whoa*."

Gura was unmoved. "This troubles you? I have already established that you are a killer, poppet. You will kill my Clarissa, as you killed Lazzaro and Chiu in the warehouse."

"Now hold on—"

"You will do this," he went on implacably, staring straight ahead, "or I will deliver you to Streinikov. What will happen to you after that does not bear thinking about."

"Bullshit. You can't hand me over to your boss. If you do, I'll spill the beans about you and Clarissa. I know the whole story now. That'd put you deep in the shit."

"Yes, I have thought of this. But you see, if you do not cooperate, I will have no choice but to tell Streinikov about my indiscretion. In that event, I can only hope that producing you at the same time will mitigate his disappointment."

"And when he finds out you offered to let me skate if I played along?"

"Come, now." He steepled his hands. "Why would he believe such a desperate story?"

He had a point there. People *in extremis* would say pretty much anything to save themselves.

She took a different tack. "Why do you even need me?

You're a big boy. Do the girl yourself if she bothers you so much."

"Impossible. I have been observed with her in Atlantic City and elsewhere. I booked the room for her in your town's hotel. I will be the obvious suspect. I must have an unbreakable alibi."

"Then get one of your mobbed-up Russkie pals to do it."

"And share with them the fact that I allowed myself to be compromised—and by a woman? In my business, you give none of your associates such leverage."

"And how can I trust you not to do me once I've offed Clarissa?"

"You cannot trust me, poppet. You cannot trust anyone." He tapped the ring he called the Roundstone. "Remember?"

"Then why should I do it at all?"

"Because if you refuse, you go to Streinikov. Whereas, if you obey, you may get to live."

"Or I may not."

"Life can never be guaranteed. Only death can be promised with certainty. To be delivered to Streinikov is death."

"Very persuasive. You got a big future in motivational speaking."

She was about sixty percent sure—okay, seventy percent—that he did plan to kill her when the job was done. It would explain why he'd gone out of his way not to be seen with her. He'd visited her office first thing in the morning, and he'd made sure not to park in the lot or wait by the building where someone might notice him.

Odds were, he was hiring her as a patsy. She would take care of Clarissa, and then he would take care of her.

She wanted very much to light another cig, but somehow she couldn't get her hand to reach for one.

"Tell me something," she said slowly. "Have you been talking to the Long Fong Boyz?"

"I? No."

"But you know who's been taking them out, right? Besides Lazzaro's people."

"It is possible I know something of this," he said blandly.

"Was Streinikov a friend of Frank Lazzaro?"

"Streinikov is a friend of nobody."

"But he was plenty pissed off when Lazzaro died, right?"

"He may have been."

"And he blamed the Long Fong Boyz. Until lately—when he started blaming me."

Gura said nothing. He didn't have to. It was the only version of events that made sense.

"There's a story going around about your boss. Word is he's been spayed. You know what that means, right?"

"I have heard the term."

"Is it true?"

"You would have to ask him."

"Well, here's the funny thing. I'm told one of the Boyz recently got neutered. Not by choice."

"Tsk, tsk. Yours is such a violent country."

"Yeah, it's a jungle out there. So does clipping this kid's nut sack sound like something your boss might do?"

"It is possible." Gura stamped out his cigarette. "It would be in keeping with his sense of humor."

"Funny guy."

"He will do far worse things to you, Bonnie Parker."

"Worse than that? He'd have to be awful creative."

"He is."

He gave her some time to think about that. Ribbons of smoke from the two extinguished cigarettes coiled around her like an enveloping net.

When she spoke, her voice was lower than before. "Even if I do the job, I won't be off the hook. When you tell Streinikov you couldn't find the hitter from the warehouse, he'll just send someone else looking."

"*Nyet.* The matter will be closed."

"How can you arrange that?"

"It is simplicity, poppet. I will convince Streinikov that Clarissa Lynch was the woman he wanted all along. I will pin the warehouse incident on her." He spread his hands. "It is plausible enough. Streinikov knows only that the killer is a blonde female who keeps a low profile while conducting illegal activities. This describes Clarissa Lynch as well as it does you."

"You think you can sell that?"

"I know I can."

Maybe he could. It was clear he'd planned it all out. There was even a small chance she could live through this thing, as long as the woman who called herself Clarissa did not.

"I really don't wanna do this," she said tonelessly.

"As your Clark Gable would say—frankly, my dear, I do not give a fuck."

"I think you got that quote pretty wrong." She sighed. "I don't have any choice, do I?"

"None." He folded his meaty hands in satisfaction. "It is decided."

"Yeah. I guess it is."

"Then you will require a retainer. How much?"

The question surprised her as much as anything he'd said. It took her a moment to get her brain in gear and remember numbers and procedures. "Um ... For a job like this, I normally charge three upfront, thirty on completion. But I was sort of assuming you'd want it done gratis."

"The laborer is worthy of his hire. Do you know this saying? It is from the Bible."

"I wouldn't have pegged you as the religious type."

"I am not. My mother was."

He removed a billfold from his vest pocket and peeled off a series of hundred-dollar bills, stacking them neatly on the dashboard. A methodical man.

"Blood money," he said, seeming to enjoy the words.

Mrs. Krauss had said the same thing. Bonnie hadn't liked it then.

She liked it even less now.

# 14

THE GARRETT TOWNSHIP public library was part of a municipal complex on Iron Town Road. Bonnie picked up a parking pass at the gate. It would cost her two blocks to drive out. Worth it if she could calm Joy the fuck down. She noticed a security camera at the gate, which she wasn't too crazy about, but there were no cameras in the lot itself.

Looking for an available space, she mused on the injustices of life. Here she was, your ordinary small-town PI and part-time hitter just trying to get by, and all of a sudden her client was losing her nerve and a made man in the Russian mob was setting her up for probable termination. The Russian thing was bad enough, but Joy's threat to go all *True Confessions* was what had really put the kibosh on her weekend. That kind of move was just willfully fucking stupid.

Finally she parked the Jeep under a leafless maple in a far corner of the lot. Before going inside, she climbed into the backseat, where she kept a hit kit.

Nothing fancy, just an untraceable .22 and a screw-on silencer. She'd hidden it inside the seat cushion, which was easy enough to do, since the cushion was already badly ripped and liberally patched with duct tape.

She stripped off some of the tape, extracted the gun, attached the silencer, checked the magazine, and stashed the item in her purse. She left the purse on the passenger seat. She wasn't going to take it with her. There was no point in toting a piece around in a place where schoolkids congregated. She wasn't going to use the gun in the building anyhow. With any luck—please, God—she wouldn't need to use it at all.

Ordinarily she wouldn't have risked a personal meeting with a client while the police were actively working the case. There was always a chance the client was under surveillance and the meeting would be observed. Under the circumstances, it couldn't be helped. She needed a face-to-face to get Joy under control—if that was even possible.

She entered the library through a sliding door and made a casual circuit of the interior. She found Joy in aisle nineteen of Reference and Nonfiction, making a poor show of studying a row of history books. Bonnie went down aisle twenty and positioned herself across from her. Through a gap in the books she could see a rectangular slice of the woman's face. In the wan fluorescent light she looked haggard and scared.

One good thing about a library was that you could talk in a whisper without drawing suspicion. While pretending to peruse a book on America's colonial past, Bonnie said quietly, "Good to see you, Joy. How you holding up?"

"How do you think?" The reply was snappish, irritable. This was a lady at the end of her string.

"Okay, dumb question." She put back the book and selected another one at random. "The main thing is you haven't made any mistakes that can't be fixed."

"They know I did it. Dan Maguire—"

"Dan's had a bug up his butt about me for years. He thinks I'm behind every bad thing that goes down in Millstone County."

"Why are we meeting like this? Do you think the police are watching me?"

"Anything's possible. But I cased the joint pretty thoroughly, and I didn't spot anybody who seemed to be taking an interest in you. Didn't see any cop cars in the parking lot, either, and I can always pick 'em out, even the undercover rides. So I think we're okay."

"I don't see how it came to this."

"It didn't have to. If you woulda lawyered up like I told you ..."

"I thought it would look guilty. And then everything happened so fast."

"It always does."

A woman toting two kids came down Bonnie's aisle. The tykes began pawing through books on the American Revolution. Bonnie moved to the far end of the aisle and stared at the wall, which displayed a chart of the Dewey Decimal System and a portrait of astronaut Russell Schweikart, for some reason. She waited for Joy to catch up on the other side.

"You said you had an idea," Joy whispered.

That was good. She was interested, which meant she hadn't lost all hope.

"Yeah, I do. You already told the cops Gil was getting threats, right?"

Joy's head bobbed behind a row of presidential biographies. "They didn't believe me. Why should they? I couldn't give them any details. It sounded made up."

"Of course it sounded made up. It *was* made up. But now you can flesh it out a little."

"How?"

"Tell them it was the Russian mafia."

"The Russian ...?"

"That's all you know. Somebody from the Russian mafia was trying to muscle their way in on Gil's business."

"That's *crazy*."

"No, it isn't. The Russkies are into a lot of oil and gas stuff. I happened to be reading about them just today."

"But Chief Maguire—"

"All Maguire knows is that your hubby was asking questions about me. Maguire just assumes that's because

Gil tumbled to you hiring me. So you give him a new reason. You say Gil must have been making inquiries about local PIs because he was looking for help outside the law. He was afraid to open up about his problem to the police, so he was exploring different avenues. He must've hoped a PI could get the Russians off his back. Or he was just desperate and clutching at straws. Whatever. Bottom line, he didn't move fast enough and got whacked."

"They'll want to know why I didn't explain all this earlier."

"You didn't even know about the PI part. Gil was doing that on his own, trying not to alarm you. But now that you've been told about it, you can see how it makes sense."

"They won't be satisfied with that story."

"Not forever. But it'll hold 'em for a bit. It gives 'em a new bone to gnaw on."

"And when it doesn't pan out—"

"Maybe it *will* pan out."

"How can it? It's not true."

Bonnie let the question go unanswered. "Did the subject of Gil's wristwatch come up?"

"His watch ..." The woman sounded faraway, lost.

"Focus, Joy. Has anyone mentioned it?"

"They asked if he wore a watch. I guess it went missing."

"I took it. It was supposed to be a robbery, and robbers take stuff like that. Do the cops know about the engraving on the back?"

"Yes. They had me describe it."

"Good. That's real good, Joy."

"What does Gil's watch have to do with anything?"

"It's going to substantiate your story. Just leave everything to me."

"I don't know. It's hard, Bonnie—it's so hard."

"Hey, it's no pony ride for me either."

"I just don't know ..." Her voice slid into a moan on the last word.

Damn. The woman was getting all weak-kneed again. "Joy, you gotta trust me. Or we are both going down. Okay?"

"I'll do the best I can."

Her best wasn't going to be good enough, not the way she was acting. Right now there was still a fifty-fifty chance Joy Krauss would open up to the next cop who looked at her cross-eyed.

And if that was the case, the only option was to go nuclear. Wait by Joy's car in the parking lot—Bonnie had identified it before coming in—and finish her with one silenced shot as she slipped behind the wheel.

Cold-blooded? Yeah. But sometimes you had to do what you had to do.

Bonnie didn't want it to go that way. There was a fine line between being an antihero and a full-out bad guy. Clipping her own client to shut her up was a pretty sure way of crossing that line. But she would do it if she had to.

Still, there could be a better way.

She took a breath, then came around the end of the aisle and faced Joy directly. If someone was watching, she was screwed. But hell, she would probably be screwed anyway; the old talking-through-the-stacks routine was unlikely to fool any investigator outside of a Hardy Boys novel.

"Look, Joy." She kept her voice even, her gaze fixed on the woman's face. "We need to work as a team on this. We're compadres, you know? Partners in—" Crime, she almost said, but caught herself. "We're partners. You took a risk hiring me. I took a bigger risk for you. I told you up front that it could get hairy, and we'd have to keep our nerve. Remember that?"

"I remember," Joy said in a tone of deep sadness.

"You're feeling guilty because you think we did something wrong. But Gil was going to *murder* you, honey. He was trolling for hitters. He was ready to hire me last night. He asked me for my price."

"Just like I did when I hired you," she breathed.

"You hired me in self-defense. He started it. You finished it."

"Yes ..."

She still didn't sound sure. Bonnie thought about the guilt in her voice and took a shot. "How'd he treat you, Joy?"

"What do you mean?"

"Did you cheat on you? Did he hit you?"

"Cheat—I don't know. Possibly."

"And the other thing?"

She lowered her head. "Sometimes."

"He slapped you around, gave you what-for?"

"That's just what he called it. Giving me what-for."

"And you forgave him."

"I didn't ... I—I don't know."

"You stayed with him. You cooked his meals and slept in the same bed."

"Yes."

"And pretended to your friends that everything was hunky-dory."

"Yes."

"And you felt ashamed."

Joy didn't answer.

"You felt ashamed," Bonnie said again, "because you knew you oughtta walk away, and you didn't. Why didn't you?"

"I ... don't know."

"I think it's because part of you thought you deserved it."

Joy's eyes flashed. "What is this, a therapy session?"

Bonnie liked that answer. It showed a spark of something other than fear.

"Sort of," she said. "You can't live the life I've lived without learning a little about human nature."

"So you think I'm ... weak?"

"I think you're inclined to blame yourself for things that aren't your fault. He beat you up, and you felt bad about it. Now for the first time you didn't let him get away with it. You made him pay. Got that, Joy? *You made him pay.*"

"I guess I did," she said slowly.

"For once in your life you said he wasn't going to treat you like shit. He could take everything else from you, but he wasn't going to take your life. You turned the tables. You showed him who he was messing with. And he knew it, too. I made sure of that."

"You told him it was me?"

"You betcha."

Joy's face worked itself into a reluctant smile. "Oh."

"He *knew*, Joy. After all the crap he dished out, he finally learned there was a point where you just wouldn't take it anymore."

"I'm glad," she said, more to herself than to Bonnie. "I'm glad he knew."

"It was a long time coming. He deserved it. You broke free. It's a *very* big deal. Now, do you really intend to throw it all away and let that miserable wife-beating bastard win?"

Joy stared at the green slice of short nap carpet between her shoes.

"I'll bet he laughed when he beat you," Bonnie whispered. "You gonna let him get the last laugh?"

Quietly: "No."

"He fucked with you six ways from Sunday. You did what you had to do. You stood up for yourself. For the first time ever—you stood up."

Joy lifted her head. "I did."

"And the police—fuck 'em. Dan Maguire—he's an ass-hole. I've played games with that dipshit for years, and I always win. Follow my playbook, that's all I ask."

"Okay ..."

"You trust me?"

"Yes."

"You with me?"

"Yes."

"All the way? I want to hear you say it."

"All the way," Joy whispered, reaching out to grasp Bonnie's arm. "It's like Ben Franklin said. If we don't hang together, we'll hang separately."

Bonnie had never heard this quote before, but it seemed curiously appropriate for the American history section of the stacks.

"Good enough," she answered. "Tell the cops about the Russian mafia. You didn't mention it before because you were scared and confused. But you're saying it now. Russian mob. That's what Gil told you. That's who was riding him."

"Russian mob," Joy repeated obediently.

"Atta girl. We'll talk later. Keep your chin up."

Bonnie walked away, out of the stacks, out of the library, into the cold clear air. She was smiling in satisfaction and relief.

For the second time in as many days, she had saved her client's life.

# 15

IN THE GREENHOUSE, among the orchids, Streinikov sat on his potting bench, pruning a *Phalaenopsis amabilis*.

He grew several species of orchid. At least two varieties were in bloom in any given season, providing him with new blossoms all year long. Holding the terra-cotta pot in one hand, he carefully snipped the stem of the *Phalaenopsis* just below the node of the last bloom. The flowers on this specimen had faded, but with precise cutting he could induce a new bloom to set, extending the plant's period of showy display by another six weeks.

He handled the orchid tenderly, as he might have handled an infant. He was a rough man in most respects, but the plants in the greenhouse were his darlings, and he would never be unkind to them.

It was good to sit here, in the humidified air, breathing the mist released by the automated sprayers—to sit in shirtsleeves, surrounded by tropical luxuriance, in a temperature of eighty degrees, while beyond the walls of tempered glass, winter hung on, sullen and desolate.

The greenhouse, though spacious, was overcrowded with foliage, a consequence of his unapologetic liberality when acquiring new plants. Along with the rows of potted orchids, bromeliads, and miscellaneous exotic blooms, there were hanging baskets of epiphytes swaying gently in the breeze from the circulation fans. Big leaf tropical plants bumped up against the benches and glass walls—ferns and palms predominated—while dense stands of bamboo rose like pillars to the ceiling.

The paved walkway bisecting the greenhouse was bordered by gravel. On each side a double row of low redwood benches, drilled with drainage holes, extended the length of the building. Floor space was at a premium, and he sometimes had trouble navigating to the farther benches. Really, he should clear out some of his plants, but he loved them too dearly. The orchids were his special favorites, but he would not part with any of his lovelies. Truth be told, he found it hard to restrain himself from buying more.

He replaced the pot on the bench and directed his attention to the next *Phalaenopsis* that was losing its leaves. He faced at least another hour of such work, but time meant nothing to him in the greenhouse. There was only the drip of percolating water through the drainage holes in the display benches, the burr of the fans, the occasional whine of the roof vents as they opened to release hot air trapped at the ridge. It was peaceful here.

In his youth there had been no orchids, no greenhouses, and precious little beauty. The city of Donetsk, where he was raised in a family of six by a gruff, overworked father and an anemic, hysterical mother, was an ugly place, a warren of factories, mines, and prisons, and smoke everywhere, and rough tattooed men cursing floridly and drinking dark Slavutich beer. One of the prisons dated to the days of the czars. On its grounds had stood a scaffold where criminals had been hanged. Ancient and rotting, it was torn down, the lumber tossed in the street. His mother had taken some of it to make a crib for him. As a baby he had slept in the wood of the gallows.

His first clear memory dated from when he was five or six years old. He found himself outside a nightclub after dark; he no longer remembered why. As he stood there, perhaps cadging kopeks from passersby, he saw a sleek black Mercedes sedan pull up to the curb. A man and two women got out, the man in a tailored suit, the women in frilly Parisian fashions. Tall women, lithe and willowy, with long legs and great manes of black hair.

Anton never forgot his sight of that sedan and the women who emerged from it. Though only a child, he knew at that moment what his life must be. He did not want to be a nobody like his father. He wanted a car like that and women like that. And to get those things, he must become a man like that.

Well, he had become that kind of man. But fate was cruel, or perhaps it merely had a sense of humor. He could have all the women he wanted now, but he had lost the desire. Long legs and black manes meant nothing to him.

"What does it profit a man," he whispered, smiling, "if he gains the whole world and loses his balls?"

The intercom buzzed, announcing the doctor's arrival. Streinikov had forgotten the appointment.

"Send him in," he said indifferently.

This was a new doctor, one he had never seen before. A replacement for old Abrutski, who had served Streinikov for several years until the two had a falling out, an argument in which Abrutski made the mistake of insulting his patient. The insult was no doubt unintentional and was quickly withdrawn, but the damage was already done. To offend a man like Streinikov, a man of power, a *vor*, was never a good idea. Abrutski had died just two days later, a victim of a home invasion in which, curiously, no valuables were taken. Newspaper reports said he had suffered greatly. His neighbors had heard no screams, most likely because the good doctor's lips had been sutured shut, a most creative touch.

This tragedy had necessitated the employment of a new doctor to administer Streinikov's weekly injections. A certain Richard Vasnev had been selected on the basis of his reputation for loyalty and discretion. It was unlikely Vasnev relished the appointment, but refusal was not an option.

He watched the doctor's progress through the main house. A monitor near the potting bench displayed a constantly changing mosaic of images from inside the residence, where a camera was installed in every room. There were, however, no cameras in the greenhouse. Nothing intruded on his privacy here.

Finally the doctor disappeared from the screen, having left the house via the sunroom. He would be coming down the path now, past the garage, escorted by Avram Lysenko, Streinikov's bodyguard, who lived on the property and controlled the front gate.

While waiting, Streinikov pruned another plant. He hummed a little tune, something from Tchaikovsky, he believed. After a few moments there was a rap on the greenhouse door.

"*Vkhodi*," he said. Come in.

The door opened, and a little man, prematurely bald and unnaturally pale, entered in Lysenko's charge.

Streinikov offered the usual pleasantries as he rolled up his sleeve. He was accustomed to this treatment, which he had received for most of his adult life. Castration would normally lead to loss of muscle tone and physical strength; the regular administration of testosterone could counteract these effects. It could also restore some degree of sexual function, but Streinikov cared nothing about that.

Lysenko stood watching in the background as the doctor opened his little black bag—yes, he actually carried one, just like a doctor in a movie—and removed a vial and a syringe.

"Do you like my greenhouse, Doctor?" Streinikov asked as the syringe was filled.

"Lovely," Vasnev said, though in truth he appeared to have noticed nothing around him except Streinikov and Lysenko and the pistol casually snugged in Lysenko's belt.

"A flowering orchid is a thing of consummate beauty, don't you think? I love very few things, but I do love my darlings."

"Yes," Vasnev said nervously, "they are very nice."

"Very nice? Is this all you can say? The orchid is a magical blossom, the flower of the gods. From time immemorial it has been linked in mythic imaginings with lust, murder, madness—and castration."

"Has it? I didn't know." He tapped the needle, not meeting Streinikov's eyes.

"*Da*. The very word *orchid* is derived from the Greek word for testicle. I have sometimes thought it was this archetypal connection that prompted a suffragette mob to destroy dozens of rare orchid blooms at the Kew Gardens in 1913—man-hating harridans performing symbolic emasculation—a monstrous orchidectomy."

Vasnev slipped the needle into Streinikov's arm. The pain was inconsequential. Streinikov had known much worse.

"And then there is my own peculiar situation," he went on. "The eunuch symbolically cultivating his replacement parts. Surely the irony had occurred to you?"

"Not at all." The doctor licked his lips, and the hand holding the syringe trembled.

"*Nyet*? To me, neither, when I began. I knew nothing of the word's etymology at first, nor of the legend of Orkhis. Do you know this tale?"

Vasnev shook his head and withdrew the needle.

"Orkhis was a young man who made the mistake of forcing himself on one of the Maenads, the female acolytes of Dionysus, god of wine and revelry. For all his merriment, our Dionysus had no sense of humor about such things. As punishment, poor Orkhis was metamorphosed into an orchid, his offending scrotum forever on display."

"Mmm." Vasnev pressed a wad of sterile cotton against

the wound. A seam of sweat wound its way down his cheek.

"I knew nothing of this, yet I chose these particular plants to cultivate. Now look at me—the eunuch guardian of an orchid harem. An unmanned man whose missing genitalia burst forth around him in a thousand blooms."

There was nothing Vasnev could say to this. He removed the cotton and affixed a small bandage to the injection site.

"Does this line of conversation unsettle you?" Streinikov asked.

"Not at all," Vasnev said. "Not at all." The phrase was his mantra.

"It pleases me to indulge in such flights of fancy. Always my mind has tended toward the poetical and, I suppose, the grotesque. I might have been a great artist, had I not been ... what I am."

"Yes, of course." Vasnev was packing up his supplies with undue haste.

"I am sure we will get along famously, Doctor. We shall have a long and happy partnership, you and I."

Vasnev tried to smile and managed only a twist of the mouth that looked like a nervous tic.

"At least as long and happy as that which I enjoyed with your predecessor," Streinikov added.

He watched with amusement as Lysenko led the man out. He did enjoy putting fear in people. One of his less attractive qualities, no doubt.

He had not always been feared. In his teenage years he might have thought of himself as a gangster, a dangerous customer, but the men who rode in black Mercedes sedans and escorted overpriced hookers on their arms were unimpressed. So little had they feared him that when his amorous diversions with Smolin's woman were discovered—a pretty blonde whore, Katya by name, a girl of no importance except as Smolin's personal property—

they had not hesitated to exact the most humiliating revenge. They had taken his manhood with the blade of a knife, cauterized the wound with a hot iron, and sent him weeping into the streets with his trousers still down around his knees.

At first, of course, he had raged and wept, thinking of suicide. But that mood had passed, and he had discovered an unsuspected advantage to his new condition. Previously, he had been forever distracted by the desire for sex, the chronic quest for relief, the embarrassing neediness that felt like weakness. Now he was rid of all that. He could devote himself single-mindedly and unemotionally to the pursuit of what really mattered, with no diversions and no need to satisfy mere animal urges.

Had that barbaric surgery never been performed, Streinikov would never have risen to his present station in life. What had been intended as the crudest revenge had revealed itself, in the process of time, to be his greatest gift. Not that Smolin and his thugs could have understood such a thing. And because they did not understand, because they had meant only to humiliate and wound, they had incurred a debt that must be paid.

It took five years for Streinikov to rise to a position of power in Donetsk. Then he sent Gura and a few others of his most trusted men to hunt down Smolin and his crew—and even Katya, by now traded to another paymaster. The prisoners were brought to him, and Streinikov himself oversaw a series of surgical procedures that deprived Smolin and his men of their balls—and their pricks also, just as he had prophesied on the night of his mutilation. He watched the men bleed out, letting Smolin linger the longest as he dangled upside down from a hook in the ceiling to keep the blood flowing to his brain.

Then he took care of Katya. Though she swore her innocence, he knew she must have betrayed him to Smolin. Under duress, probably, but that was no excuse. She had given him up and cost him his manhood, and he took his revenge personally, by his own hand. By the time he consented to let her die, she was a thing without fingers, ears, or eyes, a thing that was all screams and blood. After she was dead, he scalped her and tacked her blonde hair to the wall, a pennant raised in victory.

The story got around. People feared him after that. They had never stopped fearing him.

He would see to it that they never did.

# 16

IT WAS SHORTLY after three o'clock when Bonnie climbed the stairs to Brad's apartment. He ought to be done with his shift by now; she expected him to be home.

He was. She found him in a terrycloth bathrobe, his hair still wet from a shower.

"Bad news," she said. "Gotta work tonight."

"On a Saturday?"

"What can I say? Duty calls. Which unfortunately takes precedence over booty calls." She wandered into the tiny kitchen and liberated a Coors Light from the fridge. "Your shift go okay?"

"Same old. Dan was going on about you again."

She cracked open the bottle. "Yeah? About what?"

"Something to do with Maritime. He wouldn't give any details."

"He's a man of mystery, is Danny boy." She took a long swig.

"Don't call him that. He's my superior."

"Dan Maguire isn't anybody's superior."

"I need to treat him with respect."

"Maybe." She chugged more of the bottle. "But I don't."

He looked away, frowning.

It was at times like this that she wondered about the future of their relationship. Brad was a good guy, but he had no rough edges. Since she was pretty much all rough edges, she couldn't quite figure out what he saw in her. He wore a uniform and respected authority, and he'd seen only a certain side of life. Nobody was going to come gunning for him. He had never drawn his firearm in the field. He gave out traffic tickets and showed up to help old people who'd called 911 because they were feeling short of breath. She didn't know if he'd ever gotten a kitten down from a tree, but one time he had assisted in the rescue of a family of baby ducks from a storm drain.

Her world was a different place, a place of tight corners and no exits and sudden, savage struggles that meant life or death. Bradley Walsh wasn't meant to be part of that world. And it might not be possible to keep her life safely walled off from his. She was trying, though. Trying her damnedest.

She sighed. "Okay, okay. Don't get all miffed. Him and me just don't get along."

"He and I," he corrected automatically.

"Oh, great. I'm dating a grammar Nazi."

He smiled at that, and the stiffness of his posture relaxed a little. "Whatever he's after, he was talking about getting a search warrant."

Her stomach tightened. She put the bottle down. "A warrant? For my office?"

"And your home."

"Why? What's he looking for?"

"Told you, I don't know. But I wouldn't worry about it. You've got nothing to hide."

He said it with just the faintest lilt of a question mark. Or maybe she only imagined that.

"I don't like the idea of a bunch of jackbooted storm troopers pawing through my personal stuff," she said slowly.

"As one of the jackbooted storm troopers, I should take offense at that." He was grinning. "It's a wild goose chase. He's always after you for something. The Long Fong Boyz, or that shooting on the boardwalk. You know what I saw on his desk last fall? Your PI application. You know, the SP one-seven-one you submitted to get your license."

"He looked into that, did he?"

"I guess he was running his own background check. Can you believe it? The state police already cleared you. What'd he think he was going to find?"

Bonnie had some ideas about that. As the poet said, oh what a tangled fucking web we weave.

Thing was, when she'd applied for her license eight years ago, she'd fallen just a hair short of the state's requirements as immortalized in the Security Officer Registration Act of 1939. And by a hair, she meant a country mile. The main obstacle was that the state expected her to have at least five years' professional experience as an investigator. She had precisely zilch.

That was where a fellow by the name of Frank Kershaw came in. He created a paper trail establishing her five years of employment at a Pennsylvania insurance firm. It was impressive stuff, backed up by a list of references that would all check out, because the people Frank used knew what to say when the phone rang. Hell, she would've hired herself after reading the résumé.

Bottom line: she wasn't worried about any investigation Dan might have initiated. Frank's labors on her behalf had been a work of sheer artistry. He was like that mathematician guy—he had a beautiful mind. Only instead of solving quadratic equations or whatever, his noggin was dedicated to conning people like Dan Maguire into believing a bunch of bullshit, or at least being unable to disprove it.

"I would've told you," Brad added, "but I guess I thought it was too stupid to even mention."

She picked up the beer and tipped it to her mouth again. "Good call."

"What can I say? The guy's obsessed with you. He knows it, too. You know what he calls you? His white whale."

"Hey, I may have put on a few pounds ..."

"I think at some level he knows it's unhealthy to be, you know, so fixated. But he can't help himself. He's like a dog with a bone. This search warrant thing is just another waste of time."

"There are judges who'll okay a warrant with no questions asked."

"Not exactly *no* questions. He's got to have something. Probable cause."

The bottle was mostly empty now. She twirled it between her palms. "He could make it up."

"Dan wouldn't do that. He may be a little crazy when it comes to you, but he's not corrupt. He doesn't take payoffs. He's clean."

"Yeah, okay."

"Seriously. He's not perfect, but he's an honest cop."

"I believe you." She polished off the bottle and flipped it into the recycle bin. "If he was dirty, he could've planted evidence on me a long time ago."

"He doesn't work that way. So you've got nothing to worry about."

"Everything's copacetic." She caught him yawning. "Look, you need your beauty rest, and there's some stuff I gotta do. Thanks for the beer. I hate to drink alone."

"You were the only one drinking, so you did drink alone."

"Spare me the technicalities." She headed to the door, still thinking about that search warrant.

"You think you'll drop by after work?" Brad asked.

"I will if I can. Could be pretty late, though."

"I don't mind. And be careful, okay?"

"Always am."

Yeah, that was a lie. But what the hell. Their whole relationship was built on lies. One more couldn't hurt.

She was at the door when his voice stopped her. "You know, you never said it back."

"Huh?"

"Last night I said I loved you. Didn't get an answer."

She looked at him, feeling guilty and, for once, at a loss for words. "Oh ..."

He smiled, coming toward her. "Don't sweat it. I know that kind of thing's not easy for you."

She found she was hugging herself, classic defensive body language. "It really isn't. I'm not real touchy-feely."

He put his hands on her shoulders. Big hands. Strong. "I get that."

"It's your fault, you know." She gave up hugging herself and hugged him instead. "You should've picked somebody better."

"Well, when I find her"—he kissed her mouth—"you'll get the old heave-ho."

"I don't mind the heave. Not so sure I like the ho."

He pulled her closer. "Suddenly I'm not as sleepy as I was."

"Yeah, but I'm still just as busy." She gently pulled away. "Sorry, Officer."

"Love means never having to say you're sorry."

"Oh, yuck. You're really gonna be a pain in the ass about this, aren't you?"

"Count on it," Brad said as she went out the door.

# 17

BONNIE DISARMED THE security system at her duplex and went straight to the bedroom. In the closet she pried up a loose floorboard, exposing the floor trap where she kept her goodies. For tonight's action she needed an untraceable, disposable gun, but not the little .22 she'd taken from her Jeep. She wanted something with more of an intimidation factor. There was plenty of stuff to choose from.

In the oversized gym bag under the floor she currently stored handguns in the .25, 9mm, and 45mm calibers, along with a sawed-off shotgun, a two-shot derringer loaded with expandable dumdum bullets, and a rifle that had been illegally modified to fire on full automatic. In other words, a machine gun. There was also a variety of silencers and magazines, a combat knife, a switchblade or two, and a couple of stun guns.

Pretty much all of it was illegal, and New Jersey was serious about its weapons laws. She could get at least ten years for any of the firearms, and five years for any of the other items. It was almost like they didn't want a girl to have any fun.

She selected the Ruger .45 as most suitable for tonight's little adventure. Like all the guns in the gym bag, it had been purchased from Mama Blessing, which made it untraceable. She chose a silencer to go with it, but left it unattached for now. She wouldn't need the silencer for Clarissa. But it might come in handy later.

Now she faced the problem of what to do with her arsenal. Brad had said Maguire was trying to score a search warrant. Suddenly she wasn't so comfortable having a mass of incriminating evidence in her house, even if it was artfully concealed. Luckily, there was another option, and his name was Felix Ramirez. She found his name in Sammy's list of contacts.

"Yo, Felix. You know that favor you owe me? I'm cashing it in ahead of schedule. Can you meet me at my address in, say, twenty? Thanks."

She spent the time hauling the gym bag up into the light and adding some items from her purse. One was the .22 and silencer, and another was the .45 formerly taped to the kneehole of her desk, which she'd grabbed from her office on her way home.

Also zipped into the bag was the three grand in cash Gura had paid her. Thirty bills, each bearing a picture of Ben Franklin, who was, like, the second or third US president, right? Not sure. History wasn't her strong suit.

At four o'clock the familiar Grand Caravan pulled up outside her front door. She lugged the gym bag out of the house and shoved it into the minivan's backseat, then joined Felix up front.

"Where to, *bandida*?" he asked.

"Your place."

He lifted an eyebrow but didn't argue.

Felix lived in an apartment above a paranormal bookstore in McKendree Park—one of the better neighborhoods, where gay shopkeepers and the people who used to be called yuppies were moving in and raising property values. She'd never been inside his place before today.

Without a word, she toted the gym bag up a long flight of stairs and waited while he unlocked his door. His home was surprisingly clean for a bachelor pad, and decorated in excellent taste, with none of the tacked-up centerfolds favored by Alonzo Duchenne.

"You got a closet you don't use too much?" she asked.

"Not really. Very little storage space here. If you need a place to stow that bag, I think under the kitchen sink would work."

She removed cans of Ajax and Comet and spray bottles of Formula 409, then pushed the duffel up against the back wall. When she replaced the cleaning supplies, the dark bag was hardly visible at a glance.

"It shouldn't be here long," she said.

"*No problema.*"

"I notice you haven't asked what's in it."

"No. I have not."

She nodded. She wasn't worried about Felix. Yeah, there was a lot of expensive gear in that bag, not to mention three grand in cash. But it wasn't going anywhere. She was good at reading people, and she knew Felix wasn't going to mess with her. Besides, Felix had at least an inkling of what she did on the side, and he was smart enough not to piss her off.

He drove her back to her house, covering the silence with some golden oldies on the car radio. Tony Bennett, Frank Sinatra. This guy was just full of surprises.

"This squares us," she said when they pulled up to her door.

"Fair enough."

"You don't talk a lot, do you?"

"No."

"That's good, Felix. That's a real good quality to have." She got out of the cab. "See ya."

He tipped her a wave and drove off. She figured she was safe as far as the search warrant was concerned. It was one less thing to worry about.

Back inside, she thought about taking another shower, took a whiff of her pits, and decided she didn't need one. She changed into a dark ensemble, wet work clothes that would blend with the night. A blouse without any funny sayings, and a pair of jeans. New hat, too—a knit beret, navy blue to match her outfit. There was never a wrong time to be stylish.

After that, she reviewed her plans. And waited. She hated waiting. The worst things in life always involved waiting. If there was a hell, it must consist of an eternity on line at the DMV, or maybe at a doctor's office full of coughing rug rats.

Eventually she decided she was too restless to hang around. And the stuff Brad had said to her had put her in the mood to pay someone a visit.

Before leaving, she looked inside her purse to reassure herself that the Ruger was there. And one other item—Gil Krauss's wristwatch. She expected to have a use for that watch, if things went as planned.

Locking up, she saw Mrs. Biggs outside her half of the duplex, rearranging the plastic flowers in her window box. Mrs. Biggs was approximately a million years old, and her wardrobe consisted entirely of ladybug-themed apparel. Tonight's little number, as Bonnie could see in the slanting light of late afternoon, was a ladybug sweater.

"Hello, Bonnie. Going to a party?"

"A private party," Bonnie said with a smile.

"Well, you're only young once."

Sometimes not even that often, Bonnie thought. She said good-bye to Mrs. Biggs, and her neighbor wished her a fun Saturday night.

Unlikely. There were a lot of possible adjectives for the evening ahead, but *fun* wasn't on the list.

# 18

PILGRIM GROVE HAD begun life as a Methodist camp meeting ground sometime back around the Civil War. "God's Thousand Acres," they called it—a thousand acres of scrub pine along a wind-blasted beach. The pines had been cleared away and tents had gone up, along with an auditorium where preachers waxed eloquent on the theme of an angry God.

The auditorium was still there, and so were some of the tents, upgraded over the generations into semipermanent cottages. But these days the auditorium was used mainly as an entertainment venue—Lionel Richie had jammed there last month—and the rows of Victorian gingerbread hotels dating from the turn of the century had been repurposed as apartment buildings and rest homes.

One of the rest homes was Green Arbor, where Bonnie presently sat on the glassed-in porch, rocking slowly in a wicker chair, side by side with Frank Kershaw.

She'd brought a Jersey Mike's sub for them to share. They ate it on paper napkins unfolded on their laps, and washed it down with peach Snapple. Bonnie had given up soda after deciding it had the same basic properties as battery acid. It was no great sacrifice, except for the loss of her favorite cocktail, Jack 'n' Coke.

"So," Frank said, leaning back in his own rocker, "how are things?"

"Shitty."

She never had to sugarcoat it for Frank. She gave him

a quick recap of the accumulating catastrophes in her life. On the darkening sidewalk a bearded guy in oversized camos was checking every parking meter for loose change while arguing vigorously with himself.

"You should get out of it," Frank said when Bonnie was through.

"Hey, I'm working on it. It's tricky."

"I'm not talking about this particular situation, kiddo. I mean you should get out of this life."

She fished a stray piece of gabagoul out of the sub's oily wrapping. "It's not a bad life."

"Yes, it is. You're always looking over your shoulder. Can't trust anybody. Can't confide in your closest friend—not even the guy you're sleeping with. Am I wrong?"

"No. You're not wrong."

She reached reflexively for a cigarette before remembering that there was no smoking at Green Arbor.

She couldn't argue with Frank. He knew her too well. He'd first met her in her wild child days, when she was living on the street. Back then, she was like a feral animal, a stray who'd tasted blood. She might have stayed that way, stealing food from convenience stores, bumming smokes off strangers at bus stops, friendless, mistrustful, angry, afraid.

But all that changed on a rainy night in April when she was sixteen. She was huddled in an alley behind a hardware store when the back door opened. It was Frank's store, and he was putting out the garbage. He found her there, and for some inexplicable reason he took her in. At first she thought he wanted a quickie, and though she didn't normally do that kind of thing, she was just desperate enough to say yes. But he didn't have any funny business in mind. He gave her a room in the back of his hardware store and let her stay there rent free, no strings attached.

At first it was only temporary. A few days of decent food and a roof over her head, and then he would kick her loose. Just till the weather cleared up, he said.

He was a widower, sole proprietor of the hardware store, and he ran a credit clinic on the side. For $1500 he could supply anybody with a new identity—driver's license, Social Security number, passports, employment records, other stuff. He was discreet and smart, and he never got caught. And he knew how it was for a runaway living outside the law.

Even so, she'd never doubted that he meant to put her back on the street. But one day, over lunch, she opened up a little. She told him her story. Not every detail, only the gist—how her folks had been murdered in a cheap motel in Pennsylvania, and how she'd gone on the run and finally tracked the killers to a farmhouse in Buckington, Ohio, where she'd taken her revenge. At the age of fourteen she'd killed three men, and it hadn't even been that hard.

She didn't expect her little tale of woe to matter much. Somehow it did. There was no outward change in Frank's demeanor. He didn't get all warm and fuzzy. He wasn't that sort of guy. But he stopped talking about sending her packing. Basically he adopted her, though not in any official way.

She lived with Frank for more than a year before moving on. Even after she left, she stayed in touch, returning to visit when she could. When she set herself up as a PI, it was Frank who put up the money for her surety bond. She didn't ask him. He just did it.

Truth was, without Frank to forge her papers and pay her way, she never could have gotten her business off the ground. Hell, without him, she might still be on the street—probably hooking by now, or pulling smash-and-grab jobs. Or she'd be in jail, or dead; the two alternatives were roughly equivalent in her mind. Frank had saved her from that fate.

And all because her story must have touched him. Which was weird, because he'd always struck her as the kind of hard-bitten bastard who could never be touched by anything. But you never knew about people.

After she moved to Jersey, she tried to maintain contact. She made calls, sent postcards. Two years ago she phoned his store, and some woman said Frank had retired, selling her the business. The woman wouldn't say where Frank had gone.

So he'd moved and hadn't even let her know. Bonnie's feelings were a little hurt about that. But he'd always been standoffish around her, while at the same time doing his best to look out for her. Anyway, she wouldn't let him disappear from her life that easily.

She drove to Philly and paid the woman a hundred bucks for Frank's new address, which turned out to be Green Arbor. She never told Frank any of this. She just showed up one day with a potted plant as a gift and started chatting, as if was only natural that she would know where to find him. Since then she'd visited irregularly. She never called ahead. He was always there.

He wasn't a father figure or anything. But he was the only one she could talk to without disguising any part of who she was. And though she'd never spelled it out for him, he had to have a pretty good idea of what she did for a living. He wasn't shocked. He'd been around.

"It's no way to live," Frank was saying. "It does things to you. Gets you all twisted up inside. It can change you in bad ways. I've seen it happen. A guy breaks the rules—pushes it a little further—then a little more—and before long he's doing things he never thought himself capable of. He's crossed the line, and he never even noticed."

Crossed the line, Bonnie thought. Like she'd come close to doing at the library. Like what she still might have to do, if Joy went wobbly on her.

"Okay," she said.

"After that, there's no way out. You end up alone, and then you end up dead."

"We all end up dead."

"Some sooner than others." He tore off a bite of the sub like a mastiff working a bone. "You're young. You're smart. You can get out, start over. Live a different kind of life. No more of this horseplay."

Horseplay—he was probably the only person who'd call it that. "I know what you're saying. But I think I can make it work."

"You can't."

"I already am. I'm not alone. I've got a guy. A really good guy. I'm in a better place than I used to be."

"Does he know the truth about you?"

"Nope. And he never has to find out. I'm good at keeping secrets."

"So you think you can have it all?" Frank shook his head. "Won't happen."

"Well, aren't you a gloomy Gus."

"Just being realistic, kiddo. The path you're on is a lonely one. Take my word for it."

She wondered just how much he was revealing of himself. She knew nothing about his past, or what had brought him to Philly as a small business owner and part-time scratch man. She'd never had nerve enough to ask.

They sat for a while without speaking. Evening was coming on. Gulls wheeled against the last traces of the sunset. Only a handful of other people were on the porch, none within earshot. Two gray-haired women were playing cards. A man in a wheelchair sat alone, sipping lemonade through a straw.

A civilized atmosphere. If you ignored the cars lining the curb and the pulse of an electronic beat from across the street, it could be a hundred years ago. A simpler time, or so everybody said. Bonnie was skeptical. Life always seemed simple when you'd didn't have to actually live it.

In her purse, Sammy started singing his favorite Beatles tune. She knew who it was.

"I need to take this," she told Frank as she got up. She moved to a far corner of the porch and answered.

Gura didn't waste time with greetings. "Here are your instructions. I have made arrangements to use a boat at the Miramar marina, a boat that cannot be connected with me. It is the property of someone who owes me, shall I say, a favor. The boat is where it will happen."

She kept her voice low. "And where the hell are you?"

"On my way to Jersey City, where I will visit a bar frequented by members of the law enforcement community. Our friends in blue will provide me with an unbreakable alibi."

"It'll be hard for you to explain why you're up there when you booked a room for your girlfriend here in town." Even as she said it, she realized the obvious. "Shit. You started the fight with her on purpose. You wanted people to see you arguing with her."

"Ah, you catch on, poppet. A little slow, but at last you see the light."

He'd needed a pretext for leaving town. His story would be that he and Clarissa had a falling out, and he left her at the hotel.

"The girl does not know I have gone," Gura went on, sounding much too pleased with himself. "In thirty minutes I will call her and invite her to a friend's boat, which I have borrowed for a romantic dinner so that we can make up. You see?"

"What if she's still pissed and won't go?"

"She will go. She needs to maintain our relationship. We have already established that it is not an affair of the heart."

"Fair enough." She looked for flaws in the plan. "If there are security cameras at the marina—"

"There are none."

"The parking lot can be pretty deserted in the off-season. When Clarissa doesn't see your car, she could bail."

"My car is there. I am using a car belonging to the same individual who is lending me his boat."

"Jeez, you really got the goods on this guy, huh?" Reluctantly she conceded that he'd thought this thing through. "What boat exactly are we talking about?"

"It is a flybridge cruiser called the *Dragon's Mouth*."

"Not sure I love the sound of that."

"I did not choose the name," Gura said imperturbably. "The vessel is moored at the pier identified as C North. You will need a passcode to open the security door to the dock."

He recited four digits, which she scribbled on her palm with a pen fumbled out of her purse. She didn't have a great memory for numbers.

"You will enter before Clarissa gets there. She, too, will be given the passcode. Wait inside. She will be unprepared for any danger."

"And afterward?"

"Just go on your way."

"So I do the hit, leave the body, and skedaddle?"

"Precisely. It will be the easiest money you ever made."

"Terrific. Is the cabin door unlocked?"

"No. But the alarm system has been disabled. It will not be difficult for you to get inside."

"Would have been easier if you'd given me the key."

"I wish for there to be a break-in. When police investigate, it must appear that Clarissa or a confederate forced entry into the boat."

"The cops are gonna wonder why a woman with a room at the Prince Edward was jimmying the lock on a cabin cruiser in Miramar."

"The boat owner will take care of that. In a few days

he will find the body. Before reporting it to the authorities, he will plant drugs and related paraphernalia at the scene. It will appear that Clarissa hooked up with a drug dealer. Together they used the boat for a private party. For reasons that will never be known, Clarissa ended up dead, and the killer ran off."

"I see." She remembered the needle marks on the girl's wrist. Yeah, the police would buy her as an addict.

"Is good, yes? Simple, believable, impossible to disprove."

"You're a friggin' mastermind. How'd Clarissa or the drug guy know the passcode to the dock?"

"This must remain a mystery. *Nyet* problem. The case should not be tied up too neatly."

He was right about that. Only an amateur plotted the perfect crime. In the real world there were always loose ends.

"Is that it?" she asked, tired of talking to him.

"Just two more things. One, you will call me later tonight to confirm that it is done."

"And two?"

"Do not fuck this up, poppet."

"Quit calling me poppet."

"*Do svidaniya.*" The call ended.

She frowned. *Do Svetlana*? It must mean good-bye. She'd always thought Svetlana was a girl's name.

Whatever. These Russkies were all crazy, anyway.

She put away Sammy and rejoined Frank. "Sorry to eat and run."

"That was tonight's job?"

"Yup."

"And if you'd gotten the call with your boyfriend at your elbow?"

"Would never happen. I'm careful that way."

"You can be as careful as you please, but things will all go to shit eventually. That's the way of the world."

She smiled. "You know what you are? You're a cur-mudgeon. If you had a lawn, you'd be telling kids to get off it."

He ignored her. "Take my advice. Get out of the life. Reinvent yourself. Move away, start fresh. It can be done."

This time she was sure he was talking about himself.

"I'll think it over," she promised.

He made a face that said he knew she was only hu-moring him. As she was walking away, he said, "Watch yourself tonight, kiddo. Don't disappoint me."

"How would I disappoint you?"

He looked at her with his calm, knowing eyes. "By get-ting yourself killed.

# 19

IT OCCURRED TO Bonnie that this was the second time today she'd brought a gun to a meeting while hoping she wouldn't have to use it. The first time she'd been seeing a client. This time she was scheduled to encounter a target.

But not really a target. She'd already decided about that.

Sure, the easiest thing would be to kill Clarissa Lynch. But she wasn't going to do that. Because she only killed the bad guys. It was important to her self-image to maintain that policy. If she'd harbored any doubts on that score, Frank Kershaw's sermonette on crossing lines had dispelled them. Admittedly, Joy Krauss might be the exception that tested the rule, but silencing Joy, should it become necessary, was simple self-defense, like cutting yourself free of a drowning person who was trying to pull you under.

Clarissa was in a different category altogether. Whatever her deal was, anyone going up against a piece of scum like Pavel Gura couldn't be all bad. Clarissa was a lot like Bonnie herself, a woman making her mark in a man's game. Sisterhood was powerful, and she owed the girl some professional courtesy. And according to Pavel, she was a wildcat in the sack. So, you know, that was another thing they had in common.

Besides all that, killing Clarissa wouldn't solve her larger problem. But keeping her alive—well, that might go a long way toward fixing everything.

The marina was located off Highway 35 at the north

end of Miramar, on an inlet of the Crab River, which fed into the ocean. The parking lot was ungated and unguarded. It was also empty, except for a lone sedan parked under a streetlight. Gura's wheels, the Mercedes that had been parked near her office this morning. Black, of course. Bad guys always went for black. It was like a fetish with them.

Bonnie drove to a far corner of the lot where she hoped the Jeep would be inconspicuous, and left it there. The sun was down. She hoofed it across yards of macadam, shivering in the night chill. She'd selected a lightweight coat that she could shed easily; a few goose bumps were the price she paid for maneuverability.

A brick promenade ran along the waterfront. Most of the slips were vacant, the owners, like migrating birds, having flocked south for the winter. The remaining boats showed no signs of life. They rocked like cradles in a gentle chop.

At Dock C North, a ramp sloped down to a steel mesh security door. She punched in the passcode and hurried along a narrow pier liberally sprayed with seagull crap. It was colder here, by the water.

The *Dragon's Mouth* was moored in the last slip. A small flybridge cruiser, as Gura had said, white and sleek and new, a nice toy for anyone who'd outgrown the rubber ducky in his bathtub. Maybe thirty-five feet long, with wide windows everywhere.

She grabbed hold of the ladder at the stern and hoisted herself aboard, reminding herself to wipe down the handrail later. She wasn't wearing gloves, preferring to keep her hands unencumbered when she picked the lock.

The obvious entry point was the glass door facing the dock, but she didn't want to go in that way. If Clarissa saw signs of tampering, she might get spooked. Instead she made her way forward, passing the starboard windows. Her pocket flashlight picked out the alarm system sensors in the window frames. Gura had said the system was disabled. She hoped he was right.

At the front of the cabin there was a small door, or did boaters call it a hatch? The lock wouldn't be any obstacle, and there was no need to fret about leaving marks because Gura wanted it to look like an obvious break-in.

The wind off the water numbed her fingers. She was adjusting the tension wrench when Sammy, in her breast pocket on vibrate mode, purred against her left tit. She checked the display. Brad. She took the call, snugged the phone under her chin, and kept working.

"Yo," she said. "What's up?"

"Sorry to call when you're on the job. You free to talk?"

"Free, white, and twenty-one." It was an expression she'd picked up somewhere. Kinda racist, now that she thought about it.

"I just wanted you to know the chief's on the warpath. The search warrant didn't come through."

"No dice, huh?"

"Judge Morris turned him down. Which means he had *nada*, because Morris will greenlight just about anything."

"Good to know."

"So you don't have to worry about us jackbooted thugs breaking into your place."

"Yeah, I hate it when that happens." It looked like she had moved her arsenal for nothing. Still, better safe than sorry.

"I told you nothing would come of it. Though I almost wish Dan had gotten the warrant."

"Yeah? Why's that?"

"That way he might finally be convinced you have nothing to hide. He'd have to admit you're clean."

"As a whistle," Bonnie agreed, releasing the lock. "Thanks for the news update. I'll see ya when I see ya."

She clicked off and dumped Sammy into her purse, then got one hand on the Ruger. There was always a chance Clarissa had come early and was planning a surprise for Gura or whoever showed up. It wasn't likely, but she'd found that anticipating unlikely scenarios could significantly improve her life expectancy.

Carefully she eased the door ajar and slipped into the cabin. She took a minute to listen to the darkness. She heard no breathing but her own, no movement but the creak of the hull as the boat swayed on the tide.

Her fingers found a light switch. The overhead fluorescents came on, flooding the interior space. She had entered through the kitchen—the galley, she guessed it was called—which was adjacent to the cockpit. Beyond both, there was a decent-sized living room with a built-in sofa that probably converted into a spare bed, a sleek coffee table, and even a flatscreen TV mounted on the wall.

Pretty roomy, more so than it looked on the outside. And there was still more floor space—a lavatory to her right, and a gangway that descended below deck where the main sleeping quarters must be.

She shrugged off her coat and stuffed it under the captain's chair, out of sight. In the living area she closed the curtains over the windows. She didn't need an audience for what was about to happen, and though the boatyard seemed empty, there was no point in taking chances. The glass door at the stern was another story. She wanted Clarissa to enter that way, so she kept the drapes open and even unlocked the door. As an afterthought, she hunted down a bottle of wine in the galley and placed it ostentatiously on the coffee table alongside two plastic wineglasses. The whole setup was designed to issue an invitation: come on in.

All she needed was a place to lie in wait. Clarissa was expecting to see Gura and no one else. She was a pro, could well be carrying, and might be a tad skittish under the circumstances. If she came face-to-face with the same nosy bitch who'd tried to chat her up in the hotel restroom, her response might be to shoot first and ask questions never.

And those steel gray eyes shouldn't be taken lightly. The girl might be young and an addict, but there was something hard in her, something that could be dangerous.

Bonnie didn't want to terminate the lady, but she also didn't intend to become a casualty of war. What she required was the element of surprise. Pop out of hiding, hold Clarissa at gunpoint with a properly intimidating firearm, and let things play out from there.

The closet in the galley looked like the best option. She opened the door, and that was when things went sideways.

Wide-open gray eyes.

Tangle of ash blonde hair.

Clarissa Lynch, stuffed in the closet.

Dead, the top of her head blown off in a bloody mess and wrapped in a white bath towel monogrammed with the initials of the Prince Edward Hotel.

Bonnie took all this in eyeblink-fast, but not fast enough to escape a sudden fall of blackness as something was flung over her face—a sheet of fabric, pulled taut, smothering—while simultaneously her arms were wrenched backward.

Hands on her body, snatching the purse away before she could grab the Ruger.

She released a shout, lashed out with a blind kick that didn't connect.

The thing on her face was drawn tighter. She yelled again, an instinctive reaction, useless, because the marina was deserted and there was no one to hear or help. The stretched cloth filled her mouth, muffling the cry.

She knew immediately, without words or conscious logic, that her assailants were two or more males. One of them shoved her forward and flung her facedown on something padded but firm. The sofa in the main cabin.

He straddled her, his knees digging into her back, crushing the breath out of her.

Rough hands patting her down, searching for weapons, finding none. Then tugging at her sleeve, pulling it back. Her right arm was jerked away from her body, held palm up on the sofa.

A band of pressure on her forearm—a tourniquet being tied in place. Fingers probing her wrist, searching for a vein.

They were going to give her an injection. She couldn't let that happen. She screamed into the cushion and thrashed and kicked. It did no good. They didn't release her arm.

Pain in her wrist. The bite of the needle. She remembered the syringe in Clarissa's suitcase. Doxy-whatever-it-was. A sedative.

Arching her back, she pistoned both legs and drove herself forward, half off the sofa. The needle popped free, liquid spattering her arm.

A male voice: *"Chyort!"*

Was that Russian? What the fuck was going on?

A heavy hand struck her across the back of the head. Her ears rang. Other hands pressed her down, fixing her in place. More than two men. Three, at least.

New pressure on her arm, a new search for an injection site on her wrist. She struggled, her head whipsawing as she screamed in pure rage.

Pain again, the needle stabbing home, the syringe emptying its contents into her bloodstream.

Then it was done, and the needle was pulled free. Still they didn't let her up. Someone counted off seconds at intervals of ten, while someone else pasted a pair of bandages to her arm.

Nice of them to stop the bleeding. Then she remembered the towel around Clarissa's head. They'd done the same for her.

"Good thing she ordered extra towels," Bonnie murmured, the words garbled by the fabric in her mouth and the pressure of the cushion against her face.

That was kind of funny. She almost laughed.

Uh-oh, she was losing it. Starting to feel all spacey and weird. That doxy shit had gone straight to her head.

Ground control to Major Tom, we got a serious fuckin' problem here ...

That was funny, too. Everything was funny.

Someone patted her blouse, her jeans, searching for other weapons, finding none. The hands released her. She shook her head, and the thing that had covered her face slipped off and fluttered to the floor.

A scarf, blood red. She had seen that scarf before.

Bonnie lifted her head from the sofa and saw two young men in business suits with close-cropped hair, and just beyond them was her pal, Pavel Gura, and he was smiling.

"Greetings, poppet. Welcome to the *Dragon's Mouth*."

# 20

WHAT HAPPENED AFTER that was a succession of separate moments like links in a chain, except there was no chain. There were only the links, disconnected, scattered, leading nowhere. Things happened, but the order didn't make sense. It was like skipping through a DVD in fast-forward and reverse, stopping here and there at random.

There was the moment when she pawed at the sofa, trying to rise, and instead found herself sliding off the cushions onto the floor, boneless as a cat, while someone laughed. The floor was carpeted and smooth, and she felt the throb of engines through the wood. Everything was misty in a white glare, which seemed weird until she realized it was her vision that was screwy, not the lighting in the cabin.

There was the moment when Gura, chuckling, shut the door to the gangway that led below deck. That must be where they'd hidden, on the lower level, tracking her footsteps until she was at the closet. In the instant when she was distracted, they'd taken her by surprise.

And there was the moment when one of the younger guys returned to the boat, reporting that he'd driven Gura's Mercedes off the lot and parked it on a side street, where it wouldn't be connected with the Jeep. Her Jeep, right—the Jeep that would be found once she was officially a missing person. Impounded, auctioned off eventually or sold for parts, when the investigation into her disappearance was finally called off.

At some point Gura was at the helm, and the boat began to move. She thought one of the two goons—goons, that was a funny word, *goons*—had gone on deck to cast off the mooring lines. She was still on the sofa then, and the red scarf was on the floor.

At some other point Gura was standing in the cabin as the boat sped through choppy waters. The scarf was wrapped around his neck now. She said, "Shouldn't you be driving?" and he said, "We are on autopilot." And the other two were removing Clarissa Lynch from the closet, folding her body into a canvas sack. Gura said something in Russian, and they answered, and spray from the ocean misted the windshield and triggered the automatic wipers.

At one point Clarissa's eyes blinked alert and she gave Bonnie a hard, knowing stare. Or had she only dreamed that?

She had a conversation with Gura. She was sure of it. The conversation was disjointed and strange, but it was real. He called her *poppet* again, and then, smiling, he asked, "You know the meaning of this word?"

"Child," she said, her voice faraway.

"*Da*, maybe. But also puppet. That is what you are to me. My little puppet, dancing on my strings." He mimed the gestures of a puppeteer, fingers fluttering. "I danced you to the boatyard. I danced you aboard this vessel. I danced you to your death, Parker."

"Not dead yet."

"You will be. But first you will have a nice long talk with Streinikov."

"Gonna be a ... one-sided conversation."

"I do not think so. Harsh measures will be used. You will not remain silent for long."

"Great ... I'm a chew toy for mobbed-up Eurotrash."

"Well put." He regarded her almost sympathetically. "It is a tough situation for you, poppet."

"Been in worse."

"You have led an interesting life."

"I get around ... Why'd you pay me?"

"A pittance. It made the ruse more convincing, *nyet*? And if you expected to meet me again for the rest of the money, you would be focused on that appointment. It would be your opportunity to neutralize me. Maybe you even hoped to win Clarissa's allegiance?"

"Yeah." The word thick, like syrup. "Yeah, I was gonna ... get her on my side."

"Then have her ambush me at the payoff? Because I would be watching you and not expecting anyone else?"

"Uh huh." She thought this had been her plan, though she couldn't be certain anymore. Vaguely she remembered bringing an untraceable .45 and a silencer, which she'd hoped Clarissa would use on Gura later tonight. Something like that.

"Dancing on my strings, poppet," he said again.

The two younger men said little. One was stocky with slicked-back dark hair, the other tall and blond. The shorter one was called Gregor, but she thought of him as Butch. No particular reason. He just looked like a Butch. The blond was Sundance.

Sundance sat beside her while she lay on the sofa. He checked the bandages. She wondered why he cared, why it mattered if she bled or not. She stared up at him, seeing the black tattoo on his neck, and a thin spot in his close-cropped hair over a scar on his scalp. Then his hand closed over her breast in a hard squeeze, and his other hand slid down her jeans, between her thighs, probing with his fingers. It wasn't sexual, somehow. He was like a butcher testing the quality of a cut of beef. Gura called him away.

Clarissa must have been carried off in the sack, but Bonnie had no memory of seeing that. She did remember Gura slowing the boat to a crawl, and shouts from Butch and Sundance on deck, and a soft splash as the sack and its contents went overboard.

Bonnie was on the floor by then. Staring across the yards of carpet, she saw a purse, probably Clarissa's purse, lying under a table, forgotten. She seemed to recall seeing her own handbag, with the gun in it, stowed in a cabinet. She really ought to get her bag. With the gun she could kill Gura and the others and save herself. But she couldn't get it. She couldn't even stand up.

She wondered if they had drugged Clarissa like this before they shot her. Or had they just clubbed her unconscious or fed her an overdose of heroin or ...?

Didn't matter. Dead was dead, regardless of how you got there.

Gura lit a cigarette. She was on the sofa, and he was retrieving his scarf.

"It was cleverly done, *nyet*?" Gura said. "I was almost sure you were the one we wanted. But not one hundred percent. I had to talk to you, watch your face. You are pretty good at keeping secrets. But not from me. I know you killed Lazzaro. I saw it in your eyes."

He exhaled smoke.

"What I needed was for you to go to an isolated location. Someplace where you could be taken alive. Streinikov was very clear on that point. You must be alive. So I sent you here, to Streinikov's own boat, the *Dragon's Mouth*. It is a kind of orchid," he added.

She blinked. "What is?"

"The Dragon's Mouth. A species of the plant. He grows them in his greenhouse. All kinds of orchids. Very beautiful. You will see. It is where we will take you. Bad things happen there."

"Not ... scared."

He only smiled at that.

There were other moments. Gura shining a penlight into her eyes. Gura on his cell phone, speaking Russian. Gura at the wheel, and the lights of New York City in the starboard windows. The curtains were open now, the cabin lights dimmed.

The boat hit rough chop. Her stomach clenched, and she coughed up a yellow string of puke. They all started yelling in Russian, and the blond guy slapped her face. They were worried about the mess she'd made, the stain on the carpet. She understood about the bandages then. They didn't want her bleeding because it was the boss's boat.

She was thirsty. Thirsty and cold at times, shivering. What the fuck had they done to her? She couldn't even recall. She wanted so badly to be strong and focused, but instead she was a limp rag on the floor. They hadn't bothered to tie her hands. She posed no threat.

And she'd lost her hat. The stylish knit beret had come off in the struggle. She didn't know where it had gone. This bothered her as much as anything. She always felt naked without a hat.

The boat passed under the tall bridge between Miramar and Swansea. That was when they were leaving the Crab River Inlet, before they hit the open sea, before Clarissa was dumped in the ocean like so much waste.

"There never was any Clarissa," Gura said. He had finished his cigarette, or maybe he hadn't started it yet. "This girl, she was a dancer in Jersey City." He chuckled. "Or so she called herself. You know what she really was."

"Party girl," Bonnie murmured. "A ho-fessional."

"Precisely."

She remembered the girl's hardness, wariness. The kind of girl who was used to dealing with shady characters and rough characters. A girl who had to look out for herself.

"I hired her to play the role," Gura went on. "I had that Facebook page created, with her photos on it. It was a bad job—bad enough that even an amateur like you could see through it. Her entire—what is your word?—

persona was invented. Today she checked in at the hotel and had lunch with me. We staged a scene to justify her early departure from the hotel. She never did go back to the room. She came here, to this boat, to join my associates. They got her high—she was an addict, like all those of her kind—and then they put down towels from the hotel, and they shot her. Unlike you, poppet, she did not struggle."

"What ... was her real name?"

"I don't remember. Who gives a damn?"

"Why ... kill her?"

Gura shrugged. "Why not? She had done her job. It is best to leave no loose ends. She goes into the sea. You would join her if you did not have an appointment with Streinikov."

"Streinikov lives on the Hudson River," Bonnie recited in a monotone, "near Palisades Interstate Park." She remembered this from the e-book she'd read, though she wasn't sure why she felt the need to say it aloud.

"This is true, poppet." Gura was amused. "We return his boat to him. Undamaged—he was very clear on this point. Hence, you see, the extra towels I asked our Clarissa to order. Poor girl had no idea how they would be used."

"Big joke to you," Bonnie said. "Big fucking joke."

"*Da*, big joke. I installed the GPS tracker in the spare belt myself. I placed the syringe and vial in the lining also. The very syringe Gregor used on you. It was all play-acting and puppetry, all a joke."

"Fuck you," she whispered, because she could think of no better comeback.

"*Nyet*, Bonnie Parker." His smile widened into a giant leer made of crooked teeth, a smile that swallowed the world. "It is not me who is fucked."

# 21

HER HEAD WAS beginning to clear by the time the *Dragon's Mouth* pulled alongside Streinikov's private dock. Time had resumed its normal flow, and her world was no longer whitewashed in a misty sheen. Her tongue still felt like cotton, though, and forming words was hard. The sounds around her echoed, and gravity seemed strangely unpredictable.

Butch dragged her to her feet and pushed her out through the open door at the stern. The cold air, like a slap in the face, revived her a little more.

Sundance assisted her none too gently down the gangway onto the dock. Unlike the pier in the marina, this one floated, riding the choppy water, the separate parts chafing noisily as they lurched and listed under her feet. A wet wind whistled off the river.

Opposite Streinikov's yacht, an inflatable tender with an outboard motor bobbed like a cork. Bonnie looked at it a little too long and started feeling seasick. She bent over and retched. Sundance grabbed her arm and yanked her forward, cursing in Russian.

Somehow she made it to the far end of the pier and *terra firma*—though no *terra* was very *firma* for her at the moment. A staircase ascended a steep hill toward the lights of an estate. The climb looked impossibly hard.

"Don't s'pose you creeps could just kill me now?" she muttered hopefully.

A shove in the back was her answer.

She followed Gura and Butch up the stairs, with Sundance taking up the rear. At least they hadn't cuffed her. She could hold on to both railings and pull herself up one step at a time.

Gazing past the pair in front of her, she saw a slim silhouetted figure waiting by the gate at the top of the stairs. Had to be the man himself, the one who was throwing this party.

Her progress was too slow for the blond perv at her back. "Faster," he said with another poke at her spine. "Move your ass."

Man, would she ever like to pop that guy.

The gate swung open as she approached the summit, and she came face to face with Anton Streinikov. A tall man, impeccably dressed in a tailored suit and black necktie, with the long elegant fingers of a pianist.

"*Alyo*, Miss Parker. What a pleasure to meet you."

"Bite me."

He was coatless. So was she, but not by choice. They'd left her coat on the cruiser. She was shivering, but Streinikov didn't seem to feel the chill. Cold-blooded bastard.

Sundance pushed her again. She started walking, Streinikov at her side. They tramped along a winding path bordered by leafless trees. Flashes of the New York skyline broke through gaps in the foliage.

"Well done, Pavel," Streinikov was saying. "I knew I could rely on my *domovyk*."

"Yeah, he's a good doggie," Bonnie murmured. "Doggie wanna bone?"

"How much did you give her?" Streinikov asked Gura.

"Two capsules in solution. Fifty milligrams in all."

But she hadn't taken the full hit. The needle had popped free, and some of the solution had sprayed her arm.

"That's a high dosage," Streinikov said. "I wanted her alert."

"She was making a fuss. We had to keep her quiet. Anyway, she will be alert enough once she is on the bench."

"I hope so."

On the bench. That didn't sound so good.

Then she remembered something about Streinikov. Something funny.

"You lost your luggage." She laughed.

Streinikov glanced at her. "Luggage?"

She was giggling helplessly. "Got your grapes peeled. Extra room in your skivvies ..."

"Ah. Indeed, the stories are true. I am a castrato." He said it with peculiar pride. "I am still a man, for all that—though perhaps not quite so mannish as a hoyden like you."

She had no idea what a hoyden was, but she got the gist. "Hey, bud ... I'm all woman."

"Not for long."

She didn't know what he meant by that.

The path took another turn, and the greenhouse came into view, aglow from within. Flowers and greenery crowded the transparent walls and made her think of summer.

No more summers for her. No more nights with Brad. No more anything except a few desperate hours of pain.

It got real for her then, real enough to make her lift her head and scream.

*"Help me, I've been kidnapped, I'm a prisoner—"*

Butch socked her in the gut. She went down on one knee, gasping. The world reeled around her. Like a carousel, she thought stupidly. But then ... where were the horses?

"You waste your breath, Miss Parker." Streinikov leaned over her. "We're alone. To the north and west lie the woods. East, the river. South, there's a house, but it is empty now. The owners are in St. John at this time of year. There is no one around. No neighbors to hear you yell." He grabbed her by the hair, pulling her head back. *"Vrubatsa?"*

She choked out a reply. "Yeah, I get it, I get it."

"Good." He jerked her to a standing position. "No more nonsense, please."

His arm wound around her waist. He strode toward the greenhouse, carrying her with him, her feet barely touching the ground.

"Dickless ... asshole ..." she whispered.

"Not at all. I retain that particular piece of equipment. Shall I prove it to you?"

"Take your word for it."

"Just as well. I'd find no pleasure in using your body in that way."

"Not into girls?"

"I'm concerned only with business matters. You cost me money, Miss Parker."

"How?"

"You killed Frank Lazzaro. He ran, as you may recall, an import-export concern. He and I were in the final stages of negotiating an agreement whereby my shipments would use his fleet of container ships. The arrangement would have been mutually profitable. His death scotched the deal. It took me years to gain Lazzaro's trust. Now I must begin anew."

"Told Gura ... I didn't kill Lazzaro."

"He didn't believe you. Neither do I."

He opened the greenhouse door and pushed her inside. She fell sprawling on a strip of pavers bordered by gravel. The others stepped past her. Streinikov stared down.

"There she is—my Firebird. She raided my golden orchard. Now she is in a cage of glass. Soon to be—"

"Stuffed and mounted," Bonnie finished for him. She coughed up a chuckle. "But not in a good way ..."

Streinikov turned to Butch, pointing to a bench that

had been dragged into the aisle in the middle of the greenhouse. "Get it ready."

Butch busied himself clearing the potted plants from the surface. The bench was for her. She understood that much.

She looked dazedly around her. Glass walls framed an opaque darkness. Double rows of wooden benches crowded with terra-cotta pots bracketed the central aisle. Close to her stood a TV monitor where camera coverage of Streinikov's residence was displayed in a cycling tiled array. A thick orange extension cord drooped from the back of the monitor, snaking under the nearest bench toward the side wall.

The whole place was dense with potted flowers and luxuriant tropical plants the size of shrubbery. There were more plants suspended from the ceiling. It was like the frigging Rainforest Cafe in here.

From a bench next to the monitor—a potting bench, she thought it was called—Sundance picked up a pair of pruning shears and clicked the big blades near Bonnie's face. Snip. Snip.

"Cool it, jerkoff." She waved him away with a languid hand. "Already got my trim for the day."

The blond perv smiled. "That's what you think."

He clicked the blades again, brushing her breast. She flinched.

"*Hvatit!*" Streinikov barked. "I want her in good condition when we start."

When we start ... She didn't want them to start. She roused herself to a last effort.

"You're makin' a mistake," she told Streinikov. "I told some cops about you. I go missing ... you're suspect *numero uno.*"

"Bullshit," Gura said. "She told no one."

"Of course she didn't." Streinikov shrugged. "Anyway, it doesn't matter. The authorities cannot touch me."

Bonnie blew a halfhearted raspberry. "What makes you so special?"

"I have in my possession incriminating documents on most persons of importance in this state. The police know well enough to let me be."

"How 'bout the other Russkie big shots? They may not like it. You know ... takin' out a civilian."

"You're hardly a civilian, Miss Parker. You're a combatant on the field of battle. And if my rivals could have brought me down, they'd have done it long ago. Isn't that right, Gura?"

The other man nodded. *"Da."*

"I fear no one. I answer to no one. I am my own man. A lone wolf, as the saying goes."

"Lone wolf ..." Her head drooped. She heard herself laughing again. "Who's afraid of the big bad *vor*, the big bad *vor* ...?"

Streinikov knelt before her, cupping her face in his hands. "Listen to me. I want you to know what's about to happen. Are you listening?"

"Big bad *vor*," she mumbled.

He slapped her face.

*"Listen."*

The slap brought her thoughts back into focus. She stared into Streinikov's eyes. Eyes that shimmered, light gray, like falling sleet.

"Are you listening?" he said again.

"Yeah, yeah ... Don't s'pose I could have a cigarette?"

"There is no smoking in the greenhouse. Though you make jokes and say foolish things, I know you're not insensible to your predicament. You are sweating quite profusely."

"It's a goddamn hothouse."

"The nighttime temperature is set to a temperate seventy degrees."

"Ain't the heat. It's the humidity ..."

"*Nyet.* I think it is fear. Your brain works slowly, but it does work. Do you see that bench?"

She looked past him. The bench had been cleared off by now. Butch was securing straps to the corners, tying them into loops.

"That is our operating table. The grow lights will illuminate our work. The loops on the corners are for your ankles. Think of them as stirrups for a gynecological exam. First we will cut off your clothes. Then we will cut off other things."

Her gaze settled on his face again. He was watching her intently.

"Did you know that castration is not exclusive to the male of the species? A woman, too, can be castrated. Desexed. All that's required is the surgical excision of certain delicate body parts."

She blinked at him. "Oh, come on. You gotta be friggin' kidding me ..."

"Do you believe in hell, Miss Parker?"

"Nope." She wasn't really sure.

"I do. But I believe hell is in the mind. Hell is a state of being. You are in hell right now. Do you understand?"

She managed a lopsided smile. "Hoo boy. I think I'm in trouble ..." Her voice lilted upward on the last word.

He seized her by the shoulders. *"Do you understand?"*

"Sure, sure, Boris Badenov ... Say, did ya ever catch Moose and Squirrel?"

She giggled again.

He rose from his crouch and faced Gura. "You used too much sedative."

"Pain will revive her. When she is on the bench—"

Streinikov said something in Russian. Gura answered defensively. Bonnie didn't speak a word of Russian, but she got the gist. Streinikov was pissed off. He wanted her begging for mercy, and instead she was too fucked up to know what a pickle she was in.

That was the thing, though. She wasn't quite as totally out of it as they all thought. Some of the knockout juice had gotten spilled, and the cold air and long walk had kick-started her brain. She was a long way from being a hundred percent, but she could function. She knew she could.

And she knew something else. She was not going to let them put her on the bench. Once she was horizontal, she was all done. They would secure her with the straps, and they would go to work, and it would be nothing like *Fifty Shades of Grey*. They were going to take her apart one painful little piece at a time.

"*Cuchka derganaya,*" Gura was saying excitedly, his big hands waving.

It all came down to choosing the exact right moment. Needless to say, she wouldn't get a second shot.

She had no illusions about her physical strength. She couldn't overpower a tag team of bad guys. She had to rely on surprise and quickness. And she had to fight dirty, which was okay, because that was the only kind of fighting she knew.

Her eyes focused on the extension cord running from the monitor. There had to be an outlet somewhere. At floor level, probably, behind the second row of benches on that side.

She had an idea in mind, or at least the beginnings of an idea. It was probably best not to overthink things, especially since she was finding it hard to think at all.

"*Ya tebya dostal.*" Streinikov cut off Gura's protestations with a shake of his head. He seemed to have reached a decision. He turned to Sundance and snapped his fingers. "Get her up."

Sundance grabbed her by the back of her pants and hauled her upright. She felt a punch of adrenaline. This was it.

"Put down those pruning shears," Streinikov said, "and

get her fucking *pizda* on the bench."

She felt rather than saw the blond's hungry smile. He turned at the waist, looking for a place to rest the scissors. For just one moment he wasn't focused on her.

Now.

With a twist of her hips she pulled free of his grasp. He pivoted, reacting fast. She stepped into him—if you were smaller, you always got in close and deprived your opponent of his reach—and delivered two quick jabs to the throat. He staggered, and she snatched the scissors out of his hand and spun on Streinikov as he grabbed for her.

The scissors were large and they were sharp and they made a satisfyingly large gash in Streinikov's side as she plunged them into his torso below the ribs.

Streinikov doubled over. She jerked the shears free. The tips came out stained with blood.

Sundance was choking. She'd hit him pretty good. With a little luck she might've busted his trachea. But Butch and Gura weren't hurt, and they were advancing on her from opposite directions.

She threw herself under the nearest bench and rolled toward the side wall, still clutching the shears. She came to a stop on her stomach beneath the second row of benches.

The extension cord, bright orange, lay a few feet away. It ran to an outlet mounted on the baseboard. Two sockets.

Everyone was yelling. For the moment they'd lost her. The benches and the thick foliage provided cover.

She crawled toward the baseboard. The benches were low, barely offering enough clearance. Gravel scraped her palms. Droplets of water seeping through drainage holes pattered her hair.

Behind her, a crash of shattering pottery. Butch was overturning the benches, looking for her. Potted flowers spilled onto the floor.

Streinikov shouted something in Russian. She didn't need a translator to know he was pissed. He didn't want his goons wrecking his hothouse and bruising his precious pansies.

Closer to her, Gura was thrashing his way through the huge palms and ferns that crowded the front wall. He would reach her in a few seconds.

She scrambled out from under the bench and got her hand on the outlet. Jerked out the extension cord, hoping it powered more than the monitor. No such luck. The lights were still on, and the nearby plants rustled crazily. Gura was almost on top of her.

She swung into a kneeling pose, balancing on her sneakers. Rubber soles. And the shears had rubber handles. Insulation, right?

With her full strength she jammed the pruning shears into the outlet, the sharp tips punching through both sockets.

Sizzle in her fingers. Shout of blue flame. She dropped the shears and fell on her ass, banging her head on a bench, and the lights went out.

For a second she was too disoriented to move. But Gura was still coming, and so were the others. The sparks and noise had been as good as a signal flare. She had to move.

She scooted away from the outlet, abandoning the shears, which might still be embedded in the sockets or might have been lost on the floor. Purple afterimages swam across her field of vision. Her teeth hurt. She felt as if she'd bitten down on tinfoil.

She slipped back under the benches and started crawling toward the rear of the greenhouse, away from Gura.

The darkness around her was loud and crazy. Streinikov shouting, Gura and the two younger guys answering back, everyone talking at once, no one sure where the hell she was.

Behind her, a flashlight snapped on. She looked back and there was Gura, aiming the beam at her, his ugly orangutan face lit from below like a Halloween mask. His gun was out, and he couldn't miss at this range.

But he didn't fire. She thought she knew why. A house of glass was no place for a shooting match. If the round passed through her or ricocheted, it could bring down the whole wall.

Instead he snugged the gun into his belt, scrambled forward, and reached out with one hairy hand. His fingers closed over her ankle.

With her free leg she kicked him in the face.

He released her, dropping the flash. It rolled away under the benches, painting the darkness in spirals of white light.

She shoved herself forward, out of his reach, and kept going, snaking from one bench to the next. There was no space between them; they were butted together, each one six feet long—coffin-sized. Plants overgrowing their pots hung down in a green curtain, screening her from view.

Other flashlights came on. Gura was yelling something in Russian, presumably telling the others where he'd last seen her. One of them—Butch, she thought—leaped up on the bench directly above her, scattering the pots. His flashlight dipped down, the beam breaking into a fan of spokes as it penetrated the drainage holes.

Flashback: belly-crawling under the Brighton Cove boardwalk while a man named Pascal hunted her from above with an infrared scope.

Butch would spot her at any second. She took a chance and rolled out from under the bench into the center aisle, exposed to view if anyone turned a flashlight in her direction. On hands and knees she scrabbled across the walkway and disappeared under the benches on the opposite side.

No one had seen her. Butch and Gura were still hunting her on the other side of the aisle. They expected her to continue to the rear of the greenhouse. There was no exit at that end. She would be cornered, helpless.

More pots broke. Streinikov shouted a protest.

She turned herself around and doubled back to the front of the greenhouse, where there was a door. Another flashlight came to life. This one was close. Not Butch, not Gura.

In the bedlam she heard Sundance's voice, hoarse but recognizable. So she hadn't cracked his windpipe after all. He had joined the hunt, and he was coming her way, bent at the waist, checking the floor.

She couldn't count on the benches for concealment, not when the beam was probing underneath. She retreated to the side wall and found a dense cluster of bamboo in a giant pot. She hid herself behind it, crouching down.

Sundance's beam flitted over the bamboo stalks, paused briefly, and moved on.

He was past her now. Converging with the other three at the rear of the greenhouse. She only had to make it to the front and get out through the door. Stooped low, she ran along the side wall, counting on the lush foliage to screen her from any stray flashlight beams.

Somewhere nearby Streinikov was still shouting. He hadn't moved since she'd stabbed him. She'd hurt the bastard, hurt him badly, and she felt real good about that.

A wall came up fast, squares of damp glass. The door was to one side. She would have to risk exposure again. Now, before they figured out where she'd gone.

She crabbed her way through the big potted plants to the paved aisle and groped for the door handle, not finding it.

Brightness.

A new flashlight. Streinikov's.

He was slumped in a chair by the dead TV monitor, looking directly at her as the beam of his flashlight pinned her like a butterfly on a mounting board.

*"Vot ona!"* he shouted.

The beams at the far end of the greenhouse swung in her direction. Gura's gun came up. He fired one shot, blowing out the glass pane alongside the door in a spray of shards.

Streinikov yelled a curse. He still didn't want any shooting in here.

In the wavering circles of multiple beams, she found the door handle and cranked it down. The door opened with a rush of night air, startlingly cold.

Streinikov's men were running at her, but the bench in the center aisle was in their way.

She threw herself through the doorway and fled into the night.

# 22

"SHE'S OUT."

Ilya spoke the words, his voice hoarse and raw. He still clutched his bruised throat with one hand.

Streinikov knew it. "We'll get her. Gura, Gregor—hunt her down. Capture her alive if possible, but take no unnecessary chances."

"I'm going too," Ilya said.

"*Nyet.*" Streinikov held up a commanding hand. "You find the outlet she disabled and fix it. Then go to the garage and flip the breaker. Have Lysenko switch on all the outside lights. Tell him to monitor the front gate in case she attempts to slip out that way. And when you return," he added as an afterthought, "bring a first aid kit."

He touched his waist, dipping his fingers into a welling lake of blood.

BONNIE DARTED OFF the path and ran north. She remembered Streinikov saying there were woods in that direction. A forest sounded like a good place to disappear into.

She staggered as she ran. Adrenaline competed with the sleepytime cocktail in her system. Willpower gave her the edge. She would not be taken back into the greenhouse. She would make them kill her out here, if it came to that. She wasn't going to have a scream session on the bench with garden tools all up in her business. That party had been canceled.

She blundered through a row of bushes and came up hard against a perimeter fence, eight feet high.

Fuck.

Behind her, voices and running footsteps. At least two of her pals were headed her way.

She hooked her fingers into the steel mesh and climbed the fence, praying she wouldn't run into a line of razor wire along the top.

She didn't. Evidently Streinikov wasn't quite that paranoid. He just wanted to keep out any errant birdwatchers who wandered off the hiking trails.

She hoisted herself over the fence, descended halfway, and dropped to the soft dirt with a thud.

A shout. Gura's voice. He was jabbering in Russian, but his meaning was clear. He'd spotted her.

She launched herself into a hard sprint over a flat stretch of ground. It was cold in the night, without a coat, but she was almost too scared to notice.

A stiff breeze blew off the river, helping her to orient herself. That was good, because she sure as shit couldn't gauge her position any other way. She wouldn't know the Big Dipper from the Big Bopper. She'd never even gone camping. For her, nature was best appreciated in a TV show about when animals attacked.

Noises at her back. Grunts and jangling metal. Gura and Butch scaling the fence. Sundance, too? She wasn't sure. But she was certain the boss man wasn't in the posse. She'd put him out of commission, at least for a while.

When she glanced back, she saw bouncing starbursts of white light. Flashlights. Her pursuers had come over the fence and were following her trail.

The first shot rang out, kicking up dirt a couple of yards from her feet. They'd seen her.

A second shot landed closer. She dived into the underbrush, scrambling toward the river on hands and knees. She needed to get down to the water. That rubber dinghy with the outboard could take her across the river into Manhattan. If she could make it there ... "I'll make it anywhere," she muttered in a singsong chant.

Damn. Her head must still be pretty fuzzy if she could make a joke that lame.

The moon was a fading sliver, low in the sky. The stars were clear and bright. They helped her to see—and made it easier for her to be seen.

Ground cover ranged from ankle deep to knee deep. It was clear under the trees except for pine needles and leaves. The low branches were treacherous. She kept her head down, plunging forward, getting caught up sometimes in the thick undergrowth. At one point she lost a shoe. It was sucked right off her foot by clinging foliage. She couldn't take the time to recover it.

Insect noises surrounded her, a chorus of chirps and hums and weirdly mechanical clicks. Somewhere a bird screeched. Owl, maybe. Or a vulture. How the hell should she know?

She wished she'd been able to hold on to the pruning shears. She needed a weapon. It was bad enough being hunted, even worse when she had no way to fight back. She remembered tracking a wounded man in the Pine Barrens, a man with a bullet in him who wouldn't go down. Now she was the prey. No bullet in her, just a buttload of doxy-whatchamacallit.

Flailing through a thicket, she came upon a fallen ash tree carpeted in moss. A three-foot branch extended from the tree, stabbing at the sky. Where the branch met the trunk, the wood was rotten, but the rest of the branch was dry and hard, and the pointed end was sharp.

She grabbed the branch and wrenched it viciously, making way too much noise, until the dead wood crackled and split. The branch came loose in her hand. She hefted it. A spear, sort of. At close range it could do some damage.

As a weapon, it wasn't much, but it made her feel a little better. She kept going.

She wanted to run, but the forest insisted on getting in her way. Trees were bunched together, throwing up rough walls of bark. Bushes sprang up in her path, threatening to trip her when they were small, acting as solid barriers when they were shoulder high. Sometimes she found open ground, but it didn't last, and even then, there were ruts and gullies, loose dirt and slippery pine needles. Her progress was always slow, always impeded by some new obstacle.

Damn, she hated the woods. Couldn't somebody have laid down some nice smooth pavement around here?

There were trails somewhere, but hell if she knew where to find them. Besides, she would be too exposed on a trail. It was one of those situations where you were screwed either way—off the trails she could barely move, and on a trail she'd be an easy target. So she could blunder through the brush and lead the bad guys straight to her with all the racket she was making, or she could run into the open and become a human bull's-eye. Some days, it was hardly worth getting out of bed.

Finally she stopped. She huddled by a tree, listening. The forest seemed quieter now, almost silent. It was as if the bugs and birds had settled down to watch the show.

In the distance, a rustle of movement. A human being—somehow she was sure of it.

A shout, clear in the strange stillness: "I found your shoe, Parker. I'm coming for you."

It was Butch, the one who'd cleared off the bench. He seemed to be alone. He and Gura must have split up to cover more ground.

By now she knew any movement would make noise, and any noise would draw him to her. Needless to say, her spear wouldn't be much good against his handgun. Her best bet was to stay motionless and hope he passed by.

Maybe. But she wasn't the type to sit and wait for the bogeyman to walk right up to her. It went against her nature. And if Butch had any skill as a tracker, he could probably follow a path of broken twigs and bent grass straight to her hiding place.

The rustling sounds were closing in, and she was getting seriously antsy. A new plan took shape. If she proceeded very slowly and very carefully, moving on all fours if necessary, she might be able to double back a few yards. Get behind him, then take him by surprise.

A good plan? Or only a feeble excuse to move her ass, because, like a toddler, she just couldn't sit still? She wasn't sure, but what the hell, she was doing it. To sit and wait was just too hard. Already she could taste the sour flavor of panic rising in her throat.

Holding the spear at her side, she crept away from the tree, along a line of thick evergreen bushes that ought to screen her from sight. If there had been any background noise to cover her progress, she would have been golden, but the friggin' woods refused to cooperate. The place was as silent as a cemetery, and before long the similarities might not end there.

She was proud of herself, though. She was keeping to a steady pace, tortoise slow, invisible and silent. She began to think she would really get away with this plan.

A bullet rang out, whining like a mosquito near her head.

"I hear you, Parker."

Piss. Apparently she wasn't as stealthy as she thought.

She crawled into a grove of pines and, for the sheer hell of it, yelled back. "Missed me, dipshit."

"I shoot only to wound. You don't die so easy."

He still wanted her on the bench. Great.

She left the trees and scrambled to cover behind a tangle of underbrush. She wasn't trying to be quiet anymore. He could hear her no matter what she did, so she might as well move fast—as fast as possible in this maze of shit.

Then she spotted him. He was standing in an open space, the flashlight arrowed away from her, its beam playing over the pine grove where she'd been.

And he was close. Closer than she'd realized. Yards away, near enough that he could freakin' smell her, which wouldn't be hard because she was sweating right through her shirt.

She went down on her stomach, hugging the cold ground, tasting dirt. She risked belly-crawling a few feet.

The flashlight shifted, swinging toward her. A stripe of light painted her arm. She rolled away as another bullet struck the dirt near enough to spray her cheek with pebbles.

Damn. The guy was a good shot, even in the dark.

"I see you, Parker. You want me to kill you, but I'm taking you alive. There will be much pain for you."

She gritted her teeth. "That's what you think, comrade."

Now he was coming. His tread was rapid, assured. He had a good fix on her location, and the stars and the flashlight helped him to see, and he knew she was unarmed.

Well, she had her stupid homemade spear. Fat lot of good it would do her.

There were no good options left. She could try to fight at close range, or she could run and get cut down by gunfire. The second way offered a better chance of a quick death.

Okay, then. Do that. Run and die.

She heard her own breathing, fast and shallow. This was it, really *it*. She was punching out. She would be dead in the next few seconds—unless she was really unlucky, in which case she would die on the bench.

On her feet. Legs pumping. Twigs and branches tearing at her as she pushed her way through the dense brush.

He saw her, of course. He had to see her.

And he roared.

It was a hoarse, bellowing roar, a Tartar war cry, a shout of rage.

She looked back and saw him charging through the bushes, heedless of obstacles, his gaze fixed on her.

But not shooting. He really did want to take her alive, God damn it.

His shout pursued her as she stumbled forward, fighting the woods, a thousand spiny fingers clutching at her hair and ankles. She lost sight of him for a moment as she plunged through a wall of shrubs, but she could still hear him, closer than ever, almost at her back.

And the ground vanished under her.

She tumbled into a narrow gully, three feet deep, lined with stones and dead creepers. She landed on her back, the breath hammered out of her, staring up at a canopy of leafless branches and the blazing stars.

Dazed, she shook her head, struggled to rise.

An idea.

The spear—she'd dropped it when she fell. She groped the rough stones, searching for the feel of wood.

There.

Above, the bushes thrashed wildly as her assailant powered through. He was a yard away, still releasing his endless bray of fury.

She planted the spear in the ground, holding it upright in both fists, the sharp end pointed at the sky.

With a cascade of loose stones, he blundered into the pit, dropping almost on top of her, and his shout changed to a high keening wail as the spearpoint punched through his groin, driving upward into his belly.

His legs kicked. The gun fired. The shots flew wild, his hand spasming. Blood spattered her face. His blood, not hers.

She threw herself at him and batted the pistol away. As she watched, he slid another few inches down the spear, impaling himself still more deeply. His face twist-ed, his mouth hanging open in a gargle of bloody froth.

Her hand closed over the first blunt object it could find. A triangular rock, heavy. She snapped to a standing position and brought the rock down on his forehead—again—again—until he was silent and unmoving and nothing was left of his features.

She withdrew, shaking, and stared at the dead thing in the pit. Her voice was a ragged gasp.

"*Do Svetlana*, asshole."

# 23

GURA CAME UPON the body in the gully about five minutes after hearing the last shots and the long drawn-out womanish shriek. Until his flashlight played over the bloody remains, he had held out hope that the shriek had been Parker's. It had not sounded like a noise a man could make.

But a man whose insides had been chewed open, a man who'd been run through like a spitted pig ... Well, there was no telling what sounds could come out of his throat.

The circle of light probed the bottom of the pit, finding neither Gregor's gun nor his flashlight. Parker must have taken both. So she was armed now, carrying a Makarov. Gura had counted seven shots in all, and he knew Gregor used the newer ten-round magazine. Three rounds left.

The intelligent thing would be to return to the estate and get Ilya or Lysenko to come along. But he could not do that. It would mean he was running from a fight, and he never ran. And when his adversary was a woman—unthinkable.

Anyway, he could not allow her an even greater head start. She had been making her way toward the river, and he expected her to continue that way. Luckily she was wet with Gregor's blood. He could follow the glistening red trail.

It led him through stands of pines and sycamores, around thickets of witch-hazel and wild azalea. The moon hung near the horizon—the *molodyk*, the first outline of a new moon. The same pale sickle he had seen on that other night, in the village, when he had killed Stavitsky. He was no longer a boy, but a man in another country, yet he was on the hunt again, in the cold and dark, seeking a human life. Some things never changed.

The cliff that dropped down to the river was quite near. The trail brought him there. He saw bright splotches, like varnish, on the rocks and shrubs that checkered the steep incline. She'd scrambled down. Going to the water? No. To the boats.

He had never been an athlete, and he smoked too much. He was wheezing with strain as he went slip-sliding down the hillside. Sharp outcrops cut his hands. A patch of briars snagged his coat. Cursing, he pulled himself free with a rip of the lining.

From a distance, he heard a low cough, a brief guttural sound.

He stopped, listening. At first he wasn't sure just what he'd heard.

It came again, another cough, more prolonged this time. The sound of a motor being cranked, refusing to turn over.

The motorboat at the pier. Of course. She couldn't take the cruiser; he had the keys. But the little launch moored near it would take her down the river or across to the city.

He descended the rest of the way in a headlong tumbling rush. His shoes found the wet strip of sand and stones along the water.

To the south, the motor coughed again, still refusing to start. He had used the outboard himself. It was a stubborn beast. It might defy her just long enough to let him reach her. Preoccupied with the boat, she might not even see him. An easy target.

He had long since given up any idea of taking her alive. He did not care for torture anyway. And after what she'd done to Gregor, he was taking no chances. Three shots to the center body mass, then a coup de grace to the head. If he could get to her in time.

He ran along the narrow ribbon of beach, the muddy ground tugging at his feet with every step. He was unused to such exertion. It might kill him. Already he felt an alarming twinge in his chest. He could give himself a heart attack before this was all over. It didn't matter. He kept going. He could not fail Streinikov.

They called him the *domovyk* for a reason. He was ever the faithful servant. He had few virtues, but he was loyal and dependable. Given a task, he would complete it.

As he was rounding a bend in the riverbank, he heard the motor catch.

She was getting away. But he was almost there. He still had a chance.

He pushed his way through a mass of trees that had grown right down to the water. Ahead of him was the floating pier, bobbing gently. Beyond it, but not far, was the launch, heading due east, toward Manhattan.

Gura clambered onto the pier and staggered to the far end. He lifted his gun, steadied it against the pounding of his heart, and fired twice at the retreating boat. Each shot was a whip crack of sound skipping like a stone over the water.

He expected her to return fire. She did not. Maybe she knew she couldn't hit him at this distance.

But he was a good shot. He could hit her. If he could see her ...

She must be staying low, keeping her head down. He had no target. But he could take out the launch itself. He fired at the stern, aiming for the outboard. Kill the motor and she would be helplessly adrift. He could close in on her in the cruiser, kill her while her sad little vessel was dead in the water.

After four more shots, the boat veered, turning in a

circle. He'd hit the rudder. She couldn't steer. She would spin aimlessly. Her only chance now was to fight back. She had Gregor's gun. He waited for a shot, refusing to kneel, though it would make him a smaller target. He would kneel to no one, and certainly not a woman.

Still she did not fire. He began to think he'd hit her, after all. She might be wounded or already dead.

It was strange, though. Strange that she'd never even tried to shoot back ...

Then he understood. He was not, perhaps, the cleverest of men. Streinikov had not hired him for his brains, but for his devotion. The girl, though—she was a clever bitch. And she had never been on the launch at all.

The gun in his hand was nearly empty. It would do him no good, anyway. He relaxed his grip and let it fall.

He turned, and she was there, standing at the landward end of the dock, Gregor's pistol in her hand. She had started the launch and sent it on its way, and then she had waited for him to walk into his trap.

Clever, clever bitch.

He stared at her across a length of floating planks. He could not see her face, but he imagined she was smiling.

He smiled also. A last, sad smile.

"I hired you as a killer, poppet," he said, his voice carrying across the water. "Now you must earn your pay."

# 24

"YOU HEAR THAT?"

Streinikov asked the question with his head cocked, eyes half shut. Kneeling by him beside the potting bench, at work bandaging the pair of wounds, Ilya nodded.

"Gunshots," Ilya said in his injured, croaking voice. "Small arms fire."

They were alone in the greenhouse. The lights were back on. Ilya had pulled the pruning shears from the wall socket, then found the circuit box in the garage and flipped the switch. He had given Lysenko his instructions, then returned with the first aid kit. Like all experienced fighters, he was not unfamiliar with combat surgery.

"And a boat motor," Streinikov said. "An outboard." He sat stiffly in the chair, his jacket off, necktie loosened.

Ilya unwound a length of tape from the dispenser. "*Da*. I heard that, too."

"My inflatable?"

"I don't know. There are a lot of motor noises on the river."

"Seldom an outboard, and never at this hour. Check it out."

"I'm not done here."

"I can finish. Go."

Ilya left the greenhouse at a fast stride.

Streinikov tore off another length of tape and finished securing the bandage to his waist. The doctor, Vasnev, had been called and was on his way—reluctantly, no doubt.

So much damage had been done—to his organization, to his orchids, even to his own body. And behind it all was just one woman, young, brash, reckless. A blonde woman … What was it about blondes? Katya had been blonde. He remembered her scalp on his wall, how pretty it was after it had been rinsed of blood. She'd had long hair. Parker's hair, too, was long, and very nearly the same shade …

His phone rang. Grunting with strain, he fumbled it out of his shirt pocket. The caller was Ilya.

"Yes?"

"Gura is dead."

Streinikov shut his eyes. The *domovyk*, his obedient servant. Crude and boorish, a peasant with yellow teeth and callused hands, but the most reliable man he had.

Ilya was still speaking. "The inflatable was set adrift with the motor running, but it appears to be unmanned. It's going in circles."

"Have you checked the *Dragon's Mouth*?"

"Of course. Parker's handbag and coat are gone. She is not on board."

"Any sign of Gregor?"

"None. I called his phone. He does not answer. And Gura was shot. Parker was not armed. Not at first."

Streinikov nodded. He had heard a few scattered shots earlier, remote and muffled. Somehow Parker had out-maneuvered Gregor and taken his firearm.

"She is a fighter, this one," he breathed.

"Sir?" Ilya hadn't heard.

"Never mind."

"She took Gura's phone. I tried to track it, but there's no signal."

"She must have turned it off."

"Why take it if she can't use it?"

Streinikov neither knew nor cared. "In all likelihood, she'll proceed south along the river."

"I can follow—"

"No. She has a head start and a weapon. If she takes the high ground, she can pick you off as you approach."

"That little *dura* is no threat to me."

"So Gura thought," Streinikov said coldly. So did we all, he added to himself. "Listen. She'll make her way to where there are streets and houses, and she'll obtain a vehicle ..."

He spoke for a few moments, giving Ilya his instructions, making everything clear.

"And call up Abroskin and Kolba," he finished. "Send them over here. And Denisov, too. Hell, call them all. All our soldiers. I want the property fully protected."

"You don't think she'll risk coming back?"

"It is hard to say what a hunted animal may do. But I have other enemies. If word should get out that I am wounded ..."

"No one will know."

"We will take precautions, even so. Do you understand your orders?"

"Yes, sir."

"Good. We'll get her. That much I promise you."

"When the time comes," Ilya asked, "do we try to take her alive?"

"No. Just kill her. And bring me her head."

"Her head?"

"Her pretty blonde head. Understood?"

"Yes, sir."

"I will hang her hair on my wall and play marbles with her blue, blue eyes."

"Yes, sir."

He heard doubt in Ilya's voice. Or was it fear? Fear that the old man was losing it? Well, perhaps he was. Parker had put a blade in his belly—a sharp blade, like a scalpel—and already he might be drowning in his own blood, and Gura was dead, and she was still out there, the fucking *shalava*, slut, whore, still mobile, still alive. He wanted to smash things. He wanted to throw her carcass on the hood of his car like a damn deer.

"You know what to do," he said sharply. "Get moving."

He ended the call, breathing fast. He stared around him at the rows of potted orchids. Irrationally he was afraid for them. Such tender, delicate things. If the girl should return now, while he was alone and unprotected—

He did not fear for himself. But who knew what such an uncouth ruffian might do to his beauties? She was a grubby little savage, that one. A creature without grace or humanity, uncivilized, *nekulturny*. Even a peasant like old Gura had been more of an aesthete than that wild-eyed, bloodthirsty little tramp.

Gura ...

He felt an unexpected twinge of grief. Though he had not known it before this moment, Pavel Gura had been more than a loyal employee. He had been a friend. The only one left who remembered the early days, the glory days. The only one still with him who had been there when Smolin and Katya had paid for their sins. Gura had wielded the knife himself; he had taken Smolin's prick and balls and roared laughter at the man's stupid staring horror. He, unlike young Ilya, would have understood the significance of the blonde mane soon to be nailed to the wall.

Slowly Streinikov lowered his head, cradling it in his hands. A moan escaped him, low and desolate, like the plaint of a dying animal. A gored ox, that was what he was. A mad bull.

But he still had horns. He could gore, could kill.

Lifting his head, he picked up the phone and began to set his plans in motion.

# 25

BONNIE HEADED WEST on US-46, looking for a motel. It had to be in her price range—in other words, cheaper than dirt. There wasn't much money in her purse or in Clarissa's handbag, and she didn't want to use a credit card, either her own or the dead woman's. Card transactions could be traced.

Yeah, she was being paranoid. She'd already powered off Sammy so the cell phone wouldn't send out any pings. Only the phone company could track the phone, but she wasn't taking chances. Streinikov was the kind of guy who would have contacts in lots of legitimate businesses. Hadn't he bragged that he could buy and sell anyone in the state?

Of course, she'd killed the power on Gura's phone also. It was a safe bet that Streinikov had a way of keeping tabs on his employees; an app like Find My Phone was pretty much a given.

She'd lifted the phone from Gura's pocket after killing him with a bullet to the heart and a follow-up, at closer range, to the head. It had been quick and not too noisy. The second shot had been purely for insurance; she was almost sure the first one had taken him out, in which case he hadn't felt a thing. Not that she would have lost any sleep if he had.

She'd taken his gun, too, and then she'd gone aboard the *Dragon's Mouth* and retrieved her purse, with the Ruger still inside, and the purse belonging to the murdered dancer who'd been called Clarissa Lynch. A pair of binoculars had been left in plain sight; she'd taken them, as well. Waste not, want not. Oh, and her coat and hat, naturally. With the beret snugged on her head, she'd felt a whole lot better.

For approximately three seconds she'd considered using the *Dragon's Mouth* to make her getaway. The wide river looked easy enough to navigate, and the lights of Manhattan were awfully inviting. A glance at the cockpit, or the helm, or whatever it was called, had been enough to scuttle that idea. She'd never driven a boat in her life, and right now was not the time for a practice session. Besides, Streinikov and Sundance would hear the big motor start up. Probably they could track the vessel via GPS. Wherever she came ashore, a welcome party would be there to do a little meet-and-greet. That was assuming she didn't steer the boat straight into a coral reef or an iceberg or some damn thing.

So the boat idea was a nonstarter. She'd left the *Dragon's Mouth* and retreated down the pier, again passing Gura's corpse. Really she should have gone through his pockets for his wallet and spare ammo, but she'd been in a kind of a hurry. She'd tramped south along the riverbank and climbed the hillside to a residential neighborhood, where she'd boosted a Honda Civic and begun her search for the night's lodgings.

Up ahead a likely candidate came into view. The sign identified it as the Magic Carpet Motor Inn and promised such enticing amenities as "cable TV" and "continental breakfast." To judge by appearances, the TV wouldn't work and the breakfast would consist of a stale mini-donut and day-old instant coffee.

In other words, it was her kind of place.

One thing was certain. She wasn't going home. Her turf was off-limits until she got this whole mess straightened out. If it *could* be straightened out …

She thought it could. In fact, she'd already come up

with a plan. Like most of her plans, it was reckless and probably stupid and unlikely to succeed. But something beat nothing, and right now it was all she had.

She parked the Civic out of sight so the desk clerk couldn't get a look at her stolen wheels. The room cost her $85, probably more than it was worth. She was not asked to sign a guest register.

The motel appeared to be mostly empty. She unlocked her room, tossed the two handbags on a table, and took a quick tour of her accommodations.

She wasn't a fan of motels. Hadn't had good experiences with them. There was the dive in Pennsylvania where her parents had been shot to death while she hid in the bathroom, and the Roach House, where she'd had a not-so-fun late-night engagement involving her friend Pascal, a bathtub, and a car battery.

Now here she was in the Magic Carpet or, as she immediately dubbed it, the Maggot Armpit. Not exactly a five-star establishment. The smoke alarm dangled from a wire in the ceiling, having been disabled by a prior occupant. The carpet was littered with dead bugs, toenail clippings, and a condom wrapper. The bed had been slept in, and nobody had changed the sheets. The bathroom offered its own special ambience. She found mysterious stains on the towels and blood spatter in the sink.

All in all, this dump made the Roach House look like the Waldorf-Astoria. But she wasn't complaining. It was still better than the greenhouse.

She badly wanted a shower, but the nozzle produced only a sad trickle of lukewarm water. Okay, no shower. She washed her face in the disgusting sink and dried it with the disgusting towels. Still not trusting her cell—sorry, Sammy—she went outside and hunted down a payphone near a busted vending machine. That's right, an actual, honest-to-God payphone, like something Sam Spade would have used.

She called Felix Ramirez. "It's me," she said. "You busy?"

"I'm on duty."

"Yeah, but are you busy?"

"Guess not."

"Then I need you to pick up that bag I left at your place and deliver it to me."

"Okay, I can do that."

"It's a little more of a favor than it sounds. I'm not at home. I'm in a motel called the Maggot—uh, I mean the Magic Carpet, on Highway Forty-Six in Ridgefield. Room twenty-three."

"You need me to drive to Ridgefield?"

"Yeah. Pronto. I'll pay you for your time," she added.

"That's not necessary."

"Sure it is. But I can't pay right this minute, so I'll have to owe you. If ... well, if things work out, I'll settle up tomorrow."

"What do you mean, if things work out?"

"If I'm still alive. Can you do it?"

"Be there in a couple hours, *bandida*."

She'd figured he would come through. He was that kind of guy.

Back in her room, she started going through Clarissa Lynch's purse, methodically sorting the contents, looking for anything she could use.

In the girl's wallet, she found a driver's license bearing Clarissa's photo and the name Trudy Welch. So that was who she really was. Now she was at the bottom of the ocean, wrapped in hotel towels and probably an anchor chain. Killed for no good reason. Brought into this whole mess merely to serve as a decoy, playing a part she'd never understood. Desperate enough to take a highly questionable job offered by less than reputable people. What the hell, she must have thought. At least she would get a boat ride out of it.

"Sorry, Trudy," Bonnie said softly. "You deserved better. Probably."

She put the wallet into her own purse. There was nothing else of value among Trudy Welch's personal effects, and nothing that could identify the owner. She tossed the dead girl's handbag into a wastebasket. Well, what else could she do with it? Make a shrine out of the damn thing?

She was no sentimentalist. Trudy Welch was dead, and Bonnie Parker—for the time being, at least—was still stubbornly alive.

# 26

ILYA KVINT PICKED up two shooters on his way from Edgewater to Brighton Cove. They were Barsky and Lukin, both family men—wives and kids—guys who drove minivans and mowed the lawn on Sundays. Lukin even attended church. Ilya had caught him praying once. And yet he killed people as casually as the average person took a shit. If he believed in hell, who did he think it was for, if not for people like him?

Ilya did not believe in hell. But he wished he did. An eternity of pain was preferable to oblivion. And he was self-confident enough to think that he would rise in Lucifer's ranks. He could end up as a dungeon master, inflicting punishment on an infinite variety of victims. A pleasant prospect, he sometimes thought with a beatific smile. It was true what they said. Religion was good for the soul.

Sadly, he was a realist. His philosophy was simple. You killed and kept on killing until eventually somebody killed you. Then you were gone forever, and whatever pain and grief you'd caused didn't matter at all. Nothing mattered. A human being was a bundle of meat and nerve endings. That bundle could be made to beg and scream and do other delightful things. There was pleasure—sensual pleasure, erotic pleasure—in eliciting those screams. Ilya enjoyed pleasure. There was no reason for him to deprive himself of it during his brief span of allotted years. That was all.

He had been raised in Donetsk and had hooked up with his boss when Streinikov purchased some local nightclubs. Ilya had been working at a club, dealing cards in games of blackjack and *durak*. He knew he could be useful to Streinikov. More important, Streinikov could be useful to him. A man like Streinikov would make enemies. Those enemies would have to be dealt with, sometimes in satisfyingly creative ways.

Unlike Barsky and Lukin, he had no wife or child and no lawn to mow. He had few possessions. He kept money in several bank accounts, but seldom touched it. He bought whores, not invariably female, and he read books. Serious books in his native language—Tolstoy, Dostoevsky, Turgenev. Occasionally he put on headphones and listened to Prokofiev or Stravinsky. He had been known to attend the ballet, though he did not advertise the fact.

Alone among Streinikov's men, he did not raise an eyebrow at his boss's obsession with orchids. He did not see it as a weakness. He understood the need to balance ugliness with beauty. He was, he supposed, an epicurean—decadent, devoted to pleasure, believing in nothing. The Greeks had a saying: Know thyself. Ilya Kvint knew himself, even the deepest parts of himself, and he was content.

At three in the morning he pulled into Brighton Cove, steering his black Cadillac Escalade to Bonnie Parker's office on Main Street.

"You really think she'll be stupid enough to show up here?" Barsky asked, his tone faintly insolent.

"It's not about catching her," Ilya said. "It's about sending a message."

He shot off the lock on the front door and led his colleagues up the dark staircase.

"Place is a real shit hole," Lukin observed.

"This girl Parker is strictly small-time," Barsky said. "A fucking *peshka*, a nobody. She never should've caused this much trouble."

Ilya heard an implied criticism in this statement. "The

bitch is harder to kill than you would think."

On the second floor he found the door marked *Last Resort*. He kicked it open.

"Do some damage."

Lukin carried a Jati-Matic submachine gun in a brief-case. Barsky had a collapsible Brügger & Thomet MP9 in a shoulder holster under his coat. The Jati used a thirty-round magazine; the MP9, forty rounds.

The two men entered, sweeping the office with both guns firing on full automatic. The noise was incredible, an avalanche of percussive sound punctuated by the tinkling explosions of the windows and the shattering wood of the desk, armchairs, and sofa. They blew the desktop computer into fragments, stitched uneven rows of bullet holes across the walls, and shredded the two tacked-up posters.

In ten seconds it was all over. Ilya retrieved one of the posters and looked at it in the light of his phone. A gun moll posing on an antique roadster. He didn't recognize the image, but Barsky did.

"That's Bonnie Parker."

"No, it isn't. I've seen her."

Barsky assumed the condescending look he wore whenever he had an advantage, no matter how trivial. "I mean the original one. You know, Bonnie and Clyde."

Ilya had no idea what Barsky was talking about, but he did not wish to reveal his ignorance. He nodded sagely. "Ah."

Barsky pointed to the drooping remains of the other poster. "That's the car they were shot up in."

"Ah," Ilya said again.

He caught Barsky smirking at him. Smug in his knowledge of *Amerikosy* gangsters who must have died decades ago, small-time hoodlums of no importance to anyone living. The man had always been full of himself. An arrogant *mudak*, who just possibly might be angling for Ilya's job. As if a creature like him could ever qualify as Streinikov's right-hand man.

He threw the poster aside and led his men out of the building. Lukin, taking the wheel of the Escalade, pulled away before the first patrol car arrived to investigate the noise.

"Where to?" he asked Ilya.

"Inland. Toward the railroad tracks."

"What's there?"

"Her house."

# 27

Bradley Walsh was a little ticked off at his girlfriend. First she was working on Friday night and didn't show up at his place until late. Then she suddenly pronounced herself busy on Saturday night, leaving him in the lurch again.

Yeah, it was true they couldn't exactly paint the town red. With their relationship on the down-low, they had to avoid public places in Brighton Cove and the surrounding boroughs. But from time to time they'd gone dining and dancing in more distant spots—down on Devil's Hook Island a couple of times, or up in north Jersey. It wasn't easy, but it was doable. But lately she always had to work.

He wondered if she was getting tired of him. Or if she just wasn't that much into the relationship.

Whatever. Having decided he wasn't going to waste the night sulking, he'd volunteered to fill in for Stewart on the night watch—working the midnights, it was called. What the heck, he could use the money. And Stew, unlike himself, had a girlfriend who would appreciate his availability on a weekend.

That was how he found himself in the station house at midnight, eating a cruller from the Donut Hutch and filling out an incident report on a loud party. Exciting stuff. They should make a TV show about his life.

The phone rang. The watch commander, Sergeant Gathers, should have answered, but he was currently indisposed. More precisely, he was hanging out in the can after consuming a very questionable bean-and-cheese taco that had been in the fridge for an unknown length of time. Brad took the call.

It was Mr. Waverling on Second Avenue, reporting what had sounded like gunshots coming from downtown.

Brad dusted the remains of the cruller off his lips with a paper napkin and promised to look into it.

Fireworks, probably. It was almost always fireworks.

He got on the radio to Evans and Brace, who were riding patrol at the south end of town, and suggested they check it out. It was really the sergeant's job to call the shots, but again—taco.

The phone rang a second time. Mrs. Glazer on Willow Avenue, between Second and Main, also reporting gunshots. He put her on hold to take another call. Mr. Bascombe, also on Willow, reporting the same thing.

If it was fireworks, it must've been a hell of a show.

He'd fielded three more calls by the time Sergeant Gathers finally emerged from the lavatory, hitching up his trousers. And those were only the calls placed directly to the station. The 911 operators, based in another township, were reporting a dozen calls or more. One caller had been very specific about the point of origin of the shooting. He'd said it came from the Clarkson Building at the southeast corner of Main and Sycamore.

Brad hadn't been aware that it was called the Clarkson Building—it was amazing what some of these old-timers knew—but he was plenty familiar with the address. Bonnie's office was there, on the second floor.

That was when he started to get worried. As casually as possible, he told Sergeant Gathers he thought he'd drive over and assist Evans and Brace at the scene. Gathers okayed the idea, seconding it with a burp. That taco was still eating at him.

Tonight's duty had Brad riding solo. He was climbing into his squad car when the radio sputtered with the other unit's report. The door to the building had been forced open, and the office of the Last Resort detective agency had been shot to hell by what looked like machine-gun fire. No casualties were reported, and the perpetrators had fled the area.

Machine-gun fire?

"God damn," Bradley whispered. It was the strongest oath he allowed himself.

Someone had gone after Bonnie at her place of business. Not finding her there, their next logical stop ...

Would be her house.

He pulled out of the parking lot at high speed, racing west, while he fumbled his phone out of his pocket and speed-dialed her number. Her cell, of course; she didn't have a landline.

He counted four rings, five, and the call jumped to voicemail. He hung up. She wasn't answering—or she couldn't.

Her duplex appeared in his headlights. The front door was open. The lights were off.

Though he was worried, he was still a professional. He wasn't going to barge in on a crew of bad guys. He checked out the area, saw no unfamiliar vehicles. He was sure they'd been here—the open door proved it—but almost equally certain they'd gone.

Before leaving the car, he called in his position. "Looks like there's been some trouble here too," he said. "Better send another unit."

*Was* there another unit? Oh yeah, Thompson and Harris were working tonight. Last he'd heard, they'd been patrolling the beachfront. They wouldn't get this far inland for a few minutes. He wasn't going to wait.

He got out of the car and approached the duplex at a run, pausing at the doorway to listen for noises from inside. He heard nothing.

The door had been kicked open—the dusty outline of

a footprint was visible on the surface—after the high-quality lock had been shot off. The intrusion must have triggered the silent alarm, but the alarm system wasn't connected to the police station or to any monitoring service. The signal went straight to Bonnie's cell phone.

He snapped on his flashlight and held it well away from his body, while in the other hand he gripped his police-issue Beretta nine. He went in.

The flashlight beam ticked methodically across the living room, illuminating patches of broken glass and dozens of spent cartridge cases. Machine guns for sure. Somebody had fired off fifty or more rounds in here, blasting at random, wrecking everything.

He risked a shout. "Bonnie?"

No answer.

Too late, he realized he should have checked the garage before coming in. If her Jeep was there—

But he hadn't thought of looking, and he couldn't turn back now. He let the flashlight guide him down the short hallway into the bedroom. Though they usually met at his place, he'd been here once or twice. This was the first time he'd ever been afraid of what lay at the end of the hall.

The circle of light danced over the unmade bed and the hardwood floor. There were many more shell casings and plenty of damage, but no Bonnie. He cleared the closet, the bathroom, and the rest of the house, finishing just as a second squad car pulled up outside.

She wasn't here. And he didn't believe she'd been kidnapped. Whoever had come into the duplex firing on full automatic hadn't been of a mind to take prisoners.

He met Thompson and Harris out front. As they went in to look for themselves, he circled around to the garage and peered in a side window. No Jeep. But there was a car in the other space, a Toyota Camry.

Duplex. Two homes. Right.

He ran to the door of the adjacent unit—safely closed and locked—and laid his finger on the doorbell until a light came on in the window and the resident appeared. An elderly woman wrapped in a heavy robe like a shawl, her eyes wide, her face bloodless and shocked.

"I'm so glad you're here," she said.

"You all right, ma'am?"

"I think so, yes. I think so."

She didn't seem certain. He sat her down on the sofa and looked for any sign of injury.

"I don't think you were hit," he said finally.

"No, I'm sure I wasn't. I'm just—well, just scared."

He called for an ambulance anyway. It wouldn't hurt to have the paramedics check her out.

Her name, she told him, was Mrs. Eleanor Biggs. A few minutes ago she'd been startled awake by a horrendous racket from next door, a sound like dozens of nails being driven into the wall. Once she understood that the nails were bullets, she'd huddled in her bed, under the covers—"like a frightened child," she said—until the noises stopped and the men sped away.

"Men? Did you see them?"

"I didn't see anything. I was under the blankets. But I heard voices. Muffled voices through the wall."

"How many men?"

"I couldn't say. Two, at least. There may have been more."

"Could you make out any words?"

She shook her head. "They weren't even speaking English. It was some foreign language. Russian, I think. Something guttural like that."

Russian. What the hell had Bonnie gotten herself mixed up in? "You said they sped off. You heard their vehicle?"

"Yes, a great big *vroom*. But I don't know what kind of car it was. I didn't move a muscle, even after they were gone. I was afraid they would come back, and my heart was pounding. It's a miracle, really, that I wasn't killed."

Bradley examined the wall that abutted the unit next door. Quickly he found a more prosaic explanation for Mrs. Biggs' survival. None of the rounds had penetrated, which could only mean there was a brick firewall between the two halves of the house. Without the firewall, the shots would have easily punched through the drywall, and Mrs. Biggs would probably be dead.

Belatedly, Mrs. Biggs raised her head and asked, "What about my neighbor? Is she ...?"

"She wasn't home, ma'am."

"Then where is she?"

"That's a good question."

He pulled out his phone and redialed her number. This time he wasn't expecting an answer. When the call went to voicemail, he left a cautiously impersonal message.

"Miss Parker, this is Patrol Officer Bradley Walsh of the Brighton Cove Police Department. There have been break-ins at your residence and your office. Some damage was done. We need you to contact our department immediately, as we believe you may be in danger. You can reach me at this number or call the station directly ..."

He rattled off the main number, then hesitated, wanting to say more. But he couldn't say what ought to be said, because there was a good chance Bonnie's phone records, including her voicemails, would eventually be obtained by the police as part of the investigation into her disappearance—or her death. He had pressed his luck leaving any kind of message at all.

He ended the call and glanced out the window to see Chief Maguire arriving in his personal car with the ambulance right behind him. The chief had been off duty, of course, and probably fast asleep—but nobody in the Brighton Cove police force would be sleeping tonight.

"The paramedics are here, ma'am," he told Mrs. Biggs as he headed for the door.

She didn't seem to hear him. She stared down at her trembling hands.

"I used to think it was rather glamorous to have a woman of mystery living next to me," Mrs. Biggs said quietly. "It doesn't seem glamorous anymore."

# 28

FELIX RAMIREZ SHOWED up at midnight, gym bag in hand.

"You're in trouble, *bandida*," he said as he plopped the bag down on the carpet. It landed with a thud. Heavy.

"No more'n usual." She considered this. "Okay, maybe a scoche more."

She'd been smoking and pacing for the past two hours as she awaited his arrival. For much of that time she'd found herself thinking about an acquaintance of hers, name of Sparky. Sparky was an amateur ghost hunter. She wasn't sure she believed in ghosts. But maybe. She wondered what it was like to be a ghost. She wondered if she was about to find out.

"Someone's after you," Felix said, appraising her.

"Gee, how'd ya guess?"

"I don't got to guess. I hear Dispatch while I'm coming up here. All the drivers are being told to stay out of Brighton Cove. Someone's been shooting up your town."

She paused in the act of lighting a new cigarette. "Yeah?"

"They went to your office and your home. With machine guns."

She felt a chill, thinking of Mrs. Biggs. "Anyone hurt?"

"Not that I hear."

"Good."

She didn't get it, though. Why would the Russkies want to shoot up empty buildings? Unless Streinikov had croaked from the stab wound, and his people were all crazy for vengeance, running amok. Maybe. But she didn't believe it. If he was dead, it would be every man for himself.

"Somebody," Felix said, "sends you a message. Very loud. They do not like you."

"Popularity's overrated." She finished lighting the cig. "Anyway, I'm working it out."

"With this?" His shoe kicked the gym bag.

"Yep. You sneak a peek at what's in there?"

"No. But I have my ideas. I obeyed the speed limit all the way up."

"Smart move." Getting pulled over with a duffel bag full of illegal firearms was never a good idea.

"I'm glad to get rid of it. But not so glad to see you like this."

"Like what?"

"Scared."

She made the sound halfway between a snort and a Bronx cheer. "Puh-lease. I've handled bigger problems than this without mussing my hair."

"Your hair is already mussed."

She checked herself in the mirror. He was right.

"I see you," he added, "and I think, *a la gran chucha,* she has been through a hell."

He was right about that, too. Her face was wild. She'd been scraped and torn and dirtied in her chase through the woods, and there was a crazy light in her eyes that only a shrink could love.

"Well," she said slowly, "maybe I'm a little worse for wear. But I'm not scared. I'm ... um ... kinda jazzed, is all."

He just looked at her, his mild, serious eyes saying that he knew better.

"Psyched," she added, uncertain if she was trying to convince him or herself. "You know, 'cause ya gotta get up for the big game."

"Is it a game?"

Damn, the little guy was sharp. She'd never realized it before. "Look, I'll be fine. Don't worry about me."

"I'm not worried about you."

"Thanks. Or should I say, *gracias*?" She was pretty sure she'd mangled the Spanish word about as badly as possible.

"Don't say either. I'm not trying to give you a pep speech."

"Pep talk," she said automatically.

"I'm only saying the truth. You'll come through this. I'm a good judge of such things."

"Are you?"

He nodded gravely. "You know I grew up in Guatemala, right?"

"I knew it was somewhere in South America."

"Central America."

"Right, right." Geography, like history, was one of those things she was hazy about.

"In Guatemala there is no safety. In my lifetime there never has been. When I was born, the war was still going on. Then it was over, and the drug lords came, and they were worse. In the high country, the jungle country, there is no law. The crime lords kill whole villages. I've seen piles of the dead, old people and children, babies even, a well stuffed full of them, flowing over. Is this how you say it? Flowing over?"

"Overflowing," Bonnie said in a low voice.

"Yes. This I've seen." A crucifix glinted at his throat, somehow adding weight to his testimony. "And the blind-folded dead with their brains shot out, and the ones who lost their heads to the machete, and the ones burned alive. And many other things. I lived for twenty-five years in Guatemala, where life is always a battle. And so I learned to know them by sight. To know them with one look."

"Who?"

"The survivors. I learned to know who would live and who would not. Some people will always make it through. They have a—what's the word? A knock?"

"A knack."

He nodded. "A knack for it. You have this knack."

She thought about a man named Pascal, and another man named Frank Lazzaro. "Maybe I do. Or maybe some people are just lucky."

"They make their luck. I watched them. The ones who survived were tougher, slyer. And they wanted it just a little more."

"Wanted what?"

"To live."

She rolled the cigarette between her fingers. "If I wanted to live, I wouldn't be smoking these things."

He only smiled at that. "It'll take more than cigarettes to kill you, *bandida*. And more than men with machine guns, too."

She watched him drive off, hoping he was right.

# 29

AT 1 AM the Miramar police found a Jeep registered to Bonnie Parker in the parking lot of the Miramar boat basin. The Jeep wasn't hard to spot. It was the only vehicle there.

Brad was still at the duplex when Dan Maguire got the call. "I'm going over to check it out," the chief said. "Walsh, you're driving."

Dan had come to the scene in his personal car, and Brad guessed he didn't want the Miramar cops seeing him arrive in anything so unofficial. He probably liked the idea of being driven into the lot in a squad car, especially since a reporter from the *McKendree Park Observer* was already at the duplex and was likely to follow him there. A chauffeur and a media escort—yes, that would appeal to the chief.

Brad slid behind the wheel of his patrol car, with his boss on the passenger side. He didn't use his lights or siren; that was Hollywood stuff.

"What do you make of this?" Dan asked as they pulled away.

"Don't know, sir."

"That Biggs woman said the shooters were speaking Russian."

"She thought maybe that was the case. She wasn't sure."

"Russian." Dan shook his head. "You know what that means?" He answered his own question. "It means Russian mafia."

"In Brighton Cove?"

"Where Parker's concerned, nothing is impossible." Dan stared out the window, his expression reflected in the glass, unreadable. "If the Russian mob is after her, she's royally fucked."

"Isn't that what you wanted?" Brad couldn't suppress a note of bitterness. "To get her out of the way?"

"I want her in prison. Not dead. Vigilante justice is her thing, not mine."

"Right. Of course."

"Has anybody thought of calling her cell phone?"

Brad wasn't happy about answering, but he had no choice. "I tried it. The call went to voicemail."

Dan turned to face him. "How'd you even know her number?"

Brad shrugged. "It's listed." He hoped he sounded casual.

"Oh. Well, good thinking. How long ago was this?"

"Maybe an hour."

His boss was studying him in the chancy glow of passing streetlights. "You seem a little off tonight, Walsh. Preoccupied."

"I guess, uh, I'm kind of shaken up. I'm not really used to stuff like this."

Dan nodded slowly. "Yeah, it's not every day people start shooting off machine guns in this sleepy little burg. Truth is, we had scarcely any violence to speak of—until *she* showed up. Since then, there was that shootout on the boardwalk, and Jacob Hart gunned down in cold blood, and a very questionable suicide right across the alley from Parker's office. Other things, too."

"And you lay all that on her?"

"Damn straight I do."

Brad thought about that. The rest of the drive passed in silence.

They arrived at the marina, tailed, as expected, by the

*Observer* guy. Bonnie's Jeep was parked in the far corner of the lot, where it must have looked awfully lonely before three Miramar patrol units had encircled it. They'd left their light bars flashing. Showoffs.

The red and blue glare made flickering ripples on the asphalt as Brad and Dan walked to the Jeep. There were the usual nods and handshakes. The Brighton Cove cops were out of their jurisdiction, but everyone knew this was their case. The only known crimes had taken place on their turf.

The Jeep's passenger door was hanging open. Dan looked at it. "Has the vehicle been searched?"

One of the Miramar cops said there'd been only a brief visual inspection to be sure the Jeep was empty. Now they were waiting for a crime scene unit from the state police.

"Mind if I stick my head in?" Dan asked.

"Look, but don't touch," one of the patrol cops said, adding, "sir."

The journalist was held back. He contented himself with interviewing the Miramar patrol guys.

Dan went around to the passenger side and shined a flashlight into the car. Brad peered over his shoulder.

The interior was pretty much what Brad expected. His girlfriend wasn't exactly a neat freak. She had a tendency to discard things in her Jeep, where they would remain untouched for weeks or months. Or years.

The backseat was a clutter of fast food wrappers, empty water bottles, and loose change. The front compartment was much neater. There was only a small scrap of paper on the floor below the passenger seat.

Dan's flashlight beam rested on the scrap. "Parking stub," he said, squinting. "Garrett municipal complex. One-twenty PM yesterday. What would she be doing over there?"

Brad shrugged. "Library?"

"Parker strike you as a big reader?"

"I wouldn't know, sir." This was a lie. He knew perfectly well that Bonnie's reading habits were limited to the occasional feature article in *Guns & Ammo*. He'd never seen her read a book. He'd once asked, only half joking, if she *could* read.

"Well, you were just in her house. You see any books there?"

"No," he answered truthfully.

"She's not a reader." Dan was talking to himself now, with Brad merely serving as an audience. "If I'm right about her background, she never got past the eighth grade."

Brad was surprised. He knew something about his girlfriend's past—enough to know she'd dropped out of school for a while—but he'd always assumed she'd gone back to get her diploma. "Doesn't a PI license require at least a high school degree?"

"Not in this state. No educational requirements except some professional training or, in lieu of that, on-the-job experience."

"Even so, you'd think she'd want to graduate."

He wasn't really talking to Dan, but Dan answered. "She didn't exactly have a normal upbringing. Her folks got killed in a motel in Pennsylvania. They were petty criminals, drifters, always involved in something dirty. After they got shot, their little girl struck out on her own."

Brad knew that part of it. He'd seen it in a file he'd procured for Bonnie a couple of years ago. And in the same file he'd seen Dan's theory that fourteen-year-old Bonnie murdered the three men responsible for her parents' deaths—shot them down in cold blood. But Dan's investigation had stalled out, and Brad had always assumed there was nothing to it.

"Parker denies it, of course," Dan added indifferently. "Says she had a very wholesome childhood. School prom, cheerleader practice, the whole nine yards. Bullshit. She lived on the street, and she was a killer from an early age."

"A killer? You can prove that?"

"Of course I can't prove it. If I could prove it, she'd be in jail already. I had a witness who could place her near the scene of a multiple homicide, but he chickened out on me. Parker got to him, intimidated him. How she found out about him, I still don't know."

Brad knew. The witness was listed in the file. At the time he thought he'd been doing the right thing in passing on the info. Now he wasn't so sure.

Bonnie was always telling him Dan was full of crap, an obsessive type with a paranoid fixation. Maybe there was more to the story.

"Take me back to the duplex," Dan said, moving away from the Jeep. "I want to pick up my Buick."

"Yes, sir. You going to her office next?"

Dan shook his head. "I'm going to the police station in Garrett. That's in the municipal center too."

"Want me to tag along?"

"You? No. You go downtown and secure the scene."

Brad nodded. It had been a stupid question. He had no business in Garrett.

But suddenly he found himself intensely interested in whatever the chief could find out about Bonnie Elizabeth Parker.

# 30

STREINIKOV WAS IN pain. The initial shock of the stabbing had worn off long ago, and his body was now vociferously objecting to the insults inflicted on it. Vasnev, arriving with his little black bag three hours earlier, had recommended Percocet. Streinikov had refused. His sole concession to pain was a bottle of Yarpivo beer, a Russian import. He sipped it slowly as, nearby, Vasnev fussed with his instruments, looking anxious and pained.

The greenhouse remained a shambles. A plywood board had been hastily installed in the broken window by the door. It kept out the winter cold, at least. Dozens of his beauties lay scattered on the floor in a litter of terracotta shards. Had he been mobile, he would have gathered up the plants and begun the process of repotting. As it was, he could only curse Gregor and Gura for their oafishness.

So much waste. So much chaos. Noise, too—enough noise that shortly after Ilya left on his mission, a policeman had inquired politely, via telephone, about scattered reports of shots and screams heard in the vicinity of his address. Streinikov had indicated that it would be best not to pursue the matter. And that had been that. He hadn't lied to Bonnie Parker when he said no one could touch him. He owned the police. He owned everyone of significance in this state.

He leaned back in his chair by the potting bench and shut his eyes. Music played over hidden speakers distributed throughout the greenhouse. He had selected Bach. It soothed him. He despised Russian composers; they were far too excitable and overdramatic, much like Russians in general.

His phone rang. It was Ilya.

"We made some noise, like you wanted. We got the locals out of bed."

"So I understand. There is already a statewide BOLO on our Miss Parker as a person of interest in the shootings. Many eyes will be looking for her. Where are you now?"

"On the parkway, heading back."

"Good. Come here directly. I want all hands on deck."

There was no telling who might be needed before the night came to an end. Already things were moving very fast. All three elements of his strategy were well underway.

First, there was Ilya and his crew. By shooting up Parker's town, they had brought the police into the picture. Even the dullest small-town cop had to realize that the PI had been targeted by dangerous persons. For her own protection, if nothing else, she would have to be taken into custody. And no matter where she was stashed for safekeeping, Streinikov had ways of getting to her. He had informants scattered throughout the state police, the county sheriff's departments, and the larger municipal forces. The moment she was in the hands of the police, she was a dead woman.

In custody, she might talk, might implicate him. But he wasn't worried. The damage could be contained. The appropriate people could be bribed or coerced into forgetting what they'd heard.

Then there was the stolen car. An older Honda Civic belonging to a live-in housekeeper had been taken from a curbside parking space in the neighborhood south of his estate. If it was found, Streinikov would be told; one of the cops he owned had assured him of that. With any luck, Parker would be picked up by the police on the spot. If not, there was a good chance she would still be in the vicinity of the automobile, and his men could track her down.

His phone rang again. This time it was Denisov, one of the men who'd been pulled out of bed, calling to say that Gregor's body had been found in the woods.

"Return it to the house," Streinikov said with a shrug. "Store it in the garage with Gura for now."

Gura's remains would be shipped to Ukraine for a decent burial. A mere foot soldier like Gregor did not merit such treatment. His corpse would go into a landfill.

Where had he been in his ruminations? Oh, yes—the third leg of his strategy. Ivanov, his IT man.

Streinikov was not an aficionado of computer technology. He took no joy in pecking at a keyboard. He would rather dig in the dirt with his hands, potting his exotic plants, or cruise the coastal waterways with the salt breeze on his face.

Still, computers had their virtues. They offered new ways of tackling old problems. Keeping tabs on one's rivals, for instance, or putting out word on the street.

Ivanov took care of all that from his perch in Donetsk. His job was to monitor the bewildering efflorescence of websites known as social media. He was not interested in videos of kittens or the latest exploits of the Kardashian clan. He followed the activities of the gangs.

The major crews and sets all had their own Facebook sites, Twitter feeds, and Instagram accounts. They posted selfies and bragged about their exploits, even uploaded photos of drugs they'd stolen or weapons they'd acquired. Often they incriminated themselves; the posts led the authorities straight to them and could be used as evidence in court. Nevertheless, they kept on doing it. Young savages, they had the narcissistic need to strut and preen. Streinikov had been nothing like them in his youth. But times changed. The world grew sloppier and more decadent.

The stupidity of these foolish children could be used to his advantage. His first phone call had been to Donetsk; he had told Ivanov to post a bounty on Bonnie Parker on all the relevant Internet streams. Ten thousand dollars for information on her present whereabouts. It required only a phone call; a number was provided.

The number—untraceable, of course—belonged to Ivanov, who would screen the calls, weeding out the bad tips. Nothing in the posts could be linked to Streinikov himself, nor could the American authorities touch his man on foreign soil, even if they could locate him—not easily done, given the sophisticated ways in which he cloaked himself online. The police would become aware of the posts in due time, but that was not a problem. On the contrary, it was all to the good. It would provide them with a further incentive to find Parker before her enemies did.

Vasnev made a throat-clearing sound. Streinikov glanced at him irritably. "Yes?"

"Again, sir, I must respectfully insist on taking you to the hospital."

"Not until the present situation has been handled."

"An abdominal penetration is potentially serious. If your intestinal tract has been perforated, you're at risk of peritonitis, septic poisoning. It can be fatal."

"Pray it does not prove to be."

"I'm administering antibiotics to fight infection. But if there's significant leakage into the abdominal cavity, only surgery can help."

"I am not enamored of surgery. My sole experience in going under the knife proved most unpleasant."

"This situation is entirely different."

"It is entirely the same. A polished blade, an incision, part of me permanently excised."

Vasnev drew himself up, mustering whatever courage he possessed. "It may prove necessary, no matter how you feel about it."

"I am a realist, Doctor. I understand the eventualities. But I say again that I will not go to the hospital until I've resolved the matter at hand." He tapped his bandaged waist. "This debt must be paid."

"If you won't follow my advice, I can't be responsible for your well-being."

Slowly Streinikov swiveled his head to appraise the other man. "On the contrary," he said in a tone so empty of emotion it might almost have been friendly. "My well-being and yours are inextricably interconnected. Should I die, your own life expectancy will be, I assure you, exceedingly short."

Vasnev pursed his lips, and a visible shiver skipped across his thin shoulders. "I'll do everything I can."

Streinikov was saved from further conversation by his phone. He thought it might be Ilya again, or his police informant updating him on the stolen car, but instead it was Ivanov in Donetsk.

"I've received several calls," Ivanov said, speaking Russian, "but they were all bullshit. Until now. This one could be for real. The man is hyped up, overexcited, but he claims to know Parker personally. Says he has a personal interest in seeing her receive justice. And he reports having just seen her in a location only fifteen miles from your property. Shall I put him through?"

"*Da.*"

"He is an *obezyana*, I think," Ivanov said, using a racial slur. Before switching over, he added, "His name is Alonzo."

# 31

ALONZO DUCHENNE HAD been pissed off about his encounter with the blonde bitch all day. It didn't help that she'd broken his fucking nose, something confirmed by a trip to the ER. The result was a wide stripe of bandage across the middle of his face, not to mention two nostrils clogged with dried blood. Every so often he would sneeze out a big wad of bloody snot. Sneezing hurt. His whole face hurt. Even a couple of pills from his stash of painkillers hadn't helped much.

That was bad enough, but what really lit his fuse was that she'd robbed him in his own home. *She* had come after *him*.

Alonzo had caught this show on TV once about how shape-shifting lizard aliens were living among us in human form. They were everywhere, occupying the highest political offices and seated on the thrones of corporate power. He didn't really believe in the lizard people. But he didn't exactly disbelieve in them, either. He was, like, an agnostic on the subject. As long as the lizards left him alone, he was all live-and-let-live.

But that was the thing, see? This girl hadn't left him alone. She'd poked her pretty little nose into his business, and busted up his not-so-pretty nose in the process.

So he'd started asking around, being cool about it, just making some phone calls and talking about Blondie. He said an acquaintance had met up with her and needed to know more. Kept himself out of it. Playing it low-key, you know.

Around noon he'd hit pay dirt. Friend of his, Eddie Lemans—probably wasn't his real name, but whatever—knew exactly who he was talking about. Bitch called Bonnie Parker, a PI in Brighton Cove, with kind of a shadowy rep, like she was into some shit that wasn't strictly legal. Could be a hitter, even. She was mouthy and a hard-ass, and she matched the description right down to her baby blue eyes.

Eddie knew this stuff—Eddie knew just about everything that was going down around here—because he tended bar at Alcatraz, an establishment that could be described as either a watering hole or a shit hole with equal accuracy. He kept his ears open, and his customers liked to talk.

So yeah, he knew about Parker. Why'd Alonzo want to know?

Alonzo didn't say. He got off the phone and took a ride to Brighton Cove, where he found Bonnie Parker's office, right there on a bullshit little Main Street straight out of Disneyland. He had no intention of confronting her. Truth was, he'd been kind of shaken up by the casual way she'd put him on the floor. It wasn't supposed to go like that. He was the one who was supposed to do the beating, not the one who got the beatdown. And from a damn beavertail, too.

Anyway, he was prudent enough to think twice about tangling with her again, especially if she was a professional popper. He just wanted to check out the area. It was pure luck that he ran into Jerry Waco coming out of a high-class shoe store called Oxfords, right down the street from Parker's building.

Waco—probably not his real name either—showed off the pricey dogs on his oversized feet. Alonzo steered the conversation around to Bonnie Parker. And that was when Waco came through for him. He'd dropped by the store earlier today to check out the merchandise, but, being a careful shopper, he hadn't made his purchase until he'd researched the shoes online. A disquisition about the perils of buying expensive footwear without doing the necessary prep work followed.

Alonzo guided him back on point. Right, Parker. She was here, chatting up a cabbie right outside the store.

A cabbie. That piece of information stirred certain dark speculations in Alonzo's mind.

He asked if by any chance it was a pocket-sized Mexican in a white Grand Caravan marked *Beach Cab*. Waco didn't recall what the dude looked like, but he did remember the vehicle, and it was the very one.

Like they said in the movies: bingo.

Alonzo had it all figured out now. The cabbie was the little wetback midget he'd stiffed last night. Fucking beaner lawn jockey had complained to Supergirl, and she'd decided to make things right. All that stuff she'd told him about a client from a few weeks ago, inferior product, being ripped off—that was all smoke. His product wasn't inferior. He gave good value for the money.

Well, he might not be quite ready to face off against Parker again, but he sure as shit could take on some five-foot-nothing taco bender who wanted to make trouble.

It took him the rest of the day to identify the cabbie as Felix Ramirez and to trace him to an address in McKendree Park—unlisted because the guy was probably a fucking illegal living under the radar. His investigation might have proceeded at a more rapid pace had he not been taking additional pain pills to relieve the ache in his nose. The meds made him woozy and slow, and he fell asleep more than once. Taking naps during the day like some old geezer really wasn't his style, and he was getting pissed off about that, along with everything else.

But he perked up when he got a lead on Ramirez, courtesy of a mechanic who did repair work for Beach Cab. The grease monkey knew Ramirez, and while he didn't know the douchebag's home address, he did know a skank who'd been dating him. Which surprised Alonzo, because he had figured that scrawny little garden gnome couldn't score a woman, any woman, even if she was a prize hog.

He tracked down the girl, broke into her place—lucky for her, she wasn't home—and found the name Felix in her datebook, along with a phone number. An online reverse directory matched a street address to the number. Alonzo went there shortly after nightfall. It was a building in McKendree Park—apartments above a bookstore. He rang the buzzer for the unit labeled *F. Ramirez*. No answer. Shorty was probably out picking up fares. But he would be back.

Alonzo spent a long time staking out the building. He thought about Parker. He thought about the lizard people. He thought about who would come out on top in a throwdown between Hellboy and the Thing. His money was on the Thing. That Ben Grimm was a badass.

As the hours passed, he felt the tug of sleep yet again. There was only one way to stay alert, and that was to sneeze open his clogged nostrils and put some white powder up there. Ordinarily he would not partake of his own supply, but desperate times, desperate measures— you know the score.

By the time a white Grand Caravan pulled up outside the building, Alonzo was feeling no drowsiness and no pain. He fully intended to ambush Ramirez right there on the street, but the little greaseball Smurf was too quick for him. He bounded up the front steps and inside before Alonzo could even get out of his car.

In a hurry. Had to take a piss, maybe.

Since the cab would have to be returned to the company for the night, Alonzo knew his quarry would be back. In short order, he was. But it was funny, the way he acted. He was carrying a gym bag, moving furtively, almost skulking. He looked scared and self-conscious, like there was something in the bag that could get him in some seriously deep shit.

Alonzo lost interest—temporarily at least—in taking revenge. He wanted to see what the hell Ramirez was up to. There might be money in it, enough money to repay him for the two hundred bucks he'd lost.

After that, things got weird. The guy headed north on the parkway, with no fare, staying cautiously within the speed limit. Eventually he switched to the turnpike and crossed into Bergen County. Alonzo had used Beach Cab often enough to know that it was strictly a local operation. There was no legitimate reason for Mini-Me to drive a hundred miles out of Millstone County. Whatever he was after, the gym bag surely had something to do with it.

As he was passing the turnoff to Route 3, Alonzo got a call from Eddie Lemans. "Looks like you were ahead of your time," Eddie told him.

Alonzo asked him what that was supposed to mean.

"Only that you were so interested in Bonnie Parker. Now everybody's interested."

"What do you mean, everybody?"

"I mean, there's a price on her blonde head. Which I think is a dye job, by the way."

Alonzo didn't give a crap about her hair. "What price?"

"Ten g's for anyone who can find her."

"That's all, just find her? Not, like, take her out?"

"Just find her. And call it in."

"There's a number?"

Eddie said yeah, there was a number. "But I ain't giving it up 'less you cut me in for a slice, big man."

Alonzo didn't actually know where Parker was. But Ramirez might. And sooner or later, him and Ramirez were gonna have a conversation.

After some haggling, they agreed that Eddie would

take twenty percent, which worked out to two grand. In exchange for this deal, rendered as an oral agreement but understood to be binding between them in the state of New Jersey, Eddie gave up the phone number. Alonzo memorized it.

He thought something could come of it; he really did. To remain alert, he took another hit of coke as he exited the turnpike.

He followed the cab down a smaller highway and into the parking lot of a dirtbag motel. As he watched from a distance, Ramirez toted the gym bag to room 23 and rapped on the door.

Alonzo was very interested to see who would open that door, and he wasn't disappointed. Even across a long stretch of macadam, he could identify the woman who'd head-butted him and sent him to the ER with a nose that wouldn't stop squirting blood.

"Parker," he breathed.

In that moment he forgot all about Felix Ramirez. The cabbie wasn't worth ten grand to anybody, and Bonnie Parker was.

He waited until Ramirez had left, just to be sure Parker didn't go with him. When she shut the door, he picked up his phone and called the tip line.

As the phone rang at the other end, he inhaled another dusting of coke. What the fuck, man, he had to stay sharp.

# 32

ILYA WAS IN the passenger seat of the Escalade, sweeping past Secaucus on I-95, when his phone rang. It was the boss.

"Where are you?" Streinikov asked.

"Twenty minutes out." The words came with some difficulty. His throat was still sore from the two punches the bitch had delivered. He'd been lucky, though. A knuckle strike could have cracked his larynx, asphyxiating him.

"You need to make a detour. We have a sighting. She's in room twenty-three of the Magic Carpet Motor Inn on US-Forty-Six in Ridgefield."

"You're sure?"

"No, but the information is plausible, and our informant claims to know her personally. There may be a way to confirm it before going in. She stole a red Honda Civic, older model." He recited the plate number. "Look for it in the motel parking lot."

"I'm on it," Ilya said.

"Remember—you're to bring me her head."

"Understood."

Actually he did not understand. Streinikov's fetish about the head was distinctly troubling. Ordinarily he was above such grisly melodrama.

But Parker had wounded him. And Ilya was enough of a student of psychology to guess that the thrust of the shears into his side could have brought back memories of another blade, another kind of surgery.

He started to program the Magic Carpet Motor Inn into

the vehicle's GPS. "We may have got her," he told his crew. "This could be over very soon."

BONNIE FINISHED REVIEWING the contents of the gym bag, leaving the money in the duffel and most of her arsenal scattered on the floor. Christmas had come early this year, and it had taken her a while to choose the very best presents under the tree.

She'd pretty much decided on the sawed-off shotgun—always your best bet when general mayhem was the aim—and the rifle she'd modified to fire on full automatic. The Ruger .45 from her purse was another keeper. No need for a silencer; she was planning to make a lot of noise. The two-shot derringer would serve as an ankle gun, and the combat knife could be strapped to her arm.

The gym bag itself was too unwieldy to carry into battle; she'd have to come up with some other way of toting her gear.

At the moment the item that interested her most was the throwaway phone she'd stashed with the rest of her stuff. It couldn't be traced to her, which meant she could use it now—if she wanted to.

She wasn't sure she did. She needed to stay focused, and a conversation with her boyfriend wasn't the best way to do that.

On the other hand, there was a fair chance—okay, a real good chance—that this would be her last opportunity to talk to him, ever.

She didn't want to jinx herself, but the odds weren't exactly in her favor, even with all the goodies St. Nick, in the form of Felix Ramirez, had brought.

And by now, Brad would have questions. A lot of questions. Not that she could answer them, but at least she could let him hear her voice. And she could hear his. It surprised her just how much she wanted to hear that voice.

She powered up the burner and entered his cell number from memory.

THE HONDA WAS parked at the rear of the motel, tucked out of sight near a trash bin.

"She's here," Barsky said, stating the obvious and managing to sound smug about it.

"Room twenty-three?" That was Lukin, still at the wheel.

Ilya nodded. "So I was told. Drive around front. Slowly."

Lukin steered the Cadillac into the main parking lot, creeping past the room in question at fifteen miles an hour. Ilya studied it closely.

"The front door and window are the only obvious ways in—or out. There's a rear window, probably in a bathroom, but it's too small, I think. Anyway, we'll give her no time to run."

"We go in shooting," Barsky said, again demonstrating his limitless grasp of the obvious.

"*Da*. But not yet." He had Lukin park in the lot, midway between the targeted room and the manager's office. "I want to be sure she's in there. If we blast our way into the wrong room, she'll have time to get away."

"The witness said twenty-three," Lukin said with dimwitted insistence.

"Witnesses can be mistaken. I'll talk to the man on duty. You two wait near the door, but stay away from the window. Once I have confirmation, I'll send you in."

Barsky nodded. "*Ya ponimayu*." He understood.

"Aim for the torso. Avoid shots to the face. Streinikov wants the head."

From what Barsky had told him, Ilya gathered that the first Bonnie Parker had died in a hail of bullets. It appeared history was about to repeat itself.

~~~

BONNIE HEARD BRADLEY pick up on the third ring. "Walsh."

Naturally he didn't recognize the burner's number. In the background she heard voices and activity. She hoped he didn't give anything away when she identified herself.

"It's me," she said carefully. "Stay cool, okay?"

"Yeah." His voice was shaky. "Okay." She heard the background noises receding as he moved away for more privacy. "Are you all right?"

"Never better," she said.

Terrific. Another lie.

"What the hell's going on? Do you have any idea what's happening in this town?"

"I've been told."

"Who's after you?"

"It's complicated."

"Is it the Russians?"

"Who told you that?"

"Your next-door neighbor."

"She okay?"

"Yeah, she's fine. So is it the Russians?"

"They're Ukrainians, actually."

She heard him take a breath. "You need to get to the police."

"That wouldn't be such a great idea."

"Why not?"

"Look, I know it's sort of a mess, but I can explain it all."

He made a sound that might have been a chuckle. "Yeah, I'm sure you can. You're good at that."

"You don't trust me anymore?"

"Well, you're not making it easy, that's for sure."

He had her there. "It'll all work out," she said, wondering if this was also a lie. "Just give me a chance."

"You've got your chance. Talk to me."

"Right now?"

"Right now."

"Um, now isn't such a great time ..."

"Why am I not surprised?"

"It's just—there's something I gotta do."

"There always is. Just tell me one thing. Did you kill the three guys in that farmhouse?"

"What?" It was the last question she'd expected.

"In Ohio. When you were a kid. Dan's theory, the one in his file."

"You want to talk about that now?"

"Yeah. I do."

"At the time when Dan was looking into it, I seem to remember you saying that if it was true, you could understand."

"That's right. I did say that."

"So what's changed?"

"For one thing, I didn't really think you'd done it."

"And now you do?"

He didn't answer. "There's more than that. I'm starting to think it wasn't a one-off thing. I'm starting to think you've been lying to me the whole time. Tell me I'm wrong."

She wanted to say so, but her mouth couldn't form the words. She was silent for too long.

"That's what I thought," Brad said quietly.

"Brad—"

"I'll see you, Bonnie."

He was gone.

"Love you," she said into a dead phone.

# 33

ILYA WAITED AS his men took up position near the door, guns ready. They would make short work of Bonnie Parker—if she was in there.

When they were ready, he slipped out of the car and entered the office. No one was on duty. He dinged the bell until a sallow emaciated codger sauntered into view.

"Apologies," the man said. "I was taking a whiz."

He punctuated the statement by zipping up his trousers.

Ilya leaned on the counter. "A woman took a room here tonight. Blonde, about thirty, probably looking a little worse for wear."

"Mister, in this place, they all look worse for wear."

"This particular woman drove a red Civic."

"I never notice cars."

"She was alone. Not a regular. Someone you've never seen before."

"There might've been somebody like that."

Ilya couldn't determine if the old fool was being cagey or was merely stupid. Either way, the threat of force might stimulate more productive responses.

He drew his Makarov and aimed the pistol casually at the clerk's stubbled chin. "Try to remember."

The man focused his heavy-lidded eyes on the gun. Then he sighed.

"I'm so sick of this shit," he said with feeling.

It wasn't the reaction Ilya had hoped for. Apparently the duties of a night clerk at the Magic Carpet bred a certain indifference to firearms.

"Do you remember?" Ilya pressed.

"Yeah, I think I do. She came in, all frazzled, looked like she'd been out camping or something."

"That's her. What room?"

"Hell if I know."

"You assigned it to her."

"These days I'm lucky if I can remember my own damn name."

"You don't keep any records?"

"In this shit hole?"

"Was it room twenty-three?"

"Could've been. You gonna kill her?"

"Yes."

"Gonna kill me?" He asked the question without visible concern.

"Not unless I have to."

"You won't." The narrow shoulders lifted. "One thing I'm good at, it's keeping my trap shut."

"Then you'll get to live a little longer."

"Whoopee for me."

The fellow's indifference to life and death was somehow dispiriting. Ilya felt like shooting him just for the hell of it. Instead he waved the gun in the man's face and ordered, "Call room twenty-three."

As the clerk dialed, Ilya took out his cell and scrolled down his list of contacts. He didn't place the call. Not yet.

"What should I say?" the clerk asked as his call went through.

"Nothing. Give me the phone."

After three rings, someone picked up, and a female voice said, "Yeah?"

Parker's voice.

Ilya slammed down the phone and punched Lukin's name on the contact list.

"*Ubey yeye,*" he said. Kill her.

From down the courtyard there was the thud of a door being kicked open, then the chatter of automatic weapons fire.

"I was never here," Ilya told the old man.

The clerk only shrugged. "Nobody ever is."


BONNIE JUST HAD time to grab her purse off the nightstand and run to the bathroom before the shit storm started.

She didn't know why she'd picked up the damn phone. Reflex, probably. It rang, she answered. Even as she was doing it, she'd realized it was a dumb-ass move.

When the phone went dead, she knew exactly what was about to go down.

Had she been closer to the arsenal scattered on the carpet, she might have grabbed a gun and tried to make a stand. But the phone was by the bed, and the bed was nearer to the bathroom than to the front door. She ran.

Good decision, because approximately one second later the door blew open and machine guns were firing. If she'd tried to defend herself, she never would have gotten off a shot. She would've been cut to pieces by the first volley.

The bathroom was a dark, dingy closet smelling of mildew, but it had one saving grace—a casement window over the shower. Not a big window, but then, she wasn't a real big girl.

She hoisted herself up on the window ledge and cranked the handle. The window didn't budge. It was sealed shut by paint or humidity, impossible to open.

Piss.

Twice before, she'd nearly died in the bathroom of a cheap motel. Third time's the charm?

The main room shook with what sounded like a fire-works show. At least two guns, both on full automatic, blasting the crap out of every stick of furniture and every panel of drywall.

The noise meant the gunmen couldn't possibly hear her as she kicked the casement window again and again until it shattered.

No time to clear away the shards of frosted glass clinging to the frame. From the other room the shooting had stopped. She knew what that meant. The killers had spent their wads and were reloading. It would take them only a second to snap in new mags, and then they would be coming to the bathroom, the one place they hadn't covered.

She swung her legs over the window frame, ignoring the multiple bites of glass, and wriggled through, her purse swinging from her neck.

Tramp of shoes. They were coming.

She dropped to the pavement right before a new barrage of shots.

Luckily the Civic was close. It was parked behind the building, yards away. Unlocked, of course; she didn't even have a key.

She was opening the car door when a bullet smacked the rear bumper. Glancing back, she saw the blond perv from the greenhouse, Sundance himself. He had a pistol in his hand and he was running full tilt.

Running was a mistake. It had compromised his aim and probably saved her life.

She dived into the car as he fired again. She heard the *thwock* of an impact on the open door. Groping under the dash, she fumbled the loose wires together and made a spark. The motor turned over on the first try.

Another round drilled through the rear window, thumping into the headrest on the passenger side.

Go, go, *go*.

She shoved the car into gear and took off, the driver's door hanging open. As she swung around the corner of the building, two men in dark suits and long coats emerged from her room. They pointed machine pistols at her.

Burps of gunfire. The Civic's side windows blew out in a cascade of crumbling safety glass. She ducked low, barely able to see over the dash, and steered the Civic over a high curb and onto the highway.

Traffic was light at this hour. She sped across a bridge and took an on-ramp to Route 95, cut over to I-80, abandoned it for the surface streets, and finally pulled to a stop at the back of a big-box store that was closed for the night.

Then she leaned out of the car and thought seriously about puking. After a few moments' consideration, she decided it was unnecessary. That was good. She really hated puking.

For the first time she noticed a spread of numbness in her left leg below the knee. She took a look and found a hole in her jeans and a lot of blood. The bullet that had impacted the side door as she was climbing into the car must have passed straight through her calf.

The bone wasn't broken. But the wound was bleeding like a mother, and when the shock wore off, it would hurt like a mother, too.

She did a quick check of the rest of her body, looking for any additional damage. The glass shards from the bathroom window had ripped holes in her blouse and jeans, not to mention her skin, but it was nothing a little bacitracin and some Band-Aids couldn't fix.

Okay, get moving. She put the car into gear and drove to another neighborhood, where she found an old Saturn parked on the street. The lock was a joke, and hot-wiring the ignition took only a few seconds. She drove away, the purse still hugging her shoulder, leaving the Civic behind. In its present condition it was too readily identifiable. Plus, maybe the bastards had some way of tracking it. Hard to believe, but how the hell else could they have traced her to the Maggot Armpit?

For a few minutes she drove aimlessly, gathering her

thoughts. Her original plan—a long shot at best—was looking a whole lot long-shottier now. She'd lost her arsenal, all of it, even the gun formerly in her purse, which she'd taken out as part of her inspection. Oh, and the three grand in cash—she'd lost that, too. She had the binoculars from the boat, and Gura's phone and faithful Sammy, both still in her handbag, and the burner she'd used when she called Brad.

So, great. No shortage of phones. She could harass Streinikov with prank calls. Or she could go into his estate unarmed, limping on one good leg. Which was suicide.

But she would do it anyway. Why? Because she was fucking crazy, that's why.

And because she was majorly pissed off. These assholes kept trying to kill her, and it was starting to get on her damn nerves.

# 34

"SHE GOT AWAY."

Ilya delivered the report as Lukin chauffeured him and Barsky east on US-46, making tracks away from the motel before the police arrived.

"Can you follow her?" Streinikov asked.

"*Nyet*. She had a head start. She could have taken 95 north or south, or I-80 east or west, or any surface street. She could be anywhere." He searched for something positive to say. "She was wounded. I found blood on the pavement."

"Perhaps she'll bleed out and die."

"I doubt it."

"So do I."

"I'm sorry, sir. *Izvinitie*."

"You did your best. She's in the wind for now, but she's won only a short reprieve."

"Shall we come back?" Ilya asked.

"There's another matter to address first. Ivanov tells me our informant is making a nuisance of himself. He keeps calling to demand payment."

"The next time he calls, have Ivanov patch him through to me."

"That's just what I was thinking."

Ilya didn't have to wait long for the call. Lukin was turning off 46 at Palisades Park when Ivanov's name appeared on his caller ID display. "He's on the line again, more agitated than ever," Ivanov said in Russian. "His name is Alonzo. A dumb *shahkter*." Literally coal-miner,

218

but in this context, a racial epithet. "I think he's been using."

"Put him on."

A new voice came over the phone. "Where's my money, asshole?"

Up to that moment, Ilya had been prepared to make a
payoff. Not the entire amount, perhaps, not the whole ten
grand. But a portion of it. The tip had been accurate, after
all.

But the man's impertinence caused him to change his
mind.

"There's no money for you," he said. "The bitch ran."

"Hey, if you morons fucked up, that's on you, not me. I
came through. I sent you straight to her."

He was talking fast, his words blurring together.
Ivanov was right. The fool was high on something.

Ilya distrusted drug users. He never touched the stuff
himself. He'd never so much as smoked a joint. A man
who required artificial stimulation to face the challenges
of life was no man at all.

"Your information did not result in the resolution of
our problem. Therefore, no money."

"You fuck. You dumb shit-eating Russkie cocksucker.
We had a deal."

"Deal's off," Ilya said complacently.

He was about to end the call when the man named
Alonzo said, "I can make trouble."

"Can you?"

"I got contacts. A rep in my burg. I'm a big man in Maritime."

Ilya had passed through Maritime on his way to and
from Brighton Cove. A shitty little town, a collection of
gas stations and subsidized housing. "Most impressive,"
he said dryly.

"I'll fucking spread the word that you Russkie cunts
can't be trusted."

"Fine. Tell all your friends."

"I will. And you tell Streinikov he's fucked with the wrong guy."

Ilya paused. Streinikov. How could this man Alonzo know that name?

"You intend to be difficult?" he asked in a different tone.

"Count on it, you fucking cossack."

"Perhaps we can arrange payment after all."

"That's more like it."

"Where can we meet?"

"You know the Shell station on Route Four by Myrtle Avenue in Fort Lee? It's closed down now."

"Yes."

"Bring the money. All of it."

"No worries, my friend. You'll get everything you deserve."

# 35

ALONZO THOUGHT THE call had gone pretty well. Fuckers had tried to blow him off, but they didn't understand who they were dealing with.

He inhaled another line of coke, staying sharp. His brain was supercharged by now. He was seeing every angle, game-planning his strategy ten moves ahead. He was smarter than any mealymouthed potato-eating peasant asshole from East Assfuckistan. Smarter than the shape-shifting lizards, too, if they were real. He could outplay and outmaneuver anybody. Even Streinikov's crew.

Yeah, he knew Streinikov was behind this shit. Had to be him. He'd known it ever since he heard a Russian accent on the other end of the phone when he called the tip line. Streinikov controlled north Jersey. The other Russian mobsters were active in New York's five boroughs, but only Streinikov was operating in Bergen County.

It was probably Streinikov himself who'd talked to him after the first call was transferred. And Streinikov had agreed to pay. Now some flunky, some Junior Ranger with an ego problem, thought he could rip him off. Probably thought he could keep the ten g's for himself and tell his boss it had been paid. But it wasn't gonna play out that way.

The flunky might just decide to put him out of the way, of course. But Alonzo had already anticipated that move. He wasn't waiting in the Shell station. He was across the highway in a turnout next to another gas station, this one open for business. He had it all figured out.

He needed more coke, though. Just one more hit, to keep his head clear.

LUKIN STEERED THE Escalade into the Shell station. It was empty. Ilya's gaze panned the fuel islands and came to rest on a piece of paper flapping from one of the pumps.

"Retrieve that," he told Lukin.

Lukin got out of the car and tore off the paper, which had been secured to the pump with chewing gum. He showed it to Ilya.

In large block letters, carefully printed in pencil, were the words:

LEEVE THE CASH AND GO

Illiterate American fool.

"What do we do now?" Barsky asked.

Ilya shrugged. "We leave the cash. And go."

ALONZO LOOKED ON with satisfaction as one of the Russians, a tall blond guy, left the Caddy and placed a manila envelope on the fuel island, weighing it down with a rock. He returned to the car, disappearing behind the driver, and a moment later the SUV pulled away.

He watched it go. It could be a trap. They might just drive around the corner and circle back. But he was patient. He could wait. He spent twenty minutes fidgeting, taking an occasional hit to stay sharp, and studying the road. No one returned.

Time to risk it. Ten grand. Not bad for a night's work. Parker was still alive, and the little Mexishit Chihuahua hadn't gotten the beatdown he'd earned, but there would be time to settle those scores later.

He drove down Route 4, doubled back, and reached

the Shell station. Warily he parked between the fuel islands and recovered the envelope. For a paranoid moment he wondered if maybe they'd put a bomb inside, some kind of lightweight plastic explosive or some goddamn thing. But when he undid the flap, he saw only a stack of hundred-dollar bills tied with a rubber band. He took a whiff. New money. It smelled better than freshly cut grass.

He turned back to his car, and the Russian was there, the blond who'd planted the envelope.

But that was impossible. He'd gotten back into the car, and the car had driven away.

The Russian seemed to read his thoughts. "I've been here the whole time, my friend. I dropped out of sight, and the car left without me."

Alonzo opened his mouth to speak. Eloquent arguments crowded his brain. He could talk his way out of this. He could do anything. He was invincible.

The Russian shot him.

He was barely aware of being hit. All he knew was that one moment he was upright, and the next moment he was on his knees with his hands clutching his belly. He lifted his head and saw the Russian pick up the envelope. The man was smiling.

"Now you are paid," he said, and he pressed the gun to Alonzo's temple and squeezed off one more round.

# 36

BONNIE SAT CROSS-LEGGED on a stool in the upstairs bedroom of the home of Howard and Margot Swanson, scoping out Streinikov's compound next door.

As Streinikov had helpfully informed her, his neighbors to the south were currently vacationing in St. John. Since it seemed a shame to let such a nice house go to waste, Bonnie had taken the liberty of defeating the worthless alarm system and forcing the lock on the front door. There was only one vehicle in the two-car garage, leaving space for the Saturn she'd boosted.

She'd had plenty to do in the Swansons' house, besides checking their piled up mail out of idle curiosity to learn their names. First she'd attended to the gunshot wound in her calf. The bullet had passed clean through, and the damage was minimal, but there was a lot of bleeding and a fair amount of pain. She found first aid supplies in the bathroom and bandaged the wound, then threw down some Tylenol to kill the ache. To keep herself alert, she swallowed some NoDoz from her purse.

The bites inflicted by the glass shards were less serious but took longer to address. She cleaned them out one at a time, swabbed them with bacitracin, and applied Band-Aids.

Finished, she looked herself over in a full-length mirror. She was a mess. She'd seen corpses that looked healthier. They'd probably felt livelier, too.

The medical stuff was taken care of. She got down to business. Having lost all her gear, she had to be creative about weapons. If things went as planned, she would acquire some new firearms soon enough. In the meantime she contented herself with items scavenged mainly from the Swansons' kitchen, as well as some gasoline siphoned from their Audi, rubber gloves from under the bathroom sink, and a nylon stocking from Mrs. Swanson's underwear drawer. She stuffed all this gear into a backpack she'd found in the Saturn's backseat, which had formerly held a stash of porno magazines from Thailand. These she thoughtfully left for the Swansons' perusal.

The pack, when fully loaded, was kind of bulky, and it rattled a little because of the wine bottles, but she wasn't counting on stealth tonight.

After these preparations were made, she positioned herself at the bedroom window and tipped the binoculars from Streinikov's cruiser to her eyes. She took her time studying the layout of his estate.

The place was all lit up now. Floodlights illuminated the perimeter fence. Sentries patrolled the property. She counted five men in long overcoats, each armed with a serious-looking firearm. Probably machine guns, both full-size and sub-gun. Plus, there were three more assholes who pulled in through the front gate and parked their Cadillac SUV in Streinikov's garage. One of them was Sundance, so that had to be the crew who'd nearly aced her in the motel.

No dogs, though. She was glad about that. She didn't want to kill any dogs.

Lights burned in the windows of the main house, a sprawling ranch whose interior she remembered from the tiled display on the TV monitor. She saw no activity inside, no silhouettes in the windows, no flicker of a computer screen or a TV set.

The greenhouse was a different story. It was a safe bet Streinikov was still in there. Other people came and went as if delivering updates or receiving orders. Other than

Sundance, they were new to her. One of them must be a doctor. He carried a little black bag and looked scared.

All told, she counted eight people, plus the doc and the unseen Streinikov. There could be additional personnel in the greenhouse, but she didn't think so. Eight was probably the head count. She thought of that old TV show, *Eight Is Enough*. It sure as hell was enough for her.

She hadn't expected Streinikov to fortify his compound to quite this extent. The place had become a fortress under lockdown. Given that she'd lost her weapons stash, was wounded, and was up against greater odds then she'd anticipated, a saner person might well have had second thoughts right about now. But she was an all-in type of gal. She was committed.

She watched the strolling sentries long enough to conclude that they followed no regular pattern. They ambled along the fence, pausing to investigate any stray noise or just to take a leak. They were mainly interested in the two gates—the front gate, which opened onto a cul-de-sac, and the hillside gate, which led to the stairway she'd climbed from the pier.

She didn't think they were expecting her. Actually she didn't think they were expecting anyone. It was more like a show of force. With the alpha dog laid up and licking his wounds, the rest of the pack weren't taking any chances.

Most of these Russian mob outfits were surprisingly small, limited to a trusted few, unlike the street armies mustered by the Italians and the Asians. There was a strong possibility that the eight guys she'd spotted were Streinikov's entire crew, or at least his core membership, the ones who mattered. If things worked out, she could shut down his entire operation tonight. If things didn't work out, she was the one who would be shut down.

Funny how things came around. It had been a February night when she went into the farmhouse in Ohio in search of a man named Lucas Hatch, who'd killed her parents. The odds had been against her then, too. But she'd gotten it done. Maybe she would do it again.

The clock on the bedroom wall was showing 5:30. She had to go in before dawn.

She shrugged on the backpack. Her purse would be stashed in the Saturn—she didn't need it weighing her down. Her hat? She almost left it off; if it got lost in the action, it might be used later to identify her. Oh, fuck it. She would wear the hat. What was the old saying—they died with their boots on? Well, she would die with her hat on. You know, if she died at all. It wasn't a sure thing. She felt the need to remind herself of that.

"Okay," she said to the Swansons' empty house, "let's put this pu-pu on a platter."

As inspirational speeches went, it wasn't exactly up there with "Win one for the Gipper," but it did the trick.

She plucked Gura's phone from her pocket and powered it on for the first time since she'd acquired it. In the list of recent calls, she found a contact labeled The Man. Had to be Streinikov. She hit redial.

This ought to be a fun conversation.


IN THE GREENHOUSE, Streinikov lifted his ringing phone. The name on the caller ID screen was Gura.

"It's her," he said to Ilya. "Calling on Gura's mobile."

"Why the hell would she do that?"

"Suppose we find out." Streinikov took the call, putting it on speaker. "Miss Parker. How nice to hear from you."

"Yeah. Pleasure's all yours. I heard some assholes shot up my house and my place of business a few hours ago."

"What a shame. Your country is still very much the Wild West, *nyet*?" Streinikov switched to an app on his phone.

"It's about to get a whole lot wilder. You're gonna have a bad fucking day."

"Am I?" He scrolled rapidly through a list of names.

"Way I look at it, you're my whole problem. You go away, and my problem goes away, too."

"It sounds most logical." The app allowed him to pinpoint the location of any mobile phone used by one of his associates. He clicked on Gura's name. "Though you forget that others will avenge my death."

"You already told me you're a lone wolf. The rest of the *vory* don't give a wet fart about you. I'm guessing your closest compadres are hanging with you at your Neverland ranch right now. The others'll have bigger things than me to worry about after their boss gets snuffed."

"Colorfully expressed. I can find no flaw in your reasoning." A map came up on the screen. A blinking bull's-eye marked the phone's whereabouts. It was close. "But sadly, you've lost your arsenal. You left it behind at the motel."

"No biggie. I'm a resourceful gal."

Streinikov zoomed in on the bull's-eye. "You've acquired other weapons?"

"I got Cool Whip and Beefaroni."

He didn't know what this meant. "You're injured, also. You've been winged, my poor Firebird."

"Nah, your guy missed me."

"You left a patch of blood."

"That was chianti. I'm a sloppy drunk. So you want a preview of tonight's action?"

"I listen with interest."

"Long story short, I'm gonna go Batman on your ass. I'm busting in, and I'm gonna kill your whole crew, and then I'm gonna to kill you."

"And just when may we expect the honor of your company?"

"Any time now."

Streinikov smiled. "You've got a fucking pair on you, my friend."

"Wish I could say the same, no-nuts."

"Charming as always."

"Let's dance."

Silence on the line. The call was over.

"Think she means it?" Ilya asked.

"*Da.* But she didn't know I could find Gura's phone. She's at the Swanson place."

Ilya turned to leave. "I'll take Barsky and Lukin."

He was at the door when Streinikov said, "*Zdi.*" Wait. "She's smart, this girl. Yet she called to announce her intentions, when a sneak attack would be more effective. And she used a phone we could trace."

"She didn't know that."

"Didn't she?"

Ilya frowned. "Why give herself away?"

"Perhaps to lure some of our people out of the compound. Divide and conquer."

"It's possible."

"It's more than possible. It's how our crafty Firebird thinks."

"So we send no one?"

"One man. Just one, through the front gate. She'll assume there are three or four soldiers in the car. She'll be expecting our numbers inside the fence to be correspondingly reduced."

"All right. I'll send Barsky alone. And I'll alert the patrols."

He was gone. Streinikov stared after him, smiling. He had not expected Parker to go on the offensive. It was a wonderful stroke of luck. It would save him the trouble of hunting her down. She would die tonight, here on his property, and the whole matter would be settled.

Stupid, impetuous girl. She might have lived a few days longer, even a whole week, had she gone to ground.

# 37

BARSKY WAS PISSED off. He didn't appreciate being used as a stinking decoy. All the action would be going down inside the compound, and here he was, driving out through the main gate in Streinikov's customized Range Rover.

He'd given Ilya some lip about it, and Ilya had told him to shut up and follow orders. He didn't much like that, either. Goddamn punk treated him with no respect. Ignorant *chajnik* hadn't even heard of Bonnie and fuckin' Clyde, for Christ's sake.

It would all change when Barsky himself was Streinikov's right-hand man. Oh yes, that was going to happen. For a long time now, he'd suspected that Ilya Kvint went both ways. Sure, he'd had his share of whores like everyone else, but Barsky had also caught him sneaking glances at pretty young boys. The only thing necessary was to catch him in the act of buggering one of them. Streinikov was a man of old-fashioned morals. He wouldn't have a faggot as his aide-de-camp. And the way Barsky had it figured, he was next in line for the seat at the boss man's elbow once Kvint was out of the picture.

It was a pleasant prospect, and it lifted a smile to his lips as he parked the Range Rover outside the Swanson place.

His job was to stay in the Rover for at least ten minutes. That would give the little blonde *tyolka* enough time to attempt to penetrate the perimeter of the estate. He'd been told very explicitly not to get out of the SUV, in case she was watching. She had to believe there was more than one man inside.

A sensible plan. Still, it rankled. His MP9 was tucked into a shoulder holster under his coat, ready for business. Thirty rounds in a box magazine. He'd dearly hoped to put several of those rounds into the American whore. Now someone else would get that pleasure. Kvint, probably.

Movement.

Barsky leaned forward. He'd glimpsed a flicker of shadow by the house's side door. A slim figure slipping out.

Parker. On the move.

Barsky knew his instructions. But he also knew that if he could bag the girl on his own, he would gain favor in the big man's eyes. And he'd have the satisfaction of unloading the MP9 into her body.

What the hell. He would do it. Fortune favored the bold, and all that happy shit.

The Rover's ceiling bulb had long ago been disabled, so there was no telltale flash of light as he opened the door. He left the door ajar; shutting it would make noise. A fellow in Donetsk had made that mistake once, when coming for Barsky. That man was dead and Barsky was alive.

He unholstered the MP9 and moved quickly across the lawn to the side of the house. Tall arborvitae shrubs were arrayed along a wall of cedar shingles. The girl wasn't in sight. She had been headed north, presumably intending to cut through the backyard as a shortcut to the cul-de-sac. He could catch up with her, gun her down from behind before she reached the street.

And take the head. Right. The boss wanted it for some reason. Well, he had a banana knife sheathed in the small of his back that would do the job. Messy, but he'd never minded getting his hands dirty. It was better than digging for potatoes in the dirt, which would have been his fate if he'd lived an honest life.

He ran lightly along the side of the house, ducking behind each bush in turn, his attention fixed on the darkness ahead. She couldn't have gone far.

At his back, a rustle of leaves.

Barsky almost had time to pivot, and pain burst in the back of his neck, an electric flare of pain that shocked him into silence. It lasted less than a second.

Then it was gone, and so was he.


THE MEDULLA OBLONGATA is a hub of the central nervous system, a meeting point for all vital nerve centers. It is located at the base of the skull and can be accessed by a small sharp blade angled upward with force. The blade of a paring knife from the Swansons' kitchen, for instance.

Really, it was amazing, the stuff you learned by watching Spike TV.

Bonnie had jammed the blade into his neck and punched it home with the heel of her hand. The method wasn't foolproof; the target was small, no bigger than a chestnut, and there was the risk of a finger twitch, a spray of shots from the sub-gun. But she'd gotten lucky. He'd dropped instantly, without so much as a gasp.

She pried the gun free of his hand and checked the magazine. Thirty rounds. Nice. She was already rebuilding her arsenal, one bad guy at a time.

She wasn't worried about handling the weapon. She'd already pulled on the rubber gloves scavenged from the bathroom. And yeah, she'd wiped down all surfaces she'd touched in the Swanson house. If she lived through this thing, she would leave no prints for the bag-and-tag brigade.

So far, at least, events were proceeding as planned. Mapping strategy against Streinikov was like playing chess. At least, Bonnie assumed it was. She didn't actually know how to play chess. Frank Kershaw had tried to teach her, but she could never get the hang of how to move the little horsey thing.

But from general knowledge, she'd gathered that a good chess player anticipated his opponent's moves—not just the obvious next move, but the more subtle ones that might follow down the line.

She'd been sure Streinikov could track Gura's cell; that was why she'd powered off the phone in the first place. Once it was back on, he would know she was squatting at the neighbors' house. But he would also know—probably—that she wasn't dumb enough to give herself away like that. So he would pretend to play along by sending just one or two guys after her, keeping the rest of his force in reserve.

She'd been hoping for two, had gotten only one, but it was a start.

Now for phase two of her plan. This part was simpler and more straightforward than phase one. She would go in shooting and kill as many of the bastards as she could.

Seven of them were left, not counting Streinikov and the doctor. Seven men who had to die in the next few minutes.

It was going to be a fucking bloodbath, like the last reel of *Scarface*. Or it was going to end with only one more body—hers.

Either way, in less than five minutes it would be over.

The thought gave her a strange sort of comfort as she climbed into the Range Rover and cranked the ignition key.


"BARSKY'S COMING BACK."

The voice on the intercom belonged to Lysenko, who'd been stationed in the residence, manning the gate controls.

Streinikov stabbed the transmit button. "Too soon—

Parker hasn't made her move yet."

"He wants in. He's got his brights on and he's honking."

Even in the greenhouse on the far end of the property, Streinikov could hear the petulant blats of the horn.

"Goddamned *xyecoc*," Ilya said. "I should have sent a better man. Why the hell would he disobey orders?"

"Why, indeed?" Streinikov considered the problem. "Could it be that Parker actually was at the house, and Barsky took her out?"

"It can't be that easy."

"Why not? We're due for some *udacha*"—luck—"where our Firebird is concerned." Streinikov keyed the intercom. "Open the gate. See what he wants."

THE GATES PARTED slowly. Bonnie waited, hunched behind the wheel of the SUV with her beret down low on her face.

Someone was emerging from the house. Another guy, one of the sentries, was striding across the lawn, alerted by all the racket she'd been making.

The sentry was closer. As she watched, he stepped onto the driveway, directly into the high beams' glare.

Go.

Her foot pinned the gas pedal to the floor. The Range Rover rocketed forward, scraping one side of the gate and throwing up a cascade of sparks. The sentry was lifting his gun when she barreled into him and made him into roadkill. Her tires thudded over his body, whumpity-whump, and left him rolling on the asphalt.

The guy from the house opened fire. Reflexively she ducked, expecting the windshield to fly apart. It puckered but held. Bulletproof. Sweet.

She threw open the door on the driver's side, thrust the sub-gun through the opening, and fired a ten-second burst, blowing the asshole away.

The front door of the house was rushing up. No time to hit the brakes. She hurled herself clear, abandoning the machine pistol, which was empty.

She hit the soft grass on the side of the driveway and twisted into a crouch in time to see the SUV head-butt its way through the open door with a shout of wood and steel. It wedged itself in the doorway at a crazy angle, tires spinning.

She shook her head, mildly dazed, ears ringing.

Yowsah. Did she know how to make an entrance or what?

Her hat had come off. She retrieved it—no hat left behind, that was her policy—then recovered the second man's Kalashnikov. She checked the magazine—still about two dozen rounds. He'd been firing on semi-auto, lucky for her. If he'd gone full auto, he would have spent his whole wad.

On the run to the doorway, she pulled Mrs. Swanson's stocking out of the backpack. Her leg was probably still hurting but, funny thing, she didn't notice it anymore.

Two guys here, one at the Swanson place. Body count: three.

Five to go.

She boosted herself over the crashed Range Rover, entering the house.

# 38

"WHAT THE HELL is happening? Lysenko?"

Streinikov thumped his fist on the intercom. There was silence on the other end.

"Barsky must've gone crazy," Lukin said cluelessly.

Streinikov shut his eyes. "It wasn't Barsky, *tormoz*. It was Parker."

Ilya, pacing the greenhouse's center aisle, was on the phone. "Kolba is with Denisov and Abroskin at the scene. Parker's not there."

"Let me talk to him."

Ilya gave Streinikov the phone, set to speaker mode.

"Lysenko and Kovalenko are down," Kolba said. "No sign of Barsky. The Range Rover hit your house. The girl took Lysenko's Kalash. We don't know where she's gone."

In the background Denisov said, "She could be drawing a bead on us right now." Abroskin told him to shut up.

"Look there." Ilya pointed at the monitor displaying a mosaic of video feeds from the residence. Two of the cameras appeared to be inoperative. The third showed a slender figure in a stocking mask entering the kitchen.

Lukin snorted. "Stupid bitch. Why would she hide her face from us?"

"Not from us," Streinikov explained with infinite patience. "She knows the police will look at the video files. She's planning for her future."

"She won't have a future," Ilya said.

The masked figure turned to the ceiling-mounted camera and aimed a spray can at it. Instantly the image

236

was obliterated.

"She's in the house," Streinikov informed Kolba. "I saw her on the monitor."

"Then you can guide us—"

"No, I can't. She's already disabled three cameras. No doubt she'll do the same to the rest. You'll need to go in blind."

"*Chyort*," Kolba murmured, then added in a louder voice: "Yes, sir."

"She's avoided the east wing so far. It appears she intends to make her stand somewhere between the front door and the sun porch."

It was a straight shot along the central corridor, with detours into rooms on both sides—living room, kitchen, library, lavatory. The sun porch, which doubled as a dining room, lay at the north end, with a door that opened onto the backyard and the path to the greenhouse.

"I'll go in with Denisov through the front," Kolba said. "Abroskin will enter via the rear."

"Just do it." Streinikov licked dry lips. "Make her dead."

Lukin lifted his Jati-Matic. "I'll join the others."

Ilya nodded. "Me too."

"*Nyet*." Streinikov shifted in his seat, feeling the complaint of his ruptured side. "I want you here—both of you. This could be another feint on Parker's part. She may intend to leave the residence and come here."

His tongue scraped his lips again. He felt hot and strangely lightheaded. Vasnev placed a palm to his forehead. It came away wet with a sheen of sweat.

"Sir, you have a fever."

"So?"

"It's a sign of infection. The antibiotics aren't getting it done. You need to be hospitalized."

"Am I supposed to leave now? Parker is in the compound."

"All the more reason to absent yourself from the scene."

"You're a coward, Vasnev. I don't run from a fight."

"I'm only saying—"

Streinikov waved a hand. "*Poshyol ty!*" The polite translation was *get lost*.

"*Da, da.*" Vasnev backed away, picking up his black bag. "Yes, sir. Very good."

On the phone Kolba's rapid breathing was clearly audible. The man must be wearing a throat mic. There was a shatter of glass, then scraping noises as he and Denisov went through a broken window.

"They'll get her," Ilya said.

Streinikov nodded, his eyes hot and bright. "Parker has fought well. Now she pays the hangman."

BONNIE USED HER trusty spray can of Cool Whip to kill the camera in the sun porch, then shrugged off the stocking mask and backtracked to the library, where the camera was already blacked out.

The library was dominated by a big fireplace and the impossibly plush sofa that faced it. Heavy draperies covered the windows. The only illumination came from scattered table lamps. She went quickly around the room yanking out all the plugs.

In the dark, guided by her flashlight, she rummaged in her pack and went to work.

Not much time. She could hear the bad guys entering at the front and back, clearing the house one room at a time, converging on the library.

Three or four men, she thought.

"*BLYAD*, I DON'T like this." Denisov's voice, low over the phone's speaker.

"She's only a woman," Kolba said in a reassuring tone.

From a distance, Abroskin shouted, "Porch—clear!"

"Woman?" Denisov said. "She's a fucking *polenitsa*."

The man-killing warrior woman of Slavic myth. Streinikov, listening, couldn't help but smile. The old folklore still retained its power.

Scuffling sounds, hoarse breathing. Kolba's voice boomed, "Kitchen—clear!"

Streinikov was unsurprised that they'd failed to find her so far. He would expect her to take cover in the library. It was centrally located, the logical point on which all three men would converge. It seemed she wanted all of them together, though he couldn't see why. Ambush? His men were far too vigilant to be taken by surprise.

"Where's Vasnev?" Ilya asked, interrupting his thoughts.

Streinikov's gaze panned the jungle around him. The doctor was nowhere in sight.

"*Sukin syn* ran out on us while we weren't looking," Lukin said. "I'll chase him down."

Streinikov negatived the idea. "Let him go. We'll discipline the damn fool later."

The doctor was unimportant. Fever and infection were unimportant. Only his Firebird mattered. She had raided his apple orchard, and now she must give up her golden life.

"Library coming up," Kolba said over the phone.

"Friendly, don't shoot." That was Abroskin, meeting up with the other two. "Bathroom's clear. If she's in the house, she's holed up in the library."

"She killed the lights in there," Denisov said. "Wall switch doesn't do shit."

Kolba barked, "Get clear of the doorway!"

Three shots cracked in quick succession and somebody screamed.

"*Dermo.*" That was Denisov. "Bitch winged me. Fucking pegged my right arm."

"At least we know where she is." Abroskin sounded

unruffled, faintly amused.

"We go in shooting," Kolba breathed, "and blow her the fuck away."

Streinikov tightened his grip on the phone. Ilya and Lukin stood staring.

A beat of silence, then a roaring fusillade.

Streinikov knew what the men were carrying. Kolba used a KG-99 with an aftermarket fifty-round mag. Denison toted a Dragunov rifle. Abroskin had an AK-47.

All three weapons were unloading simultaneously into the library in a volley of furious noise.

Parker couldn't survive this. No one could.

Then it was over. The only sounds were the ragged breathing of three men and the clatter of expended magazines being dumped and new ones heeled into place.

"Use your flashlights," Kolba said, his voice pitched low. "Look for movement."

"I don't see—" Denisov paused, then emitted a low whistle. "Fuck."

Abroskin laughed. "*Boss moy.*" Oh my God.

"Do you see her?" Streinikov shouted. "Is she dead?"

"She's dead, all right." Kolba was no longer whispering. "We've got her pinned in three beams. She's on the floor by the fireplace, with her fucking brains blown out all over the fucking flagstones."

Streinikov's relief was mingled with a twinge of disappointment. He would have liked to receive her head intact.

"Good work," he said, as Ilya and Lukin visibly relaxed. "Collect the remains."

"We're going in now, sir. Damn. Fucking brain spatter is everywhere."

"Gonna need a new carpet," Abroskin said, and the others laughed.

"She's still got her hand on the Kalash."

"Lysenko's piece."

"Man, her brains stink like shit."

"Yeah, I might be losing my appetite."

More laughter.

Streinikov tried to envision the scene. Parker sprawled on the floor, clutching her firearm in a death grip, the back of her skull shot away, a mass of blood and brains decorating the hearth like so much uncooked meat.

Uncooked ...

*"I got Cool Whip,"* she'd said, *"and Beefaroni."*

He knew then. He understood.

"Kolba!" He was screaming into the phone. "Fall back! *Fall—"*

Shouts. Gunfire. A prolonged burst.

Muffled thuds. Bodies falling.

After that, nothing.

"Kolba?" Streinikov breathed.

He expected no answer.


BONNIE PULLED ON her beret as she left the house at a run. She still had her hat, and she still wasn't dead. She wasn't sure which of those two facts was more surprising.

It had gotten a little hairy back there, what with all the firepower aimed in her direction. But the big sofa had provided decent cover, and the hardwood frame and thick cushions had absorbed the lead whizzing her way. The really dicey part was playing possum on the floor and hoping they didn't pop her just for the hell of it before they got close enough for her to open up. And hoping, too, that they didn't recognize the smell of Beefaroni, which she'd artistically smeared all over the fireplace even before the action started.

Her lethal burst had emptied the Kalashnikov. Luckily one of her new kills had been toting a KG-99, and he'd thoughtfully loaded it with a full magazine.

The body count was now six. This was starting to look like a Quentin Tarantino flick.

But there were still two left, and one of them was Sundance, whose face she had yet to see among the dead.

"THEY'RE ALL DOWN." Streinikov put aside the phone he'd been using to speak with Kolba. "She outplayed them."

Lukin's eyes were wide and shocked. "How?"

"Does it matter?" Streinikov felt his strength ebbing. He was unnaturally calm.

"*Khrenoten*," Ilya whispered.

"*Da*," Streinikov agreed with something close to a smile. "A clusterfuck indeed. And she's still coming. You two are the only men I have left."

"We'll barricade the doors," Lukin said. "Make a stand in here and protect you."

Streinikov sighed, weary of the man's stupidity. "A greenhouse is no place for a siege. The walls are made of glass. Do you see? Glass! She can pick us off at her leisure."

"That's why we have to intercept her before she gets here." Ilya gestured to Lukin. "Come on."

He was at the door when he remembered propriety.

"If you approve?" he asked his boss.

Streinikov nodded. "Go. And do what you can."

"We'll get her," Ilya said, leading Lukin outside.

Fine words. But Streinikov did not believe them. The girl had invaded his home, his sanctum sanctorum. She had taken out six of his best men, his inner circle. And he, an invalid, could neither run nor fight.

All his life he had prized strength, and now he was helpless, as helpless as he had been under Smolin's knife.

# 39

ILYA WAS UP for the kill. The fact that Parker had taken out six others in the last few minutes meant nothing to him. He was no witless *mudak* like Barsky or clumsy oaf like Kolba. He was a killer, sleek and efficient, and no mere woman would write his finish.

Rounding a bend in the path, he caught sight of a distant moving figure. He snapped off two shots. Didn't connect. Then she was gone, vanished in the trees.

"That way." He didn't wait for Lukin's reply. Lukin was just another fool. Of all Streinikov's men, only Gregor and Ilya himself had been worth a gob of warm spit. And Gregor was dead. Because of this girl, this bitch, this ...

"*Shluha vokzal'naja,*" he muttered. Train station whore.

He veered off the path, crossing the manicured grounds. The crescent moon had long since set. The sky was thick with clustered stars. Their brightness competed with the lights of the city across the river, flickering through breaks in stands of pine.

Then the trees were past him. He approached the cliff. She was just ahead. Before he could fire again, he saw her vault the gate and head down the staircase.

She was climbing down to the riverbank, perhaps hoping to get aboard the *Dragon's Mouth.*

A mistake. She could never reach cover in time. On the stairway she would be exposed, and he and Lukin would occupy the high ground.

"We have her," he breathed, speaking not to Lukin but to himself.

He pounded forward. As he neared the gate, he dropped instinctively into a half crouch. There was a chance she had turned on the stairs to target her pursuers. His best course was to stay low.

He pushed open the gate and slipped through, Lukin trailing him. On the landing, they stopped, looking below.

The staircase twisted down to the starlit sparkle of the river, where the cruiser bobbed at its moorings. Parker wasn't there. She had disappeared.

"What the fuck?" Lukin whispered, superstitious fear infecting his voice.

"She's taken cover."

"Where?"

The hillside, Ilya thought. Amid the rocks and scrub. But it didn't seem right. There was something he was missing, something so obvious that he couldn't see it, though it was right under his nose.

Under. Under his ...

His gaze ticked to the landing, and the world exploded.

The planks blew apart, splinters of wood driven into his legs, large-caliber rounds blasting upward. Lukin screamed and died, his stomach ripped open like a bag of blood. Ilya felt hot needles of pain in his thighs, his groin. He made no conscious effort to leap to safety, but somehow he found himself on the hillside, crawling, bleeding, the smell of cordite in his nostrils.

Everything from his navel to his knees was a ragged tissue of gore. His balls—they were gone, just gone. He'd been castrated, like Streinikov. That was funny, somehow. A good joke. Damn good joke.

It hardly mattered anyhow. He was sure to bleed out and die.

But he would get her first.

He had dropped his pistol, but it hadn't fallen far. His groping fingers retrieved it. He turned on his side, lying parallel to the crawlspace under the landing which Parker had used as a blind. But she was no longer there. She'd moved on, taking cover elsewhere, on the far side of the staircase.

He bellied forward, snaking over sharp rocks and plants like pincushions, bristling with thorns. It was cold out here, very cold. He hadn't noticed the cold before, but he felt it now, deep in his bones, the cold like a tangible darkness eating away at his soul.

Crazy thought. His mind was going. He must be leaking blood by the gallon. Couldn't hold out long. But he only needed to spot her. If he knew where she was hidden, he could empty the gun at her. Take her with him, the bitch, whore, *suka*, *blyad*.

The stairs rose over him. He pulled himself underneath the shattered landing into the spider hole where Parker had been concealed. As long as he was in motion, she would stay hidden. But if he huddled here, still and silent, she might show herself, and he would get her. He would get her, if he was still alive.

Come on, Parker. Make a move, girl. All it takes is one mistake, and I'll have you. Just one mistake.

Brightness.

An arc of fire pinwheeling through the sky. It touched down a yard from him with a shatter of glass and a gasoline smell and a flash of flame.

Ilya knew what this was. It was a Molotov cocktail, a weapon he'd used himself in Donetsk when shopkeepers who refused to pay for *krisha* required a loss of inventory.

Already the fire was hurrying toward him, devouring the dry brush, and another bottle smashed nearby, its contents setting the wooden stairs ablaze, and another, bursting like a hand grenade at his feet and spattering his trousers with gas. And now the fire was all around him, penning him in, raging above him and alongside him, climbing onto his body, advancing along his legs, finding his shirt and surging upward, undoing the buttons like an anxious lover, throwing hot kisses at his face, clawing at him with burning fingers. It was all over him now, engulfing him, crowding out the rest of the world as his skin peeled and his hair smoked, as his lips and gums dissolved and his teeth split and popped, as his eyelids burned away and his eyeballs roasted in their sockets, until finally in a last act of mercy Ilya Kvint turned his gun on himself.

BONNIE WAS OFF the hillside and back on the trail to the greenhouse even before she heard Sundance fire his last shot.

He hadn't screamed. That was the really remarkable thing. Even while being consumed by fire, he had stubbornly refused to cry out. She kind of had to respect him for that.

Truth was, she'd gotten lucky this time. Sure, she'd meant for the pair to spot her and give chase, but she hadn't expected those first shots to come so friggin' close. One of the bullets had punched a hole through the top of her beret. An inch lower, and it would have been lights out even before she could get to the crawlspace under the stairs.

But what the hell, close only counted in horseshoes and hand grenades. By luck or skill, she'd pulled it off. Eight down.

And the doc was gone, too. She'd seen him running to his car while she was on the sun porch.

By now the first responders would be gearing up. The initial gunfire would only have confused people. Residents of upscale neighborhoods weren't used to hearing bullets fly, and Streinikov's few neighbors within earshot were doubtless disinclined to call the police anyway. The Range Rover impacting the house would have gotten them out of bed, but they wouldn't know just where the noise had come from. And the gunfire inside the house would have been muffled, perhaps inaudible at a distance.

But the blaze of fire on the cliffside would rouse even the least vigilant citizens to action. By now 9-1-1 was being flooded with calls. She had to move fast.

There was only one man left, but he was the most important one of all.

STREINIKOV SAW THE wavering red glow to the east, the false dawn. He didn't know exactly what had happened, but he knew his men hadn't set that fire.

He found himself thinking again of the old fable. On the night when he'd recited the tale to Gregor, he hadn't told it all. He'd left out the lengthy middle of the narrative, during which the czar sent each of his sons in turn to catch the trespassing Firebird. One by one, they had met with terrible misfortune. Only his youngest son, the last to be sent out, had prevailed.

Perhaps he should have remembered that part of the story—the successive missions and successive defeats.

Unlike the czar, he had no sons left to send. There was no one to defend him. No one to stand between him and this avenging angel, this blonde Valkyrie.

Too late, he realized he should have commandeered a firearm from one of his men. He never carried a gun. It had never been necessary. He had weapons stored about the premises—in the garage and the residence, and even here in the greenhouse, under a bench in a distant corner. He did not think he could walk that far. He gave it a try, straining to rise from his chair. His knees shook. His fever raged. He was not strong enough. Should he attempt to walk, he would fall on his face, and she would find him prone on the floor. That fate was unthinkable. To die was acceptable. Everyone died. But to die without dignity was shameful, unforgivable.

Slowly, Streinikov lowered himself into his seat. He sat for a moment, catching his breath and letting a swirl of vertigo subside. Then lovingly he picked up a potted orchid, a *Cattleya violacea*, one of his favorites, thankfully undamaged in the violence. He held the clay pot in one hand, while with the other he touched the tender, luminous blooms that spoke of summer and sun, two things he would never see again. And he waited.

His wait was not long.

# 40

WHEN IT WAS all over, Bonnie went out on foot through the front gate, carrying her gym bag, which she'd recovered from the Cadillac Escalade in Streinikov's garage. The goons at the Maggot Armpit had stuffed all her artillery and other junk into the bag and taken it with them, leaving it in the SUV. Her cash was in there too, all three grand. So the day wasn't a total loss. Plus with all the running, she'd gotten in her cardio.

She'd wanted the bag back, partly for the cash, partly for all the primo gear it contained, but mainly because she didn't want anything with her fingerprints on it to be found at the scene. She'd covered herself pretty well by wearing gloves and, as necessary, a stocking mask, and she didn't want to blow it now.

In the garage she had seen two corpses lying against the wall. Gura and Butch. Gura didn't look so bad, but Butch was in sorry shape.

Sirens were closing in when she left the garage. As she ran along the driveway, she came across the sentry she'd run over. Though he wore tread marks on his back and was a mangled mess, he was still alive, moaning piteously. She shot him in the head and kept going. It was more kindness than he would have shown her.

She made it off the property and into the shadowed safety of the Swansons' yard before anybody showed up. The Saturn was waiting for her in the Swansons' garage. She started up and hightailed it out of there. A fire engine passed her, charging to the scene.

Dawn set the sky aglow. A morning she hadn't expected to see.

Now that it was over, she could admit the truth. She hadn't really believed she would make it. She'd figured she would get two or three of them, maybe even four or five, but not the whole outfit. She wasn't sure if she owed the outcome to tactical brilliance or dumb luck. A little of both, probably.

Or maybe Felix was right. She was a survivor, just like Gloria Gaynor. Or a cockroach.

As she hit the highway, she lit a cigarette. She checked herself in the rearview mirror. If she'd been a horror show before, she was something worse now. But she was alive. She found herself laughing, quietly at first, then more insistently, until she had to make herself stop or risk hysteria.

Speeding south, she turned on the burner and phoned Joy Krauss. It was just past six o'clock, and Joy was probably asleep, but this news couldn't wait.

"Yes?"

Apparently she wasn't asleep. She'd answered on the second ring, sounding alert enough.

"You can relax," Bonnie said without preamble. "It's all worked out now."

"Is it?" Joy sounded a lot less ebullient than she should have.

"Yeah. You know that story you told about the Russian mob? Now there's evidence to back it up."

"How can there be evidence? It—it wasn't true."

"Yeah, I know it wasn't true." Her client was a little slow on the uptake this morning. Maybe she wasn't so awake, after all. "I'm the one who made it up, remember? But I've arranged things so Gil's wristwatch will turn up on the arm of a certain Russian crime boss."

"You gave it to him?"

"It was no big deal. He was deceased at the time."

"Oh." The single syllable dropped away into silence, like a pebble tossed down a bottomless well.

"Hey, cheer up, kiddo. This is a big deal. It means the heat's off. They can't challenge your story now. We beat the system. We won."

"No, you didn't, Parker."

That was a new voice, and it belonged to Dan Maguire.

Though she was speeding at seventy miles an hour, Bonnie shut her eyes. "Crap."

"You can say that again." Dan spoke slowly, as if wishing to draw out this moment as long as possible. "I heard everything you said. Thanks for the confession. Not that I needed it. Your accomplice already told me the whole thing."

"Joy, Joy, Joy," Bonnie muttered. "You just couldn't keep your mouth shut, could you?"

She'd said it to herself, but Joy must have heard. "I couldn't help it," she wailed. "He went to the police station by the library. He checked the security camera footage from the parking lot. He can prove we were there at the same time."

"You could have talked your way out of it," Bonnie said wearily. "I would've come up with something."

"Don't bet on it," Dan said. "I'm not that easy to fool."

"Sure you are, Danny boy. You're a fuckin' moron."

"Says the young lady who's looking at a homicide rap. Maybe more than one. And what's this I hear about a Russian mobster?"

"You can't take that seriously. I was just slingin' the shit."

"If Mr. Krauss's watch is found on the body, we can add that individual to your hit list. How long will you last in lockup if the Russian mob thinks you're good for killing one of their own?"

"That probably won't matter. He wasn't very popular, even with his fellow countrymen."

"Sure, you just keep telling yourself that. You'll run, naturally, but you won't get far. I'll put out an APB—"

"I'm not running."

"You telling me you'll face the music?"

"I guess so, if this was 1950 and people still talked like that."

"Will you surrender yourself or not?"

"I'll turn myself in at the Maritime police station at twelve noon."

"That's nearly six hours from now. Why not sooner?"

"Stuff I gotta do first."

"You're trying to play me. It won't work, Parker. I'm not as dumb as you think."

"Nobody could be that dumb. Twelve noon, Maritime. I'll be there with bells on. On second thought, I can't guarantee the bells."

She ended the call and powered off the burner, just in case Dan, or some smarter person, had the bright idea of trying to track the signal.

She hadn't been shining him on. She really would give herself up. But first she had to get a lawyer. Chase Benedict, probably. She'd recommended him to Joy Krauss, but naturally Joy hadn't taken her advice.

Joy. What a disappointment she'd turned out to be. "I probably should've killed her when I had the chance," Bonnie said philosophically.

Oh, well, you couldn't kill 'em all.

She finished the cig and patted down her pocket for another one. What she found was the top joint of Anton Streinikov's index finger.

Oh, yeah. She'd forgotten she still had that.

She rolled down the window, tossed the fingertip, and drove on.

# 41

BONNIE SPENT A couple of hours at the ER in Maritime, getting her leg patched up. Happily the bullet had passed clean through, and she was able to explain the injury as a pellet gun wound, the work of an overenthusiastic eight-year-old who'd ambushed her in the house. And the small lacerations caused by broken glass? When the tyke shot her, she fell on a glass table, which shattered. And the dirt and grime and grass stains? Well, this had all happened in the garden. *Come on, people, work with me here.* The docs might not have bought it, but they pretended to. They saw worse stuff in Maritime every night.

Despite her promise of voluntary surrender, the police were undoubtedly still looking for her. As a precaution she used the driver's license from Trudy Welch's purse as her ID. What the hell, one blonde gal looked pretty much like another. Trudy even had health insurance, which Bonnie put to good use.

While triaged in the admitting area, she watched a rundown of local developments on News 12. Ordinarily she had minimal interest in current events—she was one of those people who couldn't pick the vice president out of a lineup—but that morning she paid attention. The doings at Streinikov's place merited two and half minutes of breathless speculation and shaky video shot through the fence. The bodies on the driveway had been discreetly shrouded. The whole place looked different in daylight, suffused in an orange glare.

There was one other news item of interest, a little later

in the broadcast. It seemed that a Maritime man, Alonzo Duchenne, had been found shot to death at an out-of-business gas station in Fort Lee.

As dog-tired as she was, she didn't even register the name until a mug shot of Alonzo's scowling puss came up on the screen.

What were the odds? Too high for it to be a coincidence. Alonzo must have gone after her, gotten mixed up with Streinikov's crew somehow, and ended up dead. Tragic.

When she was done at the hospital, salved and scrubbed and looking almost civilized, she got back into the Saturn. She was all out of cell phones that couldn't be traced, so she hunted down a payphone and got Chase Benedict's number from Information. Though it was a Sunday, she succeeded in arranging an appointment for later in the morning. A few scraps of information were enough to provide the lawyer with a powerful inducement.

She stopped at a copy center and spent a half hour hour there, using up all the cash from Trudy Welch's purse. With a little time left before her appointment, she took a detour to Pilgrim Grove and parked near Green Arbor.

The residents were finishing their Sunday brunch. She helped herself to some eggs—okay, a lot of eggs—and sausage links and bacon and pancakes and ... She was hungry, all right? She'd eaten nothing since the sub sandwich last night, and she'd expended a buttload of calories since then.

With the plate on her lap, she joined Frank Kershaw on the glassed-in porch, where space heaters kept off the chill.

"Looks like you came through unscathed," he said.

"Maybe a little scathed." The bandaged wound on her leg was hidden by her jeans, and the blood on the fabric had dried dark enough to be hard to see. "But I'm still around."

"You can't keep living like this, kiddo. One of these days, it'll catch up with you. Did you give any more thought to what I said yesterday?"

"A little."

"Still think you've found a loophole in the system?"

She thought of her phone call to Brad. "No, I guess not."

He studied her. "But you're not going to walk away, are you?"

"Nope."

"You know what you're signing up for?"

"I think I do."

"There's a lot of darkness in the world, kiddo. You don't want to end up alone in it."

"What I want doesn't matter. I just have to keep going."

"And keep fighting?"

"It's all I know."

"You can't fight forever."

"It doesn't have to be forever. Only until I lose."

He shook his head. "You're too young to think that way. It's not too late to reinvent yourself."

"I guess you know about that. Don't you?"

Something flickered in his eyes. She watched him as she unfolded a sheet of paper from her purse and handed it over. He looked at it for a long time.

"Where'd you get this?" he asked finally.

"Doesn't matter."

"Well, it's all true. I wasn't always a forger. The first ID I faked was my own."

He started to hand back the paper. She waved him off. "You can keep it. Or better yet, destroy it."

"Is it the only copy?"

"Far as I know."

He nodded. Slowly he shredded the document between

his fingers, tearing it into long ragged strips.

"So he was your son," she said quietly. "The night I told you my story—that's when you knew."

"That's right, kiddo."

"But you didn't kick me out. Or kill me."

"Should I have?"

She shrugged. "I did kill him, didn't I?"

"You had a good reason," Frank said, his gaze distant.

The document that had been reduced to curling ribbons by his tremulous fingers had consisted of only a few lines of text. It said that Frank Hatch, wanted for murder in the state of Ohio, had changed his name to Frank Kershaw and relocated to Philadelphia, where he ran a hardware store that doubled as a credit clinic. His farmhouse in Buckington, Ohio, was abandoned and, after sitting empty for years, eventually sold. There was no information about his retirement; apparently the file hadn't been kept up to date, which was hardly surprising, since Frank Kershaw was not an important man. He was merely a random and insignificant scrap of data, preserved in the files in the unlikely event that he could ever prove useful to the people who mattered.

There was nothing in the document about his son Lucas. But Bonnie knew. She knew when she saw Frank's last name and the reference to a farmhouse in Buckington. The farmhouse that had served as a hideout for the three men who'd killed her parents—a convenient hideout, since they knew the owner wasn't coming back. The farmhouse where those three men had died, shot down by a fourteen-year-old girl with vengeance in mind.

"So you didn't know till I told you?" Bonnie asked. "You weren't looking for me?"

"I wasn't looking. I knew Lucas was dead, of course—him and the other two. Word had reached me about that. But I had no clue who'd done it or why. Certainly didn't think it was some shivering tomcat of a girl who I'd found in an alley behind my shop. I hardly could believe it even after you told me about Ohio."

"And you let me stay. Despite that."

"Not despite. *Because* of that. My son made you an orphan. I felt a certain responsibility. And the way I found you—well, I'm not religious, but it did give me pause. As if maybe I'd been offered a chance at, I don't know, redemption."

"You didn't hate me?" But even as she asked it, she knew he had hated her, at least a little. He couldn't help it. And yet he'd felt he was under an obligation. And so he'd maintained that mystifying balance of endearment and remoteness. He'd helped her in all the ways that he could, while never able to forget that his son's blood was on her hands.

"How I felt," Frank said as he looked at her through narrowed eyes, "was immaterial. Still is. I had to make it right. I'd done a bad thing once, but only once. Lucas—he made a habit of it. You remember me saying how it gets easier to cross those lines? Lucas crossed too many of them. So many, there was no coming back." He sighed. "If you hadn't done him in, someone else would have."

"I'm sorry, Frank."

"Don't be. You did what you did, and you were right to do it. Some men get to be like wild animals, and then they've got to be put down. It's hard, though—hard when it's your boy." His voice trembled just slightly. "But it had to be done. Hell, if I'd had the chance, I'd have done it myself."

She doubted it, but she didn't say so.

"As for you, kiddo," he added softly, "I felt there was a debt to be paid. I tried to pay it."

"It's paid," she told him. "In full."

He nodded, but she knew he wasn't listening. He was thinking of the farmhouse, and the body of Lucas Hatch on the bloody floor.

She left him after that, waving once from the front steps. He didn't wave back. Maybe he just didn't see.

Back in the Saturn, she set out for the law office of Chase Benedict. Time was running short, and there was still a lot left to do.

# 42

FROM PILGRIM GROVE, she went to Maritime. She spent an hour talking to Chase Benedict in his office. After that, she was really dragging. He let her crash on his sofa. She only had time for a catnap, but it did the trick. By the time she and Benedict pulled up to the Maritime police station in the attorney's Infiniti, she was wide awake.

Benedict parked in the lot at the rear of the building, a procedure he'd arranged in a phone call to the authorities while she slept. A small crowd waited there. Cops, all of them. The story had been kept out of the press so far.

Bonnie scanned the crowd. Dan was there, of course, an ugly leer riding on his mouth and making him look stupider than usual. Brad had not made an appearance. She wasn't sure how to feel about that.

Nobody slapped cuffs on her. That was something, at least. A lieutenant named Van Zile, who introduced himself as the head of Maritime's detective division, led her into a conference room with pale green walls. Everybody took a seat at a long mahogany table under a fluorescent panel. Dan and the other cops sat on one side; she and her mouthpiece sat on the other.

Danny Boy just couldn't stop staring at her and grinning savagely. She'd never really understood the old expression about the cat who swallowed the canary, but she got it now. She could practically see the tail feathers sticking out of his mouth.

"Miss Parker," Van Zile said, "you and your counsel need to know that the allegations against you are very serious. We have a sworn statement from Joy Krauss. We've also recovered her late husband's wristwatch from the scene of a multiple homicide, and we have reason to believe you had something to do with that."

"Why? Just because of a watch on Streinikov's wrist?"

Dan leaned forward. "No one said anything about Streinikov. You're the first one to mention his name."

"Yeah, I know. I heard myself. I was here." She took out a cigarette and lit it. "I was also there. I planted the watch on him to back up Joy's bullshit story about the Russian mob."

Van Zile glanced at Chase Benedict, who sat mute and expressionless. "That's an interesting admission."

"I figured you'd think so."

"You can't smoke in here, by the way."

"Who made you the tobacco czar?" She exhaled a long plume of smoke. "You notice anything else about Streini-kov?"

"We noticed he was dead."

"Very perceptive. I made him that way."

"And the top joint of his right index finger had been removed postmortem. With pruning shears."

"I did that too." She blew out another breath of smoke, aiming it in Dan's direction. She was gratified to hear him cough.

Chase Benedict still hadn't said anything. Van Zile's eyes kept ticking to him, then sliding away.

"You've just confessed to a homicide, Miss Parker. Are you prepared to make a formal statement?"

"My statement is that whatever Joy told you is true. Plus, I killed Streinikov and the other guys you found on his property. I counted eight goons plus the boss man. Oh, and a couple other stiffs they were storing in the garage. I took care of them earlier."

"You've been busy."

"I like to stay active."

"I suppose you'll say it was self-defense," Van Zile said with another glance at the lawyer.

"The two in the garage were self-defense. The other ones were more like a revenge thing. I mean, I had to bump 'em off in order to stay alive in the long run. But technically, you know, I should've gone to the cops or something."

"And why didn't you?"

"I don't like cops." She sucked down another long line of smoke. "No offense."

"So you took it upon yourself to murder eleven people?"

"Yep."

"All by yourself? Just you against Anton Streinikov and his whole crew?"

"Admit it. You're impressed."

"She's a sociopath," Dan said. "I've been saying it for years. Who knows how many people she's killed?"

"Have there been others?" Van Zile asked.

Bonnie blew a smoke ring. "No comment."

"Suddenly you're clamming up? Isn't it a little late for that?"

"Nah, I think it's just the right time. Counselor?"

Benedict snapped open his briefcase and removed a thick sheaf of photocopied pages. He plopped it down on the table.

"These are Xeroxes," Bonnie said. "The originals are someplace safe."

Blinking, Van Zile flipped through the sheets, casually at first, then with greater urgency. The muscles of his face did not move, but she heard a thick swallowing sound in time with a jerk of his Adam's apple.

Bonnie finished the cig and stabbed it out on the tabletop, leaving a burn mark. She leaned back in her chair, hands behind her head.

"Let's deal," she said.

~~~

AT THE END, she had found Streinikov in the greenhouse, shirtless in a chair by his potting bench, his side heavily bandaged. His face was flushed with fever, but he seemed strangely calm.

"My men?" he asked indifferently.

"They're dead," she told him. "Everybody's dead. It's just you and me now."

"Well, get on with it."

"Not so fast, buckaroo. You told me you've got the goods on everybody who matters in Jersey. Was that true?"

"*Da.*"

"Where's your stash?"

"A bargain, is it? If I tell you, you will spare my life?" He was smirking.

"We both know it doesn't play out that way. No quid pro quo. You're a dead man."

"Then why should I give you the keys to my kingdom?"

"'Cause if you don't, I'll burn this fucking hothouse to the ground."

"You think I hold my lovelies so dear?"

"Let's find out."

She flicked her cigarette lighter and touched the flame to a leafless orchid with a single bright pink-purple flower. The bloom caught. It burned slowly, shriveling, depositing a thin layer of ash on the bench.

"What do you call this thing, anyway?" she asked.

"*Equisetum telmateia.* Colloquially, Dragon's Mouth."

"Oh. Like your boat."

"Indeed."

"Is it rare?"

"Extremely."

The petal was gone now, the stem burning down like a candle wick.

"Burns real good," she said.

Streinikov's mouth twitched. "You really are a malicious, dirty-minded little bitch."

"Yeah, I get that a lot. Now—spill."

Still he hesitated. Apparently more persuasion was required.

"Who's next in line? How about this little darling?" She pointed at another plant, one with complicated tiger-striped petals.

"That is a Rothschild's Slipper," Streinikov said, his mouth barely moving. "It takes fifteen years to grow."

"Really? How long will it take to burn?" She thumbed the lighter and held it threateningly close to the plant. "Let's find out."

*"Nyet!"* In his agitation he lifted himself half out of his chair. With a wheeze he sank down. "Don't," he added in a whisper.

"So talk already. Or I'll burn 'em all, asshole. Every last one."

He took a long moment to raise his head, but when he spoke, his voice was steady. "In the main house, in the den, there is a sliding panel on the left side of the fireplace, level with the mantelpiece. The items are in a fireproof lockbox within."

"What's the combination?"

"The lock is paired to the index finger of my right hand."

Her gaze slid to the pruning shears on the bench.

"Then it looks like you're giving me the finger, Anton." She aimed the gun at him. "Last words?"

"Fuck you, *pizda*."

There were worse epitaphs.

She shot him. Then she picked up the shears and went to work.

Before leaving the grccnhouse, she removed Gil Krauss's wristwatch from the backpack and placed it on

Streinikov's arm. Not exactly subtle, but she wanted to make it easy for the boys in blue.

There was a small chance Streinikov had lied about the safe. She wasn't completely sure until she retracted the panel in the den and released the lock. Inside, revealed in the glow of her cigarette lighter, was an attaché case, and in the case was a pile of papers, along with assorted flash drives, DVDs, and even some old-fashioned audiotapes. The labels bore a lot of familiar and semi-familiar names. She didn't follow politics much, but even she knew who some of these people were.

It was one hell of an insurance policy. And since she wasn't a hundred percent sure the wristwatch ploy would get her and Joy out of deep water, she felt the need for an insurance policy right now.

Skimming the labels, she saw one name that shouldn't—couldn't—be there. She took out that file—it was just one page—and put it in her pocket. She would read it later, when she had time. Right now she had to book.

She stuffed the contents of the attaché case into her backpack, locked the safe and closed the panel. She left the room, taking care to avoid tripping on the bodies she'd dropped in the ambush. She felt no particular emotion in their presence. They meant nothing to her. They were not even people, really, just pieces on a game board. Toppled pieces, victims of her superior skill. Had the game played out differently, she would have been on the floor, and they would still be upright. That was all. Different outcomes, but the same game.

Always the same game.

# 43

IT TOOK THREE hours to work out an agreement with the Maritime police, but the outcome was never in doubt. There was enough dirt in Streinikov's files to sink every politician in the Garden State, and a whole passel of media big shots and corporate chieftains to boot. Maybe a fearless hero with a rebel streak would have risked releasing the info—someone like Jimmy Stewart in an old movie—but Bonnie had been willing to wager there weren't any Jimmy Stewarts in the Maritime PD. There were only jelly-spined paper pushers who would piss their trousers at the thought of even touching a scandal this hot.

Besides, one of the names in the files just happened to be that of Maritime's chief of police. Married with children, but he kept not one but two girlfriends on the side. One of them was a lap dancer at an establishment called the Boobie Trap.

Basically she had their dice in a vise, and they knew it.

Chase Benedict, silent until the documents were produced, came to life after that. He did all the talking. The upshot was that no charges would be filed against Bonnie Parker in connection with the Gil Krauss shooting, which would be officially explained as the work of the Russian mafia. Nor would any charges be filed against Joy Krauss, whose sworn statement would simply cease to exist. Oh, and of course Miss Parker had nothing whatsoever to do with events at the Edgewater home of the late Anton Streinikov.

Confidentiality was part of the agreement. Not a big stumbling block. The authorities wouldn't want it known that they'd made this kind of deal, anyway.

"The Jeep," Bonnie said as negotiations were wrapping up. "Don't forget the Jeep."

Right. Miss Parker's Jeep would be released from the impound lot and driven to Maritime. Any items confiscated from the Jeep, or from her office or home, would be returned, with no questions asked.

When all of this had been guaranteed in writing, the originals of Streinikov's files, including the audio recordings and flash drives, would be handed over to Lieutenant Van Zile, who could do with them as he wished.

"The material will be destroyed," Van Zile said grimly. "All of it."

Bonnie nodded. Some men would have wanted to keep their hands on a trove of incriminating data. Not Van Zile. He didn't want any trouble. He would keep his head down and retire with a pension.

"You'll still have to deal with the Russians," Van Zile added. "They'll want payback."

"Nah. Streinikov was a lone wolf. The other Russkie bosses wanted him dead. I did them a solid."

"So you had it all worked out."

"I'm a problem solver. It's what I do."

"This ... is ... bullshit."

The words, long simmering, came from Dan. The smirk on his face was gone, and in its place there was the frozen snarl of a Halloween mask. "Fucking bullshit."

"Chief Maguire—" Van Zile began.

*"Bullshit!"* His fist banged the table. His eyes, fixed on Bonnie, appeared to have actually changed color, becoming red—really, for God's sake, *red* with rage.

No one in the room wanted to look at him. Well, except for Bonnie. She was a kind of enjoying the view.

"You can't let her skate on this. You just can't. She's a

murderer. An assassin for hire. Mrs. Krauss told us. She's a goddamn hit man, and she's been getting away with it for years, and she's in *my town*."

"It's my town too," Bonnie said mildly.

Dan let out a choked scream and lunged at her across the table. But the table was wide, and he came up short, his clutching hands full of nothing but air.

"Sorry, Danno." Bonnie lit another cigarette, her sixth of the afternoon. "Better luck next time."

She thought he might really snap then, might draw his gun and try to shoot her, or shoot himself, or something. She wasn't worried. He probably wasn't a very good shot.

But he didn't do that. Slowly he sank back in his chair, all the anger hissing out of him. He seemed to become physically smaller, a used-up, withered thing. His face sagged. His eyes lost their red glare, lost all color, becoming gray and empty.

"God damn you, Parker," he whispered, but the words had no force. They were said by rote, a formula without meaning.

Beaten again. Defeat snatched from the jaws of victory. It had to sting.

At a time like this she almost felt sorry for old Dan. Okay, maybe not. But if she'd been a better person, she would have.

# 44

THE JEEP, DELIVERED to her at the rear exit of the station house, wasn't much worse for having been pawed over by the police. There might have been a few extra rips in the upholstery, but it was nothing a little duct tape couldn't fix.

As she was leaving, Van Zile offered a parting word. "This doesn't buy you any freedom from prosecution for other crimes—past or future."

Bonnie nodded. "I'm aware."

Dan, loitering nearby, lifted his head when he heard that. He sidled up to her, his voice low.

"I'll be keeping an eye on you, Parker. Now that I know what I know, I'll be watching you closer than ever. One slip-up, and you're mine. Just one."

"Great, Danny. Hold on while I change into some boots, so I can shiver in 'em."

He only stared at her as, very slowly, a ghost of his old grin materialized on his face.

On the move in the Jeep, she powered up Sammy for the first time in hours and retrieved her voicemails. Brad's was the only one that mattered. She could hear his concern and fear, though he'd done his best to sound coolly professional. He knew the message might be heard by cops investigating her disappearance or death, so he'd covered himself. Smart. She respected someone whose instinct for self-preservation remained paramount at all times.

Yellow crime-scene ribbon was strung across the

front door of her duplex, which was still guarded by a bored cop. Some lookie-loos were hanging around at a safe distance, as if the place was radioactive and they were afraid to get too close. Enough of them were local to ensure that she was recognized. Their reaction to her was less than positive. She saw a lot of scowling faces.

Jeez, she was like friggin' Typhoid Mary all of a sudden. You would think they'd be grateful to her for bringing a little excitement into their lives.

She felt their cold stares on her back as she approached the door. "Take a picture," she muttered, "it'll last longer." Then she noticed that some of them actually were taking pictures with their cell phones. Shit. They were one step ahead of her.

The cop on duty checked her ID before letting her in. He warned her, "They trashed it pretty good."

"Well, I've been meaning to redecorate."

She went inside and surveyed the damage. The windows had been shot out, and the place was cold. Bullet holes were everywhere. Broken mirrors—that was seven years' bad luck right there. TV set shot to hell. The laptop computer on the dining table had been plugged multiple times. She was guessing that kind of thing probably wasn't covered by the warranty. The kitchen floor was littered with shattered plates that had formerly been stacked in the cabinets. The cabinets themselves had been blasted apart, the doors hanging on busted hinges.

They'd even shot up the freakin' toilet. The bowl was cracked, the tank leaking.

It was lucky she didn't collect Fabergé eggs, or she'd really be ticked off.

Basically the place had been totaled. Her office must be pretty much the same. Fixing all this crap was going to be a real pain in the ass. If she'd known Streinikov's boys had been this thorough, she might have clipped his finger while he was still alive.

Outside, she saw Mrs. Biggs leaving her unit. The older woman didn't notice her at first.

"Eleanor," she said.

Mrs. Biggs flinched. She turned slowly, her face unreadable.

"Sorry about all this. It was a big mix-up, but it's all taken care of now." Even as she said it, Bonnie realized how inadequate it was.

Her neighbor said nothing.

"I'm just glad you didn't get hurt," she added pointlessly.

A beat of silence passed between them. When she spoke, Mrs. Biggs kept her voice low and flat.

"This is a small town. Things like this don't happen here. Or at least—they never used to."

She walked away.

Bonnie shut her eyes. If even Mrs. Biggs had turned against her, then she'd lost her last friend in Brighton Cove.

# 45

OUT OF HABIT she parked several blocks from Brad's apartment and walked there in the cold wind. She expected him to be home on a Sunday, and he was.

"So," he said, opening the door, "you slipped out of it. We should call you Houdini."

She stepped inside and let the door swing shut behind her. "Houdini was a piker compared to me."

He wasn't smiling, wasn't amused. Not that she'd expected him to be.

"So I guess Dan's brought you up to speed?"

He gave a curt nod, his eyes fixed on her face. "That's right."

"We were supposed to have a confidentiality agreement."

"He'll honor it. But he had to vent to somebody. I was elected."

"Lucky you."

He kept staring at her, as if he'd never seen her before. "You shot that man Krauss in cold blood."

"He was trolling for a hit man for his wife."

"Then he should have been arrested. Not—executed."

"I guess it depends on how much faith you've got in the legal process."

"I guess it does. And there were others, weren't there? Other hits?"

She was sure—almost sure—he wasn't wearing a wire, but she still wasn't going to incriminate herself. She remembered Van Zile's warning about the limitations of her immunity. "No comment."

"The other night—the last night when we ... You'd come directly from killing him."

"Not directly."

"You still had blood on your hands."

"No. I'd washed it off."

"Some things don't wash off."

"Yeah. I kinda knew you'd see it that way."

"You think you're so smart, but you're just a killer. A sociopath, like Dan says."

"Dan's a moron. He couldn't even spell *sociopath*."

"You are one, though. Or something worse. You're evil, Bonnie."

"I'm complicated."

"You're evil. Evil all the way down."

"Bad to the bone," she whispered.

Brad nodded, his face grave. "Yeah."

He just stood there, arms folded, giving her the old stink-eye. It was starting to piss her off.

"I did warn you," she said. "I told you to keep your distance. I tried everything I could to push you away for months and months. For years. You think you can make me feel guilty. You can't. I know what I am. No delusions. You're the one who doesn't want to deal with it. You're the one who kept looking the other way. You even read my file and you still didn't want to believe it. You wouldn't believe until it was pushed right up in your face."

"So it's my fault?" he said in a toneless voice.

"It's nobody's fault. It is what it is."

"And you are—what you are."

"Damn straight, buddy. I'll kill whoever needs killing, and I won't lose a minute's sleep over it."

Yeah, she said it. So what if he was wired up? Fuck it. She could always beat the rap.

"You're as bad as Dan says," he told her. "It's just that simple."

"Things are never just that simple. They're never just good or bad."

"They are, for me."

Bonnie nodded. Of course they were.

She figured she ought to leave now. This conversation felt extremely over. But he surprised her by speaking again.

"You're just like her, aren't you?"

She almost asked who he meant, but it wasn't necessary. The subtle stress on the word *her* gave it away. Her namesake, the first Bonnie Parker.

"I don't know," she said honestly. "I've lasted longer. And I don't rob banks."

"Do you write poetry? She did."

"I ain't Shakespeare." She frowned. "He wrote poems, right? Not just plays?"

"He wrote poems. Think you'll end up like her?"

"Blown away in an ambush?" She considered the question seriously. "Yeah, probably."

"I do, too. She had Clyde Barrow with her when she died."

Her memory flashed on those dreams she sometimes had—blood and broken glass, and Clyde's screams mingled with her own. "I know."

"Who will you have?"

She took a breath, let it out, felt her body sag with the finality of surrender. "Nobody, I guess. Nobody at all."

He seemed satisfied with that. Like an inquisitor, he'd wrung a confession out of her.

"Get the hell out of here," he said.

She let him have the last word. He deserved that much.

In her Jeep, heading back to the bullet-pocked mess she called home, she took out a cigarette. Her hand shook only a little as she thumbed the lighter.

So it was over. No surprise. It could never have lasted.

Bradley Walsh believed in rules and order, things making sense. She didn't. She knew what life really was—the insanity of it, the biting cruelty. Life was a blade, and it cut deep. Streinikov had known that blade, and so had she.

And she couldn't change, no matter what Frank Kershaw thought. She'd crossed too many lines already. She'd gone too far to ever double back.

The road she was on—it was a rough road, and it led to a bad place, but it was her road, the only one she knew. She would travel that road all the way to the end of the line.

And she would travel it alone.

# Author's Note

As ALWAYS, I invite readers to visit me at www.michaelprescott.net, where you'll find links to all my books, news about upcoming projects, contact info, and other good stuff.

*Bad to the Bone* is the third book in a series that began with *Cold Around the Heart* and continued with *Blood in the Water*. A fourth book featuring Bonnie Parker is in the works.

Many thanks to Diana Cox of www.novelproofreading.com for her usual fine job of proofreading the manuscript. I made some changes after she read it, and I probably introduced some new errors; so if you find any mistakes, they're all mine.

The lines of poetry at the front of the book were written by the historical Bonnie Parker, partner of Clyde Barrow. Two weeks before her death, she gave the poem to her mother. It was published posthumously.

—MP

# ABOUT THE AUTHOR

After twenty years in traditional publishing, Michael Prescott found himself unable to sell another book. On a whim, he began releasing his novels in digital form. Sales took off, and by 2011 he was one of the world's best-selling e-book writers. *Bad to the Bone* is his most recent thriller.